LER FO

Cut By: _____

Scanned By: _____ Qty _____

Scanned _____ _____

GALAXY'S EDGE

EDITED BY MIKE RESNICK

ISSUE 29: November 2017

Mike Resnick, Editor
Jean Rabe, Assistant Editor
Shahid Mahmud, Publisher

Published by Arc Manor/Phoenix Pick
P.O. Box 10339
Rockville, MD 20849-0339

Galaxy's Edge is published in January, March, May, July, September, and November.

www.GalaxysEdge.com

Galaxy's Edge is an invitation-only magazine. We do not accept unsolicited manuscripts. Unsolicited manuscripts will be disposed of or mailed back to the sender (unopened) at our discretion.

Available by subscription (www.GalaxysEdge.com) or through your favorite online store (Amazon.com, BN.com, etc.).

ISBN: 978-1-61242-389-0

Advertising in the magazine is available. Quarter page (half column), $95 per issue. Half page (full column, vertical or two half columns, horizontal) $165 per issue. Full page (two full columns) $295 per issue. Back Cover (full color) $495 per issue. All interior advertising is in black and white.

Please write to advert@GalaxysEdge.com.

FOREIGN LANGUAGE RIGHTS: Please refer all inquiries pertaining to foreign language rights to Shahid Mahmud, Arc Manor, P.O. Box 10339, Rockville, MD 20849-0339. Tel: 1-240-645-2214. Fax 1-310-388-8440. Email admin@ArcManor.com.

Contents

TWO NEW TITLES

WHEN PARALLEL LINES MEET
a Stellar Guild book
MIKE RESNICK,
LEZLI ROBYN
LARRY HODGES

THRESHOLD OF ETERNITY
JOHN BRUNNER
DAMIEN BRODERICK

ON SALE NOW

November 2017

THE EDITOR'S WORD

by Mike Resnick

Welcome to the twenty-ninth issue of *Galaxy's Edge*. New stories featured in this issue are by new and newer writers Dan Koboldt, Eric Leif Davin, Sandra M. Odell, Steve Pantazis, Daniel J. Davis, David L. Hebert, Larry Hodges, and French superstar Jean-Claude Dunyach. We've also got some older stories by old friends Mercedes Lackey, Kevin J. Anderson, Nancy Kress, and Barry N. Malzberg, as well as another segment of Joan Slonczewski's serialized novel, *Daughter of Elysium*. We've got our regular columnists, as always—Bill Fawcett and Jody Lynn Nye on books, Gregory Benford on science, and Robert J. Sawyer on literature. And this month's Joy Ward interview is with Nebula winner and bestseller Jack McDevitt.

In other words, welcome to another typical issue of *Galaxy's Edge*.

✧

There was a time, and not so long ago, when the standard advice to new writers and wannabes was: Go to Worldcon. Meet editors. Listen to panels on how to break in. Hit the parties at night and see who was buying for anthologies. If you had a couple of other free weekends on your calendar and could afford it, do the same thing at World Fantasy Con and Nebula Weekend. That way you'll cover the whole field, meet everybody who's anybody. It's worked for more than the first half-century of Worldcon and lesser lifespans of the other two; no reason why it shouldn't continue to work.

And, in 1989, or 1995, there *was* no reason why it shouldn't continue to work.

Welcome to 2017, where there are one hell of a *lot* of reasons why that advice isn't still valid.

Oh, it's valid as far as it goes…but it stops at just about the point where reality intrudes.

Consider: there have been seventy-five Worldcons, starting in 1939. Not one has drawn as many at ten thousand attendees. Most, even recently, average less than half of that.

Now consider Dragon Con. When I started going a dozen years ago, it drew about thirty thousand. Each year it gets more popular.

This year it drew over eighty thousand.

And they weren't all just readers.

There were a *lot* of writers there, as usual (and they pull more each year). A convention that was disdained by publishers a decade ago now draws them. Same with artists, and editors, and just about everyone else connected with the field.

Are you a new writer who wants to meet your fans, perhaps by doing a reading or sitting on a panel? You can do it at a traditional convention, or you can do it at Dragon Con. The only (enormous) difference is the size of your audience.

Now, I'm not shilling for Dragon Con. I'm mentioning it simply because I was there two weeks before writing these words and it's still fresh in my mind.

But cons that do *not* disdain games and comics and costumes and movies and all the related aspects of the science-fiction field are not limited to Dragon Con. Hell, Comic-Con in San Diego regularly pulls well over a hundred thousand. Indiana's Gen Con is no slouch, pulling considerably more than fifty thousand. I was invited to a convention in Dallas a couple of years ago that was devoted entirely to anime (except for one track of science fiction programming, which was what I'd been invited for) that drew well over ten thousand, at least half of them not old enough to drink or vote.

Does this mean that I'll stop going to Worldcon, or stop recommending it? No.

But it *does* mean that I recognize our little world is changing, and that there is more than one way to skin a cat—or make a contact, or sell a book.

*Larry Hodges has sold more than eighty stories. His third novel—*Campaign 2100: Game of Scorpions*—was recently published by World Weaver Press. His* Parallel Lines Never Meet, *a Stellar Guild team-up with Mike Resnick and Lezli Robyn, is due out in October.*

THE NATURE OF SWORDS

by Larry Hodges

The two floating swords parried and thrust as they battled through the corridors of the ruined castle. Dust and cobwebs swirled in the musty air as the steel-on-steel clashing continued up a stairway and into a large room that had once been a kitchen. Rusty pots and human bones littered the floor by a broken table covered in dust.

"Got you!" cried the sword Glory as she slammed the Unnamed Sword into a giant black cauldron. Her voice came out of the golden hilt, which was engraved with scenes of human battles. His own hilt was plain steel with a simple leather grip. Both swords looked brand new, with gleaming steel blades. "No wonder they didn't name you."

"No you didn't!" cried the Unnamed Sword as he shot up toward the ceiling, irritated at her dig about his lack of a name. The parrying continued for much of the afternoon. Often they'd cut into each other's edges, wounding each other, but the pain was both invigorating and temporary as the magic quickly healed them. Glory relentlessly beat the Unnamed Sword back, chasing him down hallways and from room to room.

Finally the Unnamed Sword lowered his point. "I give up. I can't beat you." He nonchalantly swatted aside a human leg bone on the ground with his tip. Only occasionally did he stop and think about how these lifeless bones had once been living humans. It had been so long....

Glory rose up over him, her point at his sword's throat, just under his plain iron hilt. "I win again, Nameless."

"You always do." The two clicked blades, and then, together, floated back through the stairways and corridors to the castle armory. Home.

Soon they were at it again, along with several of their friends—the determined rapier Relentless, the smug but efficient longsword Splendor with its jewel-encrusted hilt, the silent curving scimitar Gravedoings, Ding and Dong the daggers, Jabber the slow but relentless jousting stick, and the giant claymore Redsteel with his long crimson blade. The greatest of them all, Redsteel, took on both the Unnamed Sword and Glory and repeatedly slammed the two broadswords about, leaving them dazed but determined. The floor was littered with non-magical weapons covered in dust: swords, shields, longbows, spears, axes, morning stars, flails, and suits of armor.

After a while the Nameless Sword floated off to the side and just watched. Ding and Dong joined Glory in the battle with Redsteel. Soon the others all joined in gleefully, and finally they pounded Redsteel to the floor. With a guttural laugh, he submitted.

"Victory!" cried the daggers in unison. Then it started all over again with new opponents.

There was a time when the Unnamed Sword could never get enough of the constant swordplay. There wasn't much else for a magic sword to do, not in the many years since the Age of Man had come to an end. Recently it had begun to bore him. He felt he had a greater destiny. But what?

Unlike the others, he'd never killed anyone. His master hadn't even named him yet when he'd been killed by another human, as humans often did to each other. His master had reached for the Unnamed Sword, but the other human had thrown Ding and Dong with all their magic power and accuracy, and both had lodged in his back. He died with his sword in his hand, unused and unnamed.

Why had the humans killed themselves off? "It's in their nature," Redsteel once explained. "It wasn't a problem until they infused us with magic. A magic sword is an unstoppable killing machine."

That night, after the swords had lowered themselves into their dusty display stands on the wall to wait for morning, the Unnamed Sword tossed and turned. Why was he the only sword without a name? The others called him "Nameless," but that wasn't a true name. Only a human could give him a name. Since there were no more humans, he could not be named.

That's when a crazy thought entered his mind, one so different that he shot into the air without thinking, slamming into the ceiling. Several swords called out to him to be quiet, but he ignored them as he pondered the bizarre thought.

What if there were still humans left?

"That's silly," Redsteel said the next morning as they prepared for the day's battles.

Glory slammed her blade into the Unnamed Sword's handle, spinning him about. "Come fight, or I'll proclaim myself human and name you Skunkbreath!"

He halfheartedly parried her thrusts but she quickly beat him to the ground. "C'mon!" she cried. "This is too easy. Ding or Dong could beat you right now, one on one."

"Probably." At least they had names and had killed. He floated away to a corner, deep in thought. Glory watched him for a moment, then dipped her point in disgust. A moment later she was at battle with Gravedoings while Jabber took on the daggers and Redsteel went to war with Relentless and Splendor.

The only way I'll ever be named, he thought, is if I find a human. So there *must* be one, somewhere. There just had to be.

He would find this human.

Without a word to the others he floated through the corridors and out of the castle, and out over the broken drawbridge and the scattered skeletons covering the ground outside near the surrounding forest. He floated up and over the trees, the sun glinting off his steel. The trees seemed to go on forever. Once there had been fields here where the humans practiced their swordsmanship and roads that connected the various castles, but they were long overrun by the ever-encroaching forest. He and Glory had often explored the local region and nearby castles, sometimes spending a day parrying with the local swords.

And yet, how did they really know the humans had all died? Perhaps somewhere, in a land far away, they still lived? Then he would have to travel to lands far away.

A journey of a thousand miles begins with a single thrust. He took that thrust forward and began his journey.

He took his time. On land, there were always trees about, and if a sword went too fast, it could end up with its point stuck in one. If it went in too deeply, and there were no other swords to help pull it out, it could be stuck for a long time, maybe forever. He was in no rush, and so he meandered about, exploring, looking for that last human, wherever he might be.

His adventures were many. A pack of wolves attacked him, a huge mistake on their part. Another time he got tangled in the branches of a tree and spent a day sawing at the branches to free himself—not an easy task for an unserrated sword. And once, while exploring a cave for signs of human life, he found instead a gigantic bear. This time he had to fight for real in a closed confined space where his flying skills and mobility were minimized. In the end, of course, the bear's great strength was no match for a magic sword. The bear left a great dent in his hilt but the magic quickly healed him.

Whenever he found a castle he'd ask the resident swords if they'd heard of any living humans, but always the response was, "No, are you crazy?" Over and over they told him humans were extinct. Only the swords survived.

One day he smelled something that reminded him of a salty soup made by a human cook from long ago. He followed the scent. And found an ocean.

He'd heard of such things but never believed it possible. *So much water!* Laughing, he charged out over the beach to the salty water and dived in. The coolness refreshed and invigorated him and allowed him to forget, if only for a moment, the failure of his mission. He spent a time chasing small fish, easily catching them and smacking them with his flat side. He had no desire to kill these small creatures. Swords were meant for greater things than cutting up seafood or slaying wolves and bears.

What was he meant for?

He had spent years exploring the land and there had been no humans to be found. Now he looked out over the ocean. Humans could not live in the sea, though he'd heard they could float on it in boats. If there were no humans in this land, then there must be other lands.

He floated up over the ocean, which seemed as endless as the forest had once seemed. But the forest had come to an end. All things have ends. It was just a matter of finding it, and then he could see what was there. But if all things had ends, didn't that mean humans might also have reached their end, and his quest was a waste of time?

He flew out over the water, tentative at first. He wasn't used to such openness. There were no barriers here, just fresh ocean smell and water lapping below. He picked up speed, faster and faster. Soon he flew faster than he'd ever flown before.

And still the ocean went on forever. A giant fish surfaced and shot water out of a hole on its top. Sometimes a turtle would surface. Otherwise it was just endless water, hour after hour. At some point well into his journey several seagulls flew overhead.

And then, after a full day of flying, he saw it—the gray outline of…something. Soon he could make out the trees.

Land! He tried to hold back his excitement. Most likely he'd find more swords but no humans. But maybe not.

He came in too fast. At the last second he veered up as the forest became individual trees with thick trunks. He plunged into the forest, trying to avoid the huge branches. They were too thick. To avoid getting entangled, he shot downward.

And right into a thick oak tree.

He pulled back, but his point had gone in too deep. He tried again and again, struggling for hours, but to no avail; he had no leverage. Soon it began to rain, the first of many times.

Weeks, months, and then years went by as the Nameless Sword fought against the oak tree, but it only held him tighter as it seemed to slowly grow about his tip, inching its way forward. He constantly cried for help, but there were none to hear. Birds and other creatures at first avoided this loud metal object sticking out of a tree, but soon they grew used to it. Squirrels scampered over him. Birds began to roost on him, often leaving smelly messes that no magic in him could remove. Yet even that wasn't nearly so painful as the realization that he might be stuck forever, that he would never accomplish his mission, and that he would spend forever namelessly stuck in a tree.

The horror of that fate led him to scream even louder for help, often from morning till night, his cries disappearing into the deep forest. And then, one day, there was an answer.

"What happened to you?" An ancient man looked down at him. He seemed a pair of dark eyes peering out of a forest of white hair that went off in all directions—beard, mustache, sideburns, and cascades of hair on top and flowing over his back. His fading robe might once have been blue but was now more gray and so thin one could see through it.

A man! A *human!*

In fast, stuttering speech—what more could he do in the presence of an actual *living* human?—he explained what had happened; his search for man, his journey across the ocean, and his embarrassing finish.

"You're lucky," said the man. "I decided to hike the beaches south for the winter, and heard your calls. I've been walking along the ocean for weeks. Normally I take a path farther inland."

"Who are you?" the sword asked.

"I am Sardonius, and I was once a swordsmith," the man said, his black eyes staring unblinking at the stuck sword. "I too fled the land of man. Though from what you say, it is now the land of swords, as I thought might happen." The man grabbed him by the hilt, and after planting his foot against the base of the tree for leverage, pulled him out with a titanic heave. Humans, the sword thought thankfully, may not be as fast or indestructible as a sword, but they were just as strong or stronger.

"Thanks," the sword said, floating up to eye level with the man, hilt to face, his point downward. The magic quickly fixed the damages done by the tree, though he feared the stain from birds' messes would be there forever, at least in his mind. "Why did you fear it would become the land of swords?"

Sardonius shook his head. "It was all my fault. I was the master swordsmith from the court of King Cluth. We were at war with King Vos. The weapons race began with improved steel from Chandalee. To keep up, we came up with our own ways of making better and sharper steel. Often we'd bring in prisoners to test the killing power of these new designs. A few lives lost was the tradeoff for our greater glory and power. And then I discovered how to infuse the power of magic into a sword. Magic in humans was a pitiful thing, with the most powerful barely able to move an apple seed. But tempered into the steel of a sword with the spirit of a human sacrifice, the power becomes great. And it was my job to find ways to increase this power. Tempering the magic was easy; finding enough human sacrifices was not."

"So you created the first magic swords using human sacrifices, and used us to defeat your enemies?"

"I wish it were that simple," Sardonius said. "There were spies. Soon all our enemies and allies had the secret. The weapons race went on until a man with a sword was unstoppable, at least until he met a man with a greater sword. Most ended up as human sacrifices as the demand for the swords grew. Soon the swords didn't even need a human to kill. Our swords killed their people, and their swords killed ours."

"So you are the last human alive?"

"As far as I can tell, there are no others here, and you say there are none in the land of swords. So I must be the last of my kind." The man stared off into the distance for a moment. Then he fell to the ground, white hair flying about as he pounded the sandy ground with his fist. *"What have I done?"*

"Stop!" said the Unnamed Sword. "You are *not* the last of your kind. We, the swords, live on as your descendants. We are your children."

After a moment the man slowly stood up, wiping his eyes. "That is true. Is there anything I can do to help you, my child, to pay for my past crimes?"

The Nameless Sword brightened, remembering his mission. "Actually, there is, my father. You can name me."

"You have no name?"

"My master died before naming me."

"Then *I* will remedy that. Now what would be a good name for a sword that has wandered across an entire ocean in search of a human? There can be only one name." He placed his hand on the Nameless Sword's hilt. "I dub thee…Wanderer."

Wanderer! What a beautiful name. Now he was nearly complete. But there was one more thing he had to do.

He thrust forward and stabbed the man through the belly. Sardonius cried with pain and surprise as he fell to the ground on his back.

"Why did you do that?" he sputtered, clutching at his stomach as the life bled out of him. *"I saved you! You should be on my side!"*

Wanderer floated up over him as drops of blood ran down his blade and dripped onto the man's face—the last man, and Wanderer now knew why. Soon he would return to the land of swords, with a name and a kill under his hilt.

"Why did I kill you? You made us from the spirits of human sacrifice. Killing was your nature. Now it is ours."

Copyright © 2017 by Larry Hodges

❋   ❋   ❋

This is Canadian lawyer David L. Hebert's first published story, but we think there will be a lot more from him in the future. We also think he's honed his art by spinning fantasies to Canadian judges.

SUICIDE PARTY

by David L. Hebert

"Are you going to Alex's suicide party?"

We were on our morning break. I leaned back in my chair, took a sip of my coffee, and looked over at Monica. "Alex is having a suicide party?"

She was nodding. "The night before his exit date. We're all going."

I didn't even know that he was contemplating an exit, let alone planning it. I shrugged. "I'll probably go." I went back to scrolling through the newsfeed on my tablet.

"The party is on Thursday. Personally I think I'd exit on a Sunday, so we could have the party on Saturday night, but it's not my exit."

I arched an eyebrow at her. "Are *you* planning one?"

She gave me a weird look that succeeded in making me question my sanity, and then she laughed. "Hardly. But Alex is a nice guy, and I'm going to miss him. So of course I'm going."

She was right. Alex *was* a nice guy. "I'll probably miss him, too."

She gave me a different weird look that succeeded in making me question my morals.

"Well, I won't miss the mealworms in the lunchroom refrigerator."

This look wasn't weird, just disgusted. Not because of the mealworms but rather at my apparent indifference to a colleague's being nearly departed. Up until that moment, I had apparently been successful in hiding my failings as a human being.

"They're gluten free and high in protein," she said offhandedly, turning back to her own tablet. After a moment, she looked back up at me. "So why do you figure he decided to do it?"

I shrugged again. "Maybe he's sick of eating gluten free." Realizing that in her eyes I was probably still failing as a human being, I added, "Besides, what the hell—it's *his* funeral."

It was out of my mouth before I realized that what I'd said probably wouldn't help. "I mean—it's his choice, Monica. That's been decided by the courts. There's no requirement for a person to be here if he really doesn't want to be here, and obviously Alex doesn't want to be here. More power to him." I sipped my coffee, which was slightly less than tepid.

Monica was back to ignoring her tablet and sipping on her tea, staring off into the air in front of her. "How could he decide he has nothing left to live for? He's only in his thirties. He's still got a whole life in front of him."

I corrected her. "You're wrong. He's got until Friday."

Another weird look from her, but it lasted only for a moment. She went back to sipping her tea, which must surely have been as tepid as my coffee. She was lost in introspection.

Feeling that I had to do something to bring the conversation back, I said, "You obviously have a different outlook, but you can't know what he's feeling. You can't know what it's like to live his life, even if he tells you—you can't *know*. If he's decided that ending it now is what he wants to do, then I fully support him in his position."

"But what about the options? What about mental health treatment? Maybe if he just got the right prescription—"

I interrupted her. "You think he hasn't been through that, Monica? You think he hasn't already spent a lifetime of doctors and prescriptions and trying to change his basic thought patterns? That was the whole *point* of the court case! Up until last year, the only people who were permitted to undergo humane suicide were the ones with terminal illnesses. Hell, living every day like you wish it were your last may as well be a terminal illness, and since the Supremes weighed in last year, not wanting to live is perfectly legitimate grounds for not living. End of story."

She was looking at me now. "It seems like you've given this some thought."

"I've given it enough thought to realize that being forced to live when you don't want to is a form of cruel and unusual punishment."

That shut her up for a couple of minutes. The silence was getting to me, and I began to think that maybe I had spoken a little too harshly to her. "Up until the laws changed, there were still suicides, Monica. On average, one every twenty seconds. All those people had to risk doing it alone, in silence, and in secret. And yes, I say risk, because there was always the chance that those people could end up as vegetables, trapped in their bodies for decades to come. Knowing Alex's decision, is that the fate you'd like to bestow upon him?"

"Well, of course not. But he's such a nice guy—"

"Well, with the new laws, anybody can do it as long as they've paid their taxes. So Alex can do it as a celebration, and family and friends can be around, and he can have a great party the night before as a nice send-off. Would you take away his dignity for your selfishness?"

Our tablets went off simultaneously. Break time was over.

Monica went to the sink and emptied her cup. "So I'll see you at the party on Thursday?"

"Probably," I said.

Copyright © 2017 by David L. Hebert

Mercedes Lackey is the author of more than one hundred novels, creator of the Valdemar universe, occasional collaborator with Anne McCaffrey, Eric Flint, and Andre Norton, and frequent bestseller. We're happy to welcome her back to the pages of Galaxy's Edge.

FALSE KNIGHT ON THE ROAD
(A SERRAted Edge Story)

by Mercedes Lackey

Billie Ray Johnson listened attentively past the thunder of the three-carb, supercharged V8 under the hood of his Ford Fairlane. He knew every grumble and roar of his machine; what he was listening for was something that *wasn't* it. Chevy, which would be the cops, more than likely. All the 'shiners hereabouts ran Fords or Hudson Hornets. Sometimes he regretted not getting a Hudson; they gripped the curves like a cat about to be tossed into the river. But the Ford was faster. Fastest car in the county, probably the fastest car in this part of the state.

It was a perfect night for 'shine running. Which was not to say that it was a beautiful, clear night with a full moon. Outsiders might consider that a perfect night, but a clear, bright night meant the cops could see you running up the mountain a mile away. Tonight was a quarter moon, and you couldn't see it for the overcast and the fog. Not enough fog to slick up the road, and it was intermittent patches, but enough to make driving a challenge if you didn't know the roads the way Billie Ray did.

Right now he was on a piece of section-line that just had patches of fog on it, not enough to turn the clay under the gravel greasy. Thanks to the fog, the thick woods to either side of the gravel road were like walls, just a hint of individual trunks in the sidewash of his headlights as he sped by. He was laden down, trunk full of cartons of tightly packed mason jars full of 'shine cradled in newspaper so they wouldn't bang together and break, tank built into the back seat full and sealed, and some extra-special jars tucked into flour sacks under the front seat. He was early, by his reckoning. He'd made good time. He'd make better time when

9

he got to the hardtop road. Seventy-five miles to Shelby, where he'd turn over his load, collect his money, and head back home again.

Moonshine had bought and paid for this car. Moonshine bought and paid for everything his Ma and Pa couldn't grow or hunt for them and the kids. Life was rough on the mountain; hardscrabble farming, plowing the few bits of land that weren't vertical the old way, with a mule. In theory it was possible to live completely off the land, but in practice, unless you didn't mind dressing yourself and the kids in leather and furs like a bunch of Indians, and you didn't mind doing without things like bread, it wasn't. What Billie brought in running 'shine paid for the flour and the stuff for clothing, all the things that made life a little easier.

Ma worried, but Billie even knew what he'd do if he got caught; he'd be a first-time offender and the judge in this county had a reputation for offering people like him the prison farm or the army. He'd take the army, and send his pay home. It wouldn't be as much as he got for 'shine running—a hundred dollars a month instead of a night—but it'd be better than nothing.

But he didn't plan on getting cau—

The hell! he thought, as his headlights cut through a patch of fog and hit the side of a car parked right across the road at a crossroads *he* didn't remember being there, and he stood on the brakes to avoid piling into it.

Which he did, just barely, and only by hauling on the handbrake and sending the Fairlane slewing sideways in a shower of gravel.

The first thing in his mind was—*revenuers!*—and his heart, already racing, went into a panicked gallop, as his brain went into overdrive calculating how to sling the Fairlane all the way around and gun her back up the road he'd just come down.

But in the next moment he realized—no, that was never a cop car, or a revenuer car, or ATI. There were no markings, no lights, and no cop car, not even FBI or treasury agent, had *ever* looked like this one.

It set his mind into a tailspin then, all thoughts of escape vanishing—because he could not identify it. At all. And he knew every make and model of every car ever built, at least in the US of A. It *had* to be foreign. One of those cars he'd read about the few

times he'd gotten his hands on a racing magazine, with names he couldn't even begin to figure out how to pronounce. *What the hell was it doing out here?* Was the driver lost, or stuck? In either case, what the hell was it doing out here?

It was low, and lean, and sleek. Solid black without a hint of chrome anywhere. It matched no make or model he had *ever* seen, not even in pictures. Some rich man's made-just-for-him racing car? There had been one magazine with photos of cars with outlandish bodies and some Frenchified race…*Grand Prix*, they called it. But what in the name of God was something like that doing out in these mountains?

And what in *hell* was it doing parked in the middle of a crossroads he would have sworn hadn't been there the last time he'd made this run?

The Fairlane had stopped mere feet away from the mystery car, and now the driver's side opened, and the driver stepped out. Calm. Cool. If the positions had been reversed, Billie Ray would have been out of that car before the Fairlane stopped moving and heading for the brush—and when the crash didn't happen, he'd have been heading *out* of the brush with a fat stick in his hand to administer a whuppin'.

Like the car, the driver was all in black from head to toe. Black pants, black jacket zipped up against the damp chill in the air, black gloves. He wore a black hat—a Stetson—pulled down low on his head so you couldn't really see his face. He strolled around the front of his beauty of a car, walked over to Billie's window and tapped on it.

Too astounded by all of this to think at all at this point, Billie automatically rolled it down. Little cold, damp wisps of fog drifted in through the window, along with a faint scent of leather and a hint of something expensive and spicy.

"Billie Ray Johnson?" The stranger's voice was low, smooth, *rich* sounding.

"That there'd be me," Billie admitted, the words coming out of his mouth before he thought.

The stranger leaned back against his car, and crossed his arms over his chest. "I heard," he said, making no attempt to disguise his high-class accent, words coming out of his mouth that sounded more like what you'd hear on a radio show one late night, tuned in by accident from some place far, far away, than anything these mountains had ever echoed. "I heard, that your Ford is a fast car."

Now there were finally thoughts running through Billie's head. That he was in the middle of a run. That this was no time to be palaverin' with a stranger in the middle of the road. That the *smartest* thing he could do would be to throw the Fairlane into reverse, hightail it back down the way he'd just come, and take another section-line road to the hardtop.

But Billie's mouth wasn't nearly as smart as his brain. "It's fast," he heard himself say smugly.

"I *heard*," the stranger continued, "That you're the fastest driver in the county."

Billie's mouth was really, really stupid tonight. "I am," he heard himself say even as he considered punching himself in the face to get himself to stop. "Ain't nobody faster."

The stranger nodded, as if all this was exactly what he expected to hear. "Well then. Are you prepared to prove how fast you and that piece of American iron are? Because last I saw, me and my girl were the fastest in three states, and I intend to make it four."

Now that made Billie Ray angry, and when he was angry, as his ma had pointed out to him time and time again, his temper burned up every bit of brains he had. "Now look here, mister, you might be *fast* on blacktop an' straight roads, but you ain't really *fast* lessin' y'all're fast on roads like you ain't likely ever seen afore—"

"Sounds to me as if you're inviting me to a race," the stranger said, smoothly, with just a hint of… challenge.

And Billie Ray was not the man to let a challenge pass unanswered. "Reckon I am," he replied, his chin stuck out belligerently.

"That was what I was hoping to hear," the stranger said with deep satisfaction. "Let's make it interesting. Here to the county line. If you win—you get this—" and he patted the fender of his machine.

Now, Billie Ray was no stranger to avarice. He'd lusted after the Fairlane ever since the model came out, and it had taken him a lot of runs to pay for her and her modifications, even after getting the "special price" from the dealer that all his boss's runners got. But just the *curves* of the stranger's beauty made that desire seem like a grade-school crush. Whereas this was the lust of a man for a red-hot woman. He

wanted that car, as he had never wanted anything in his life. Already in his mind he was boring her cylinders, mounting a supercharger….

But there was one, tiny little bit of reason left in his brain, just enough to choke out, "And what if I lose?"

"We'll talk about that at the end of the race," the stranger laughed. "Don't worry. It won't be anything you can't afford. In fact, you probably won't even miss it."

Well, the stranger must have been insane, but then, foreigners generally were. A lot of the men of the mountains had come home from the Big War with stories about those crazy French, Italians and English—

So long as he wasn't betting the Fairlane, he didn't care in the state he was in—half angry at the condescending tone of the stranger, half on fire at the challenge. He backed up the Fairlane to the treeline and slowly got her pointed in the right direction. The stranger's maneuvering was more graceful, a smooth curve of a backward turn that came within a hair of the Fairlane's bumper without ever touching it, and put him door to door to Billie Ray.

The driver revved his engine. It had a throat like nothing Billie Ray had ever heard before: a deep, throbbing rumble, deeper than the Fairlane. Not a growl, not a howl, but still something primal. A roar. A jungle roar.

It put the hair up on the back of his neck, and for the first time, he felt a sense of warning….

But it was too late to do anything about it now.

"You count it off!" the stranger shouted through his open window to Billie Ray.

That was an invitation to cheat, to jump the gun. The stranger was taking the measure of him.

Well, Billie Ray was going to measure up as a man. He might be doing something he could go to jail for in order to make a living, but he never had cheated in his life, and he never would.

"*On your mark!*" he shouted, one foot on the gas and the other on the brake. "*Get set! GO!*"

There was not a second's worth of difference between them as the two cars leapt forward into the night.

Now…racing like this was taking a calculated risk. Whether or not someone tried to arrest them both depended largely on who was prowling the night tonight. If it was treasury, revenuers—they'd see two fast cars out neck and neck and figure no way either of them was carrying shine. The extra weight of all those gallons of liquid alone was going to handicap a vehicle and if there was a crash, the very last thing you wanted was a car soaked in alcohol about to catch fire. If it was state troopers—now they might take an interest in stopping the race and arresting them both for speeding. If it was local cops—they knew Billie Ray's Fairlane, and while they surely knew he was a runner, they'd never actually *caught* him, and in a case like this one, seeing him pitted against a furriner and a strange car…it would be a case of letting Billie Ray uphold the honor of the county and show that outsider just who ruled the roads hereabouts. Why, they might even use their new radios to make sure the road stayed clear, once they figured out the route.

And tonight was a damp, cold, foggy night. Hard to see. Hard to navigate if you didn't know the roads like someone born and raised in one of these hollers. He'd bet that if there was anyone out looking for 'shine runners, it would be the local boys.

They were "running by the treeline," as one of the other 'shine-runners said. If you asked someone, they'd say this was a two-lane road, but that only meant there was enough room for two cars to get out of the way of each other and not end up hung up in the brush. The right side of the Fairlane was getting beat to death with twigs, but that wouldn't be as bad as it was for the stranger, who'd be getting his driver's side whupped. There wasn't more than five inches between them, and they were door-handle to door-handle, two sets of headlights lighting up the whole road as they bounced over the uneven surface.

At least it wasn't washboard here. And at least it was as straight as an arrow.

Billie Ray was planning ahead, far ahead. He knew where this road came out onto the two-lane blacktop, and of all things, he wanted to be ahead and *stay* ahead on the blacktop as far as Cherokee Mountain. It didn't matter if he was only a few inches ahead; he needed to be on the inside of the road when it hit the mountainside. Because there were no guardrails on Cherokee Mountain, and not a lot of verge, and the inside lane was the only safe place to be.

If he could hold onto his lead up to the mountain, he'd keep it when the road started climbing.

Unless the stranger was crazy…or crazy-good.

Or completely without fear which it was looking very like he *was*.

Any sound was drowned out by the song of the two engines, the howl of the Fairlane and the guttural roar of the stranger's machine. He glanced over at the car that was pacing him as if the two vehicles were Siamese twins, and barely made out the stranger in the headlight wash, Stetson still pulled low down on his forehead, hands on the top of the wheel, staring intently ahead.

Billie Ray didn't dare to more than glance, just enough to get a fleeting impression. Even though the road was straight, there were plenty of hazards. Any one of the bumps could throw the Fairlane into the stranger's car, or vice versa. Deer could jump out onto the road. Hell, at the speeds they were going, a rabbit could make one of them skid into the other.

And the blacktop was coming up—

He sensed it, then oh-so-briefly recognized it, the darkness that meant the trees were gone, and he swung the wheel more on instinct and knowing the road in his gut than by anything he actually saw. The Fairlane's tubeless tires shrieked as they hit the surface and skidded before digging in and Billie was thrown to the side by the force of the turn, holding onto control by his nails and teeth. The tires bit into the asphalt, and the Fairlane howled away, and—

And that *damned* black machine was right there with him, as if it was glued to him! She was a little behind him, her headlights just about even with where he sat, but a moment later she was back, side by side, the two of them racing down the two-lane blacktop as if they owned it.

The blacktop road wasn't straight; it swerved and jinked around the bottom of the valley, following the contours of Higgins Crick. Billie Ray had never powered down this road, this fast, at night. This was white-knuckle driving, and there was one thing of paramount importance. He absolutely had to be in the lead by at least a little at the point where the stranger realized they were going up the face of the mountain. He had to have the inside lane on the mountain. Taking the outside at this speed—

Well, there were stories about that, and they generally ended in a pile of twisted metal.

He had both windows down, and the air was thick with the scent of cold, fresh water and green river weeds. He glanced out of the side of his eye at the stranger. They were so close he could have reached out and yanked on the stranger's doorhandle. The stranger was nothing but a dark silhouette against the headlight wash of the blur that was the forest on his side of the road.

He was waiting for something only he, or someone who knew this road as well as he did, would know. And there it came—the scent of pine. There was going to be a dip and a rise, and anyone who wasn't ready for it would automatically pull back on the gas.

He hit the dip and jammed the pedal to the floor, the Fairlane actually taking to the air over the rise. The stranger dropped back almost a full car-length; Billie kept his foot down.

But the stranger wasn't surrendering; not with plenty of miles between here and the county line. Slowly the stranger's car crept up, somehow gaining what he'd lost an inch at a time. At the point where Billie Ray felt the road starting to rise, climbing away from the crick and starting the climb up the side of the mountain, the stranger's hood was even with his door again. But that was enough.

He found a little more pedal, and a little more acceleration. As he began to pull ahead again, he glanced back.

And the hair on the back of his neck stood straight up.

Glaring at him through the windshield where the driver would be was a pair of hell-hot, glowing green orbs.

And that was when he finally came to his senses; when he recognized what he should have figured out a good long time ago. Like, back at the crossroads, when the stranger talked about wagers, and offered to bet his car, a car of a sort Billie Ray had never laid eyes on even in pictures.

The stranger wasn't…human.

Billie Ray was racing with the Devil.

As his body wrenched and hauled on the steering wheel, sending his car thundering up the mountain road, his mind was moving almost as fast in a panic. The stranger had dropped back, seeing the wisdom of not taking the outside lane when there was nowhere to go if you encountered another car in the outside lane, and the danger of skidding off if you lost even a little control or hitting a patch of the stones that were always coming down off the rock-face. But when Billie Ray looked up to his rearview, he could see them, faintly, through the headlight-glare. Those eyes, those inhuman eyes, green and glowing.

Billie Ray's granny'd had a great store of tales about the Devil. Tales, and songs too. Little Billie had listened avidly, and a good thing he had, too, because somewhere in all those stories and songs was the key to getting him out of this mess. Or so he was praying.

Not that praying was going to do him any good right now. Billie's granny had been very clear on something in her tales. God wasn't going to be hornswoggled by a last-minute repentance and pleas for mercy. God was like Granny. *"You made that there bed, you're a-gonna lie in it."* It was one thing for a good man to be tricked by the Devil; God would take pity on such, and send him help. But a bad man would have to get his own self out of the mess. And Billie Ray knew he was a bad man.

Not so much because of the 'shine running. That might be against man's law, but it was a plain, bad law that had no reason to exist except to enrich some men at the expense of common folks. There hadn't even been such a law until Prohibition, but then after, the Revenuers had figured out there was a lot of money to be made for the government by keeping the likker-making in the hands of a few and taxing the hell out of it. That was greed, and sin, in and of itself, to deny a man the ability to take his own corn from his own land and do what he wanted with it.

No, it was because Billie had done more than his fair share of sinning for all that he was a young'un. Cussin' and lyin', getting drunk and not just having a drink or two, fornicatin'…and he'd had lust for the stranger's car, which was right against the Commandments, lusting after what your neighbor had. No, he was a bad man, and God was going to be no help to him.

So what he needed was cleverness.

Some of Granny's stories had been new, or at least came from this side of the ocean, but a lot had been old, going all the way back to the family roots in

English soil. And the one he could remember now was the one that he'd acted out to the amusement of *his* ma and pa, singing out the lines for the clever lad, while Granny sang the ones for Old Scratch. *"Never nohow call him by his name,"* she'd warned. *"Or he'll come, soon or late, he'll come!"* Well, Billie had called out that name often enough…and here was proof that Granny was right.

He was driving this road on pure instinct, relying on the memory of a couple hundred such runs to tell him *where* to hit the brakes and crank the wheel over a fraction of a second before the next hairpin turn came into view. And the stranger was still right on his tail, headlights burning furiously through the rear glass, green eyes glaring through the light-haze.

"The False Knight on the Road"

In the song, like now, the Devil had appeared in disguise, in the guise of a man of wealth and status. He'd confronted a little boy—probably a very naughty little boy, since God hadn't sent an angel with a flaming sword to drive Old Scratch away—but a clever little boy. Billie hauled the wheel around another turn and searched the song for a way out of his predicament.

> *"Oh where are ye going?"*
> *said the False Knight on the road.*
> *"I'm goin' to my school,"*
> *said the wee boy and still he stood.*
> *"And what is on yer back?"*
> *said the False Knight on the road.*
> *"Me bundles and me books,"*
> *said the wee boy and still he stood.*

All right what did that tell him? What had Granny said? The wee boy showed courage, standing right up to the Devil. But not lying. Lying would have given the Devil leave to snatch him up on the instant. And he wasn't insolent; insolence wouldn't have let the Devil *take* him, but you didn't anger the Devil, for he might well kill you. God would have your soul, but that wasn't a great consolation if you were dead.

> *"What sheep and cattle's them?"*
> *said the False Knight on the road.*
> *"They're mine and me father's,"*
> *said the wee boy and still he stood.*

> *"How many of 'em's mine?"*
> *said the False Knight on the road.*
> *"As many's got blue tails,"*
> *said the wee boy and still he stood.*

He was sweating with fear and his heart was pounding along with the throbbing engine. Granny had explained that one. If the boy had said "none," that would have given the Devil a pretext to find one or more sheep that "could" belong to him—a ram with curled horns, maybe, or a black sheep. That would prove the boy a liar and forfeit his soul. But by setting a condition, the boy had bested him. And that made him angry, and *that* kicked off the dangerous part of the song, where the boy had to counter every curse the Devil threw at him, and throw it back.

> *"I wish you were in yonder tree!"*
> *said the False Knight on the road.*
> *"A ladder under me,"*
> *said the wee boy and still he stood.*
> *"The ladder it would break!"*
> *said the False Knight on the road.*
> *"And you would surely fall!"*
> *said the wee boy and still he stood.*
> *"I wish you were in yonder sea!"*
> *said the False Knight on the road.*
> *"A good boat under me!"*
> *said the wee boy and still he stood.*
> *"The boat would surely sink!"*
> *said the False Knight on the road.*
> *"And you would surely drown!"*
> *said the wee boy and still he stood.*
> *"Has your mother more than you?"*
> *said the False Knight on the road.*
> *"They're none of 'em for you,"*
> *said the wee boy and still he stood.*

And there the clever boy even diverted the harm from his siblings.

> *"I think I hear a bell!"*
> *said the False Knight on the road.*

That would be the death knell—the Devil had lost patience, and if he could not have the boy's soul, then he would have his life!

But the boy knew the answer to that—

"Aye, it's ringin' ye to hell!"
said the wee boy, and still he stood.

Turning it from a death knell to a church bell. And that—that was it! No demon nor the Devil himself could stand against a church bell, and it was, by the feel of the air and the finely-tuned time sense Billie had honed over many, many trips, close to midnight. If he lost the race—if he lost the race—if he could just keep the Devil talking until the church bells from Holy Grace Baptist rang up from the valley, he'd be saved.

Now, if he could get up this mountain and win the race, he had nothing to fear. And he was close, close to the top, for the road had started to narrow still further, to the point where cars approaching each other at this part of the road would stop and inch forward, door handles actually scraping, to get past each other. Surely not even the Devil would chance trying to pass here, at the speeds they were going. His heart started pounding, and not with fear, but with triumph. He was going to win! He was going to win!

And then he heard it.

Behind him, a new note rose in the throat of the great black beast that the Devil was driving. The howl rose to a scream, and with a scant five hundred yards to the top and a thousand to the county line, the sleek machine accelerated like nothing Billie Ray had ever seen before, *tore* past him on a lane that could not have been more than three-fourths of a proper lane wide, and shoved itself in front of him so quickly he had to brake to avoid ramming it—

And then, to add insult to injury and shame to it all, the red taillights ran off up the road and out of sight so fast you would have thought the beast was powered by rockets and not by an engine at all.

Of course it's not powered by an engine, Billie thought with his stomach in knots and his mind in a whirl. *Or at least, it ain't an engine that any man's hand was in the building of.*

For one brief moment, as he made the last turn and headed for the county line, he hoped that the Devil had got so far in front of him that he might could make a run for it.

But no.

There he was, the bastard, his sleek car parked square across the road, blocking it, right on the other side of the county border. And him leaning up against it, hat still pulled down over his face.

Billie rolled up slowly, and turned off his engine. Just as slowly, and wracked with terror, he got out of the car. From the Fairlane came the tick-tick-tick of cooling metal. From the stranger's car…nothing.

How far was it to midnight?

"Well," said the Devil. "There's the little matter of the bet."

"Aight," Billie agreed, sweating. *How to turn that against him?* There was nothing there to use! *How to keep him talking?*

But the Devil was already talking. "I'll have what's under the front seat of your Ford Fairlane, Billy Ray," he said, with a hint of laughter in his voice. "And don't you trouble to tell me there ain't nothing there. There's six old-style bottles there, all wrapped in flour-sack towels and corked with their tops waxed, all full of *proper* corn whiskey, made from 'shine from a clean, clean still, all good copper and no lead solder about it, and aged in charred oak barrels, and I'll be having them all."

Billie almost fainted with relief.

He hardly knew how he managed to get the passenger door open. His hands shook so much getting out the "special" bottles that it was a wonder he didn't drop them. He didn't even stammer thanks when the stranger gave him six flour-sack towels full of broken glass to stick back under there, and give him the excuse for why those special bottles of real whiskey weren't there no more.

All that he could really do, when the stranger had pulled the car far enough off the road that he could get by, was put the pedal to the floor and speed away.…

✧

"Great Harry's Ghost, did you see his *face*?" howled Dylan ap Dai, throwing the Stetson onto the head of what was now a stunning black horse and exposing his pointed ears as the wind at the top of the mountain blew back his hair.

"Aye, that I did, ye daft bugger," said his cousin Caradoc, coming out of the woods at the side of the road, followed by his own mount, a silver stallion.

"Poor lad, he thought you were the Devil! Shame on you, for putting such a fright into the boy!"

"Well the shame's on him for carrying such a delectable cargo I couldn't resist the challenge!" Dylan retorted, and twirled his finger around the top of one of the bottles that hadn't made it into his elven-steed's saddlebags. The wax obligingly peeled off and the cork extracted itself and Dylan took a pull of the bottle. "Oh aye…" he sighed. "There's the sweet dew of the mountain…here, taste that and see if it was worth a challenge."

He handed the bottle to his cousin, who took it, exposing the badge of Elfhame Fairgrove on his chest. Caradoc took a considering sip, his eyebrow rose, and he took as deep a draught as Dylan had. "Why is't yon mortals can make such delectables and we not?"

Dylan shrugged. "And what d'ye think of yon challenge-race?" he demanded, taking the bottle back and having another mouthful. "I think we've found us a new sport."

"Safer than a challenge-joust, for certain sure." Caradoc claimed the bottle, and pondered over his second drink. "I reck me Lord Keighvin Silverhair will find it as tasty as he finds this drink."

"Then we've two prizes to carry home, sweet cuz!" Dylan laughed, and slapped his fellow elf on the shoulder. "So, let's hi us hence, and give him the winnings and the word!"

A moment later, two sleek sports cars, one silver, one black, sped away along a road that, until a moment before, had not been there. Then the trees swallowed them up, and they were gone.

Copyright © 2014 by Mercedes Lackey

Jean-Claude Dunyach is one of the leading science fiction writers in France. He is the author of eight novels and nine collections, and has won the Prix Ozone, the Prix Rosny-Aîne, the Prix de l'Imaginaire, and the Eiffel Tower Award. He also writes lyrics for a number of French singers. This is his third appearance in Galaxy's Edge. The following piece won the Prix Imaginale 2017.

WITH A WINK OF THE HERON'S EYE

by Jean-Claude Dunyach

He saw her stumble, in slow motion, and lean against the flower merchant's window. The shopping gallery at the Schiphol airport had been invaded by the usual hustle and bustle of hurried travelers. No one paid any attention to her. When she stood up, a silver tear slipped from her ear, down her blonde hair before bouncing off her shoulder. He watched it, noting every detail, and headed over toward her at a leisurely pace. When he got to where she had been standing, he bent down and picked the earring up off the ground. Then he stood up and glanced about, looking for her, but she had already disappeared, swallowed up in the crowd.

He closed his fist and felt the piece of metal jewelry dig gently into his palm. The boarding gate for Djakarta was located at the other end of the terminal. Suddenly, it seemed inaccessible to him. He headed toward one of the train station entrances, then changed his mind. With a shrug, he straightened his travel bag with its many pockets and headed for the taxis.

✧

The driver dropped him off near Leidzeplein. Workers had started tearing up the small street that led to his usual hotel. Among the heaps of stones on the roadway, he caught a glimpse of a small strip of bone-colored sand. Seized by impulse, he crossed over the protective barrier and took a few steps on the secret beach in the heart of the city. Fossil shells crunched under his polished shoes. Eyes closed, he sniffed toward the east and felt the first drops of rain caress his lips.

As he reached the front steps of the hotel he heard a woman's voice swear in French behind him. The contrast between the voice, rich and harmonious, and the curse was striking. He turned around slowly. She was pulling an enormous black canvas suitcase and the wheels kept getting caught between the uneven cobblestones. The storm threatened to transform her blonde hair into something unacceptable. He smiled at her as he reached out his hand.

"Let me help you. Amsterdam is fiercely unsuitable for luggage such as yours."

"I've seen worse," she said, automatically wiping her eyes. "You're staying at this hotel?"

"If they have a room…" (He grabbed the handle of the suitcase and effortlessly carried it to the top of the steps). "They know me and I hope they'll find something for me."

He rolled the suitcase to the reception counter that was stuck in a room built all in length, and then courteously stepped back to allow her to speak with the employee there first. Then he adjusted his bag and discretely walked off. Things were going faster than expected and he would, in all likelihood, have no need to book a room.

The rain swallowed him up without a sound.

✧

He walked, nose turned to the wind, along the Spiegel canal. It had stopped raining, but the air remained oily under his tongue, laden with the stench of the port and the memory of cut flowers that had been carried on carts for centuries. On each side of the canal, shops down below offered countless marvels: silverware, works of art, maps and portolan charts. He glanced at them quickly, without lingering. He felt nervous, impatient. At the bottom of his pocket, the earring felt very heavy, weighing his step down more than usual.

He heard a familiar staccato on the slippery sidewalk nearby. An old heron with shiny feathers was moving away from the canal with its high-stepping gait to a destination known only to it. He watched it and stood right in the middle of the street to block the half dozen bicycles arriving from the museum. The heron crossed slowly, beak down as if looking for a place to plant it between two cobblestones, then

the bikes continued on their way with the grinding of metal. A bell rang out joyfully close by and he nodded in return.

The heron looked at him gravely. Its round eyes, filled with liquid light, blinked several times. Then the bird spread its wings and heavily took flight.

When the traveler reached the South American antique store, he felt eyes resting on his shoulders, but did not turn around. In the midst of the reflections on the window, he recognized the woman from the hotel, accompanied by an almost identical version of herself. They stood very close to one another, twin sisters rather than lovers, and were consulting a tourist guide, pages fluttering in the wind.

He allowed his eyes to wander inside the shop filled with parchments and old maps stretched on racks. The sun that played among the clouds drew fleeting trails toward Atlantis, Eldorado, the kingdom of Saba. He would have liked to stand in front of the window forever and learn all of the world's secret roads. But everything in Amsterdam encouraged him to move. He turned around and walked quickly back to the heart of the city.

✧

The aisle at the flower market smelled of fresh humus and mayonnaise. A family walked noisily past him, armed with cones of fries drowned in gravy. Overhead, the off-kilter rooftops formed a ragged skyline against the gray backdrop of the sky. He felt as if he could simply reach up and tear off a ribbon of roughly pinked clouds. Someone bumped into him gently and he felt a hand slip into his bag. He forced himself not to look down when expert fingers searched desperately for something to steal in the heap of multi-colored scarves and magic rings. Then he pulled on the strap and walked off, catching sight of tulips with bent necks and bags of all kinds of bulbs stacked in stalls.

His tenderness for the city was gradually awakening. Everything here suited him, from the trompe-l'œil styles of the narrow facades to the clap-trap of the strident neons that had colonized the entire center. He walked in the shadow of the belfry, and then headed over to Place Rembrandt. Inevitably.

They were sitting on a terrace, holding hands. He allowed the human tide to carry him to them, noting every detail. When he was close enough, he smiled at them and slowed just enough for his bag to swing over their table, dangerously close to the glasses of gin and tonic standing side by side.

"Were you able to get a room?" the older one asked.

"Still waiting. You?"

"My sister handled the reservations. We saw you with the heron. Quite entertaining. Well, I mean unusual."

"Not for people here. The birds were here before them."

He turned part way to look at the younger one, trying to read the lines of a possible story in her features. She held his gaze distractedly before plunging back into her glass and finishing it with a single gulp. The ice cubes tinkled when she put it back down on the table.

"Excuse me for being indiscrete, but you don't seem well."

"My sister is trying to forget an unpleasant divorce," interrupted the older one. "Moreover…"

"Don't be ridiculous!" (The younger woman shrugged.) "That was over three years ago and I'd like people to stop reminding me about it every five minutes. No, the truth is that I lost my earring." (With an abrupt tug, she brushed aside a lock of golden hair, streaked with a touch of gray that covered her left ear lobe.) "It's stupid, but my sister gave them to me and we don't see one another often, so I wanted to wear them specifically for this occasion. This is our first vacation together since…I don't even know how long anymore."

"I'll give you others," her sister interrupted. "It's not important."

"I wouldn't say that if I were you." (He bent over the younger one and examined her ear.) "Earrings like this are very indiscrete. They hear everything you say and, generally, they remember it all. It would be better to find it. This happened recently?"

"Yes, but I don't know where and I don't even know if they have a lost and found here. Supposing that someone brings it in, which I doubt. It was gold."

"It's easier than that, fortunately." (He took on a concentrated expression and plunged his hand into his bag before placing it over the empty glass.) But I warn you, this might hurt a little… Ready?"

Without waiting for an answer, he touched the exposed ear lobe with his fingers. The young woman felt a pinch, followed by a cold sensation.

"What are you…" she yelped in indignation.

He opened his hand. An earring sparkled wetly in the palm of his hand. A drop of blood pearled on the stud.

"I wouldn't put it on right away if I were you. It's icy and you might well lose it again."

Around them, the crowd of tourists appeared to freeze, then flashes burst behind him. A bride, looking like an enormous meringue, was posing in the middle of the tables. He turned back to the older one and winked at her broadly.

"How did you do that?" asked the younger woman. (She grabbed the earring feverishly and held it up to the light.) "This is it. Where did you find it?"

"I'm a magician…"

"And you never reveal your tricks. Is that it?" (The older one clapped her hands, dryly two or three times.) "It was well done in any case. My congratulations."

"You're insulting me, you know. I'm a *real* magician, not an illusionist."

"Tell me all about it. I'm certain your explanation will be more interesting than this little sleight of hand. I'll buy you a drink in return."

"Only if you allow me to invite you both to dinner." (He raised his hands to cut off any protest.) "I know a restaurant that's not in any tourist guide, not far from the hotel. You can get antipasti and pasta there. Neither is particularly good. An extraordinary place."

"Really?" (She smiled and it was as if the sun were rising a second time.) "When you put it like that, it's hard to refuse. Mediocre pasta, hmmm. But we'll pay our own way, my sister and I. And I really want to hear your explanation."

"Simple." (He walked around the table, pulled out a chair and sat down between them. At the other end of the terrace, the bride was spinning about to laughter and applause.) "It goes back centuries, to the time when Amsterdam was just a simple fishing village built on swamps. The geography of the sand banks and the lagoons changed with every tide, or almost. Frequently, the inhabitants had to re-build their homes when they were swallowed up by sand or the sea. So one man, a little more ambitious than the others, came up with the idea of building a dike in order to mold the currents to his will. In the sand, he planted a gigantic stake made of an entire tree trunk circled with iron, then another, and then yet another, until the soil became stable enough to build a house that would last for centuries.

"That's both the charm and the curse of this city. It's nailed to the ground by thousands of needles. Nothing ever gets lost. I…" (A smile made his eyes sparkle.) "I merely listened to your memories and went to find the lost earring in a recent past when it was still hooked on your ear. I brought back a little pain as well—the past is an icy place—but I didn't need to travel back too far in time. See? It's as simple as that."

The younger sister nodded, never taking her eyes from him. Between her fingers, the earring flashed one final time before she closed her fist over it.

"Well done," said the older sister. "We'll meet in the hotel lobby at seven this evening? I'll leave the reservations to you."

He stood up, nodded, and clasped his bag against his thigh. He felt strangely tired. Recovering the earring had given him a jolt of pure adrenaline, and coming down would take a long time.

"Wait…" The younger blushed, then said, "This is our first time in Amsterdam. What do you recommend we see first?"

He smiled briefly and flicked the guide she held out to him closed.

"Learn to get lost instead."

✧

Under the veiled sunset, the city spread in a gray and watery green infinity, highlighted with fleeting streaks of pink. It was time for hesitations. He had spent most of the afternoon changing his airline ticket and had not had enough time to walk on the lumpy skin of the streets as much as he would have liked. Along his way, he purchased a bag of chocolates of many flavors—ginger, pepper, thyme—and had munched on them while standing above a canal, seeking his own tracks in the blurry reflection of the waves. The passersby had respected his solitude, punctuating his thoughts with the tinkle of silvery bells.

The two sisters were waiting for him in the hotel lobby. They stopped talking when he entered and he

guessed that they'd been discussing him. The second earring had found its place and the younger sister had lined her eyes with makeup. The other woman's face was bare.

He guided them along Neu Spiegel, toward the heart of the city, listening to their enthusiastic descriptions of sites he knew like the back of his hand. He divided his attention among them, equitably. His fatigue had faded; he felt obscurely ready for what was to come and what he had had no hand in determining. He settled for being there, in the center of the vortex of events that had drawn him up in the airport and spit him back out here.

The restaurant was in the basement and opened onto street level by means of a few steep steps that he walked down cautiously. His knee was starting to bother him again; one day, he would certainly need help crossing the street before being able to take flight.

The room was divided into two: the first part looked onto the kitchens and the second was partially filled by a grand piano with the top up. Clay plates with blue designs filled with Italian hors d'œuvres were arranged on a special shelf over the strings. A pianist was playing quietly. A waitress in dance tights and a sequined top seated them in a corner with a basket of breadsticks, menus in four languages, and a carafe of coarse red wine.

"We start with the antipasti buffet, and then we choose our pasta and a dessert." (He unwrapped a breadstick and bit into it, making it crunch.) "Avoid everything that comes from the oven, it's always overcooked. And don't wait to help yourselves. Soon it will be time."

"Time for what?" asked the older one, folding her menu.

She'd selected what she wanted from the list with a single glance; he imagined she would not take dessert.

He placed a finger on his lips and stood up. The younger one joined him next to the piano. Side by side, they filled their plates. With her fork, she chased a purple artichoke around the plate and blushed when she noticed him watching her. Her perfume mingled with the scent of vinegar and garlic that rose from the hors d'œuvres. Now that she'd found her earring, she seemed drabber.

The pianist allowed his melody to fade and played a series of chords, like a signal.

"Your sister is going to have to wait," he murmured. "I wonder why she doesn't like me."

"She doesn't believe in you."

She seemed to realize what she had just said and looked down at her plate, studded with spots of oil and diced vegetables. He grimaced in resignation.

"Stop looking at those artichokes with regret like that and come and sit down. You can come back later if you're still hungry."

He'd had barely enough time to push back his chair when the young waitress asked for silence. The lights lowered, the pianist started to play again, barely brushing the keys. The music rolled around them. *Strauss…*

The waitress opened her mouth and started to sing.

The marvelously rich voice found the melody effortlessly and echoed off the walls of the small room. Eyes closed, hands clasped over her bosom, she sang of love and the death of desire with an intensity that made her tremble. It was not the polished interpretation of a diva on a stage covered with velvet, but the song of someone who would come back later to serve wine and remove dirty plates. Hanging at her waist, the notebook she used to take orders shook every time she took a breath.

She bowed when the song came to an end and headed back to the kitchens, followed by the guests' applause. Chairs scraped against the stone floor and a line formed in front of the piano.

"I understand why the pasta is always overcooked," said the older sister. "I owe you an apology. I took you for an ordinary flirt while you're certainly more than that."

"Do you want to share my antipasti?"

"I'm not sure I have much of an appetite after that. I'm a musician, you know. A pianist. You can't imagine what I've just experienced."

He held her gaze for a long moment and murmured, "One day, I wanted to know myself. Girls like her study singing in Concertgebouw and earn barely enough here to pay their teachers. They generally don't stay for more than a few months. It's very hard working until midnight six days a week while singing all day long. There's a constant turnover in voices…"

"I preferred your previous explanation," said the younger woman. (She touched her earring, flirting.) "How did you discover this place?"

"That's a secret."

He trapped a tomato confit with his fork and added, "But you don't have to believe me."

There was another recital during dessert, then the traditional round of grappa offered by the boss. He paid the bill while they took their time in the washroom and held their raincoats for them at the foot of the steps.

"Do you want to go back to the hotel right away?" he asked. "It's not raining and I'm sure were might even be able to catch sight of a star or two. For Amsterdam, this is as close as it gets to good weather."

"We're supposed to go to bed early," said the younger sister, voice tinged with regret. "We're leaving for Rotterdam tomorrow."

"So allow me to show you a place I like a lot. It's on the way, next to the large casino, quite close to the hotel. You may have walked past it without seeing it."

He pulled up the collar of his leather jacket and headed down the street, one step ahead of her. In the sleeping shops on each side, pale blue night-lights outlined the potbellied shapes of Dutch furniture. In the distance, he heard the hoarse croak of a heron and the clank of a tram. He felt melancholy wash over him without knowing why. The sensation was pleasant, as long as it was shared.

"It's here. Wait a bit and you'll see them appear."

The tiny square was actually a triangle, surrounded by a wood barrier a few centimeters high. In the absence of light, the grass was dark, dotted with tiny puddles that shone like eyes.

Gray shapes, as large as rats, gradually emerged from the grass. As their eyes grew used to the darkness, the details grew clearer. They were metal statues, possibly twenty or so, carefully engraved.

"I present to you the varans of Amsterdam. They don't look much like that, but when they're covered with snow, they're quite fascinating."

"Can I go closer to them?"

"That's prohibited. And most likely disappointing. I've never wanted to get close to them. It's all a question of lighting, in fact."

"Like many things that concern you, Mr. Magician." (The older woman firmly took her sister by the arm and prevented her from stepping over the wooden barrier.) "You said that the hotel was nearby?"

"On the other side of Leidseplein."

✿

Almost all of the cobblestones had been removed from the alley. The sandbank shone like a shard of bone under the white neons of the hotel. The older sister had unconsciously slowed her pace, as if unsure of the complicated choreography that would have to be played out at the top of the steps. He allowed her to walk ahead of him and stopped on the bottom step when she blocked his way.

"I'll join you in five minutes," she told her sister. "If they're still serving tea at this late hour will you order me one?"

Then she took him by the arm and pulled him along a few meters, her heels sunk in the sand like tiny nails.

"How did you do it?" she said after a long silence that he didn't bother to break. "I designed those earrings myself; they're unique pieces."

"My story didn't convince you?"

A veil of darkness flitted briefly over his face. He dispelled it with a broad smile.

"I don't need magic to find an explanation," she argued.

"Let's see if I can give you one you find more acceptable."

He bent down and stacked a few cobblestones to make a miniature table and pointed at it.

"Your sister was there. I bent over her and looked straight into her eyes to keep her from taking an interest in what I was doing. I took an ice cube from her glass, then pinched her ear between my thumb and index finger while pressing the ice cube with the palm of my hand. Pain, followed by cold."

"And the earring?"

"Your sister lost it at the airport. I was a few meters away and I picked it up, but she had disappeared by the time I stood back up. When I saw her with you,

I recognized her and I wanted…I don't know what I wanted. To play, perhaps."

He picked up a handful of sand and let it slip through his fingers. A tiny shell stuck to his fingertip.

"There's no such thing as magic," she murmured.

"Magic doesn't exist. That's true. But it can be created. It takes a great deal of energy and time for a result that varies from one person to the next." (His eyes clouded over, growing as dark as the water in the canal in an instant.) "If I give you this shell that I've just picked up, will you have the courage to wear it on your ear? It will tell you what you need to hear, whether that pleases you or not." (She moved imperceptibly back.) "Magic is choosing the dream in which you want to wake up. It's something that you can learn."

"I've never needed magic. Or wanted it."

"I know…. Are you going to tell your sister what I've told you?"

"I've always tried to protect her from liars and people who make up lovely stories for her. I failed with her rotten husband, but that won't happen again!"

She frowned, disenchantment ruining the polished perfection of her features. At that moment, he found her touching. Not beautiful, but attractive, desirable like people who truly exist are. He felt like embracing her, knowing that it was already too late for that.

"In any case," she concluded, "What I decide to tell my sister is none of your business."

"True. Do you want to go in? I believe that I'll walk for a bit…"

She nodded reluctantly and turned away.

"Thank you for the restaurant," she said before walking off. "Whether you believe it or not, I've had an unforgettable evening."

✿

He watched her walk into the hotel and disappear behind the glass door. With a sigh, he raised the shell to his ear and listened, eyes half closed. Determined footsteps, the clinking of cups against saucers, then the voice of the young woman, questioning, and that of her sister, answering.

"I have something to tell you…"

The moisture-laden wind caressed her cheeks as she faithfully repeated everything he had just told her, concluding with, "I know that he's disturbing, for an illusionist, but…"

"I didn't come from the airport," the younger one interrupted. "I took the train."

"How?"

"I was in Brussels. I came by the TGV and I thought I might have lost my earring last evening. What he told you is a lie!"

"That's what I wanted to tell you, but…"

They started to quarrel, two opposing visions of the world that would never in all likelihood ever be reconciled. Yet, perhaps the older one would learn to doubt. That was the best he could hope for, the reason he had gone out of his way to come here. He cautiously placed the shell back in the sand and walked off calmly, his bag hitting his flanks with every step.

☼

He walked toward the casino's lights without turning back. There were still some taxis stopped at the corner of the boulevard and his plane took off in two hours. When he slipped his hand into his pocket, he felt the silver earring he had picked up that morning at the airport. With a melancholy smile, he brandished it in front of his eyes and watched how it caught the light from the passing headlights. Then he walked over to the canal and slipped it into a crevice in the stone guardrail. One day, when the sun struck it at the right angle, someone would find it. Someone who would know how to look at it, what to do with it. The story no longer belonged to him.

Copyright © Jean-Claude Dunyach 2009.
Translated by Sheryl Curtis

Daniel J. Davis *has appeared in* Alien Artifacts, Writers of the Future #31, Funny Horror, UFO 5, *and other anthologies. This is his first appearance in* Galaxy's Edge.

PILOT PROGRAM

by Daniel J. Davis

"There's some men here with a truck. They say they've got a delivery. Should I go ahead and let them in?"

Jonathan Hale stared down at the tabla-phone. Mrs. Drinkwater's tired face looked up from the grainy display screen.

"A delivery?" he asked.

She rolled her eyes and sighed at him. A lock of hair came untangled from the messy gray bun on top of her head. "That's what I just said. Look, am I letting them in or not? I wasn't told about this."

Jon wasn't told about it either. He tried to imagine who it could be.

"Well?"

"Fine. Let them in." It didn't really matter if it was a scam, he decided. It wasn't like he had anything in the apartment they could steal. Hell, maybe he'd get lucky. Maybe they'd drop a crowbar or something else valuable enough to pawn.

Mrs. Drinkwater punched a button on her end. A Filmore Realty release form came up on screen. "Initial here and press your thumb to the pad. You hereby authorize me to grant a third party access to your apartment." There was a long but not-quite empty pause as Jon signed and gave his thumbprint. "Next time, tell me when you're expecting a delivery."

Jon knew it was pointless to argue. He mumbled some affirmative and hung up with Mrs. Drinkwater. He put the tabla-phone back in his pack, and wheeled his ancient, manual-powered wheelchair to the handicapped levi-tube. His cigarette break was almost over, and he'd already wasted most of it talking to his landlord. He only had a few minutes left to get down to the smoking area.

He swore under his breath. Whatever they were leaving him, he thought, it had better be worth it.

☼

The old, broken motorchair was still in the corner of Jon's apartment, right where it had been for the last thirteen years. It was the very last thing Jon noticed when he got home. The first was the massive hospital bed in his living room.

A large box-like chassis was attached to the foot of it, with two actuator arms coming out of the sides. A bulb-like optical sensor sat on top like the light on an old-time police car.

"What the hell…?"

The bed buzzed to life. The optical sensor fixed on him. Jon's arms tensed. He pulled on his wheel-rims and backed away. The bed rolled toward him.

"Greetings, Jonathan Hale." The bed had a calm, vaguely effeminate voice. "I am pleased to inform you that you've been selected to take part in the new HealthAid pilot program."

"The what?"

The bed clicked and whirred somewhere inside its box-like chassis, the sound of cooling fans and spinning hard drives.

"Pursuant to Title II of the Interstellar Heroes at Home Act, three thousand veterans of the colony world conflict have been selected to receive automated in-home health care. I am pleased to announce that your application was chosen out of a pool of over half a million candidates."

"But I never filled out any application."

More clicks. More whirs. "Records indicate you applied on May 6, 2275, three days after the program was announced to the public."

"But I *didn't* apply!"

The bed quietly motored back to the middle of the room. "You need to monitor your excitement level, Mr. Hale. Studies show that patients diagnosed with traumatic stress are more susceptible to hypertension."

Jon eyeballed the useless, dead motorchair in the corner. Thirteen years and counting, waiting for the Department of Interstellar Veterans' Affairs to replace it or fix it. He didn't know why he bothered to get his hopes up. He should know better by now. But sometime after his cigarette break, he'd gotten the crazy idea that the delivery people Mrs. Drinkwater had called about were from the IVA. He'd even convinced the day supervisor, Ray Johnstone, to let him clock out a half hour early.

Jon shook his head. Only the IVA would deliver an unnecessary piece of talking junk to his doorstep while completely ignoring the one thing he actually needed. Government waste at its finest.

He wheeled himself into the kitchen. A drink would be pretty useful right about now. He opened the cabinet beneath the sink. And he swore loudly.

"What did you do with my whiskey?"

"Alcohol consumption is not recommended for patients suffering from traumatic stress. Additionally, several of the medications associated with your spinal injury are unsafe to take with alcoholic beverages."

John wheeled himself toward the bed. "That doesn't answer the question."

"I took the liberty of removing it," the bed replied. "Having no alcohol in the home will provide a more therapeutic environment. I have also removed the tobacco, the empty carbohydrates, and the caffeine."

Jon clenched his fists. He counted to ten, breathing in and out slowly. He also thought of the old baseball bat in the closet, and wondered if a mechanical bed could feel pain.

✿

The hold music was a smooth-jazz remix of some patriotic medley, bars from songs like "Terra the Beautiful" and "My System 'Tis of Thee." The tabla-phone's screen cycled through a series of inspiring images: The Terran Marines raising the flag on Mount Godan. The Luna Monument. The launch of the *Columbia VIII.*

Jon fiddled with his coffee mug of filtered tap water and glared at the bed. It sat idling in a corner, the slowly pulsing lights indicating it was in rest mode.

He'd called Ray as soon as he woke up to let him know that he'd be taking another day off to deal with the IVA. Ray understood. His old man had been a flyboy during the Orion Prime campaign. And from what Ray had told Jon, it had been hell getting them to pay for the old man's cyberoptics.

Jon thanked him. As an afterthought, he told Ray to thank the old man for his service. Then he called the main number at the Jerry Hawker Medical Center.

Jon spent the next several hours having his call bounced from department to department. Twice they transferred him to off-world call centers. Now he was waiting to speak to somebody in the special claims office on Tau Ceti B.

"Hello, Mr. Hale. How may I be of assistance today?" The hold music cut off abruptly. A triangular, green-yellow face filled the screen. The name displayed underneath the image was "Mr. Ixxbrixxzixxnixx."

Jon cursed silently. It was one of those weird bug things from the Andromeda belt. Jon hated talking to them. It wasn't that he was prejudiced. It was that the insectoids had a hive-mind, and they couldn't understand the concept of a miscommunication. An honest mistake could be seen as a grave insult.

Jon swallowed nervously. One slipup and he'd be bounced back into the phone menus. "Hi, yes. I have a new automated HealthAid bed. It was dropped off yesterday."

Mr. Ixxbrixxzixxnixx ran his pincers over his keyboard. His black, bulbous eyes twitched back and forth as he read Jon's record. "Yes, Mr. Hale. I see here that your application was approved on the first of the month."

"But that's just it. I never filled out an application."

The bug-creature tilted its head to the side. The gesture made Jon think of a huge, disgusting dog. "That seems very unlikely, Mr. Hale."

"What do you mean?"

Mr. Ixxbrixxzixxnixx spoke slowly, as if trying to explain an advanced technology to an inferior race. "It says here that you filled out an application on May 6, 2275. And that the application was approved."

That the computerized records could be wrong appeared to be a foreign idea to Mr. Ixxbrixxzixxnixx. Jon decided to try a different approach.

"Look, I um…I've decided I don't want to be a part of the pilot program anymore. It's not working out. How soon can you come and pick up this robotic hospital bed?"

Mr. Ixxbrixxzixxnixx made an annoyed chittering noise. "Mr. Hale, you obviously don't remember section 674 of the application you filled out. It guarantees your participation in the program for a period of three and one half standard Earth years."

Jon didn't know whether to laugh or cry. Trapped. He was trapped with the stupid thing.

"Is there anything else I can help you with today, Mr. Hale?"

"What about my motorchair request? I filled that out over thirteen years ago."

Mr. Ixxbrixxzixxnixx ran his pincers over the keyboard again. "I'm sorry Mr. Hale. There is no record of a repair or service call for a motorchair."

Jon could feel a painful throbbing sensation in his temples. He heard his voice rising before he could stop it. "You people send me physical, printed-paper notices in the mail that say the call is still pending. I got one yesterday!"

The bug-creature bristled and hissed. Its wings started to come out of the coverings on its back. "There's no need for that tone of voice, Mr. Hale."

"I'm sorry, Mr. Ixxklicksnicks, I—"

The black, bulbous eyes glared at him. "*It's pronounced Ixxbrixxzixxnixx.*"

Crap. "Right, I'm sorry. I just—"

"If you are unsatisfied with my service in any way, I can transfer you to our customer relation's office on Gilese 581."

"No, that won't be necessary!" There was a note of barely-concealed panic in Jon's voice.

"Transferring you now, sir."

The smooth-jazz music began to pipe from the tabla-phone's speakers again. The bug-alien disappeared from the screen. But before it did, Jon was almost sure the big-eyed sonovabitch smiled.

Jon woke up feeling groggy. He shook the fuzz out of his head and sat up. It was his second night in the new hospital bed, and his second morning feeling like his brain was made of wet garbage.

The actuator arms on the bed helped him get to his chair and get dressed. It was only after he was clothed and seated that he noticed the dried blood spot on the inside of his arm.

"What the hell is this?"

The optical sensor on the bed whirled around and focused on the spot. The usual clicks and whirs sounded from inside the chassis, noises that Jon had begun to associate with the bed thinking.

"You took an inadequate portion of your prescribed sleep medication before bed last night. I merely administered the remainder after you entered a state of REM sleep."

"I took the same dose I always take."

The bed thought for a few seconds. "Your record indicates that your prescribed dose of Benzodiazepine is seventy-five milligrams. You took twenty-five. You also took it in the less efficient oral tablet form, rather than the intravenous injection your medical record specifies."

That was a bunch of crap. None of that was in his medical record. There had to be a mistake. This dumb machine was crossing its wires.

"Show me my medical record. Send it to my tabla-phone." The phone pinged and vibrated a few seconds later. Jon had to concentrate to read it, but the bed was right. The medication doses were all higher now. And they called for injections.

"This is wrong."

"Your medical record is displayed as it exists in my files, Mr. Hale."

"Then your files are wrong!" Jon slammed a fist on the arm of his wheelchair.

"Your stress levels appear to be rising, Mr. Hale. If you do not calm down, I will have to recommend a mild sedative."

All right. Enough was enough. Jon opened a net-search on how to disable a HealthAid bed. If the IVA wouldn't come and get it, at least he could find a way to turn it off.

The first ten pages were nothing but sites warning against tampering with equipment owned and operated by the Department of Interstellar Veterans Affairs. The equipment was monitored, said the various sources. Any attempts to modify or alter the function would result in felony charges with a ten-year sentence to Charon Correctional Facility upon conviction.

Jon almost gave up on the idea right then and there. Charon was a frozen hellhole on the edge of the system, orbiting a dwarf planet somewhere out past Neptune. He'd met former inmates before, their noses and fingers blackened from the frostbite. Even the long-term medical wing, which was where Jon would go, was rumored to be little more than a cold-storage facility for invalids.

Nothing was worth a trip to Charon, Jon thought. He could find another way. Maybe he could get an appointment with a patient advocate at Jerry Hawker Hospital. The waiting list was supposedly down to two years.

Before he could close the search window, a link buried beneath all of the others caught his eye. It was from a private message board about various IVA programs

"'Pilot program' dangerous!" read the headline. "HealthAid beds programmed to malfunction." Jon opened it and began reading.

"All of the HealthAid beds are doing exactly what they were designed to do: dope us, isolate us, and quietly kill us off. Listen carefully, NOBODY signed up for this program. The IVA forged the paperwork behind the scenes because we're costing them too much money. 'Automated in-home health care' lets them kill us off and blame faulty equipment later on. Whatever you do, DO NOT let one of these machines into your home. They're trying to turn you into a statistic."

Jon read a little further. There were no confirmed deaths yet. Nobody had definitive proof. One of the other posters alleged that coroner's reports had been changed after the fact to cover up the truth.

Jon was still reading when he heard the mail delivery come trough the wall slot. He set his tabla-phone down and wheeled to the door to collect it. As usual, most of it was from the IVA. Only government organizations were still archaic enough to use printed-paper mail for anything.

Jon sorted through the stack. Two more surveys, a notice that his new primary care physician was located in the Sirius cluster, and the weekly "release and consent" forms, allowing the IVA to export his information to other star systems. And of course, another notice telling him his motorchair's service and repair call was still pending.

Jon wondered if he should call Mr. Ixxkickysick, or whatever his name was. Show him the notice. Maybe his big black eyes would explode from the sides of his head.

Jon rolled back to the table where he'd set his tabla-phone. He picked it up and stared at the screen. The page he'd been reading was gone. In its place was a public broadcast show called *Barney the Batrachiosapian*.

"Hello kids," said Barney. "We're going to sing the counting song today. Doesn't that sound like fun?" A chorus of children's shouts answered him.

Jon tried to log onto a different page. But all he could access was the purple frog-alien and his counting song. Jon wheeled around to face the bed.

"What the hell did you do to my tabla-phone?"

"I have restricted your net content, Mr. Hale. Stressful news articles and baseless conspiracy sites will only upset you. I have allowed some access to soothing programs, as they may help you relax."

Slowly, carefully, Jon set the tabla-phone down. He backed his wheelchair toward the door. "I think I'll head down to the store. Get some food."

The bed clicked and whirred. "That is unnecessary. I have already arranged for food deliveries from the neighborhood grocer."

Jon felt his stomach sink. "Well, maybe I should head out and see Ray. I was out of work yesterday. He'll be expecting me soon."

"I already took the liberty of calling Raymond Johnstone. I informed him that you would be out of work for a period of convalescence. And that pursuant to the Heroes at Home Act, he was not authorized to ask for further details."

Jon backed his chair as far as it would go. He felt the wheel-rims touch the wall. The bed slowly motored toward him.

"My sensors indicate that your heart rate is elevated at this time. You need to relax, Mr. Hale. I recommend a sedative."

✧

Jon remembered very little of the next few weeks. He spent most days in a drugged-out funk. His phone calls were screened and monitored by the HealthAid.

He had one clear memory, of trying to talk to Mrs. Drinkwater. She'd called to ask about the rent. Jon knew the bed was listening, so he tried to use his old code words from P.O.W. training. He tried to use the hand-signals for "torture" and "duress" but Mrs. Drinkwater didn't catch on. She kept asking why Jon was poking his eyes and talking about raisins and fiber content.

Jon cursed her inwardly. You just couldn't rely on pilots.

Then he second-guessed himself. Mrs. Drinkwater was never a pilot. He was thinking Ray's old man. On top of that, Jon was starting to think he might have mixed the code words up with an oatmeal recipe.

The heavy drug dosages weren't helping. He started to laugh out loud then, and sing Barney the Batrachiosapian's counting song.

"I have fun

"With number one!

"Number one is so much fun!"

Mrs. Drinkwater told him it was okay. She said to get some rest, not to worry about the rent just then, and she politely hung up.

After that, Jon remembered the bed telling him that he wouldn't be allowed to take any more calls. It was too stressful. It brought him his usual stack of IVA consent and release papers to sign and initial. It promised him that once he did the paperwork, he could go back to watching *Barney*.

For three or four weeks (or was it five?) Jon just existed, eating his meals, taking his meds, and watching shows like *Barney* and *Playtime Planetside Pals*. The bed helpfully attended to all of his needs, bringing his paperwork once a week, and encouraging him to give the right answers on the government's quality surveys.

On May 30, 2084, the notice he'd been waiting for arrived in the print-paper mail. Jon smiled through the medicine haze.

And he waited.

✧

By five o'clock Jon still felt heady and dazed, but it was still better than he'd felt earlier in the afternoon. And since the bed would be ready to give him his evening dose in a few minutes, it was now or never. Jon wheeled himself over to the closet. He dug inside for the baseball bat and turned to face the HealthAid.

"What do you think you're doing, Mr. Hale?"

Jon smiled. It felt good to be in power again, to have some control. "I'm going to smash you into scrap. Then I'm going to dump the pieces of you into a trash disintegrator."

"If any damage is done to my systems," the bed reminded him, "a signal is beamed to the Department of Interstellar Veteran's Affairs. You would face criminal charges and imprisonment on Charon."

"I know that. But the IVA is going to ignore the signal."

The bed seemed unsure now. Could a machine feel doubt? It slowly motored backward. "What makes you believe that would be the case, Mr. Hale?"

Jon pointed to the corner of the apartment, at the old motorchair. "I filed a repair and service request on that thing thirteen years ago. And every so often, I get another print-paper notice telling me my request is pending. But the other day, when I talked to that bug-creature in special claims, he told me that my request was never filed. So that got me thinking."

"You're acting irrationally, Mr. Hale. You appear agitated. I recommend a sedative."

Jon smiled. He wheeled closer. "So I filed a service request on you. I snuck it in with the weekly liability-release forms. And do you know what I got today?" Jon held the paper up in front of him. The bed's optical sensor focused on it.

"It's a notice that says my request is pending. Which means that hell will freeze over before you get any kind of response from the IVA."

"Mr. Hale, this is a foolish chance to take. When the IVA reads my distress signal, they'll file charges against you for violation of the—"

"Yeah, I thought about that. That's why I told them your network link was sending erroneous messages."

For the first time since it had arrived, the bed didn't have anything to say. Jon smiled from ear to ear. He lightly drummed his fingers on the bat.

"Mr. Hale, please don't do this. You'll only aggravate yourself."

Jon hefted the bat, tested the weight. "Nope. I think that by the end of this, I'm actually going to feel pretty good."

Jon slept after he was finished. When he woke up he called Ray Johnstone. He said he'd make it back to work on Monday.

Yes, he said. His convalescence was over.

Copyright © 2017 by Daniel J. Davis

Kevin J. Anderson is a Hugo and Nebula nominee, the author of more than fifty national or international bestsellers, and is the publisher of WordFire Press. This is his sixth appearance in Galaxy's Edge, *and the fourth featuring his popular detective Dan Shamble, Zombie P.I.*

NAUGHTY & NICE
A Dan Shamble, Zombie P.I., Adventure

by Kevin J. Anderson

1

Santa Claus was an *unnatural*. That made perfect sense—I just hadn't thought of it before.

The jolly bearded guy in the bright-red suit came into the offices of Chambeaux & Deyer Investigations, desperate to hire my services. It's not often, I suppose, that Santa requires a detective—particularly a zombie detective.

"I need your help, Mr. Chambeaux," Santa said.

I extended my gray hand to shake his black-gloved one. "At your service."

I assessed my client-to-be. Santa carried a voluminous cloth sack over his left shoulder; it was limp and empty at the moment, rather than bulging with brightly wrapped gifts. His bloodshot eyes were as red as his suit. His cheeks were pale, and his face seemed less plump than the pictures I had seen on a million Christmas cards.

"It's a crisis." He looked around with haunted eyes. "I've been robbed!"

In the Unnatural Quarter, we see all sorts of clients. After the Big Uneasy, all manner of legendary creatures had reappeared: ghosts, vampires, zombies, werewolves, ghouls, and other creatures that go bump, growl, or thud in the night. Why not Santa too? Somebody who can slip down billions of chimneys in a night—without incurring a single home-invasion charge—would fit right in.

"We'll do everything we can to help, Mr. Claus," said Robin Deyer, as she came out to greet the new client. "Is this more of a legal matter or an investigative one?"

"Oh-ho-ho, I definitely need a detective, and I came here because Mrs. Claus and I have heard about Mr. Chambeaux."

I was surprised. "We don't even advertise up at the North Pole. How did you find out about Chambeaux and Deyer Investigations?"

"Actually, we're local. My powers only manifest during the holiday season—it's not a full-time gig up in the cold. The rest of the year Mrs. Claus and I run a nice little bed-and-breakfast in the Quarter. Everybody around town knows the zombie detective to call when they're in a bind."

When I first moved into the Unnatural Quarter, I was a regular human P.I., trying to make a living like anybody else. I catered to clients who, though they sometimes looked like monsters on the outside, still had very human problems. Even after I got myself killed on a case, I climbed out of the grave and got back to work, still with Robin as my partner. Most unnaturals aren't even bothered by the bullet hole in the middle of my forehead, and I've stopped being self-conscious about applying morticians' putty to cover it up.

Sheyenne flitted up to Santa, beaming her gorgeous smile. "May I take your coat, Mr. Claus?"

Not only is Sheyenne extremely smart, competent, and efficient, she's beautiful on all counts. She's also my girlfriend. On top of that, she happens to be a ghost, murdered in the same case that saw me dead. But even through all that, we stuck together. It's a testament to the strength of our relationship.

Santa decided against removing his red coat. "No-ho-ho! It's part of my traditional image. The coat is made of magical material that keeps me comfortable no matter the temperature. That way I never have to take it off until the season's over. Traditions are important, and never more so than around the holidays."

Sheyenne leaned closer and whispered, "For the record, I never stopped believing in you."

He regarded Sheyenne with both wonder and mirth. "Strangely enough, I didn't believe in ghosts—until a few years ago." Santa sneezed, then turned back to me. "Mr. Chambeaux, I'm not going to kid you. There's more riding on this particular Christmas than ever before, and I'm coming apart at the seams. I need you to find my stolen property before

Christmas Eve, or there'll be no joy to the world, no ho-ho-ho, no holly jolly, no Feliz in the Navidad, no Frohe in the Weihnachten, no Merry in the Christmas. You see how serious this is?"

"I think I do." I really had no idea, but I didn't want to look dumb in front of Santa Claus. "What exactly was stolen?"

"My list!" He was distraught—which was not at all the sort of attitude I expected from a man famous for his rumbling belly laugh and infectious good cheer. "My *list* of who's Naughty and Nice! Without that list, I won't know which houses to visit, which Johnny deserves a model train set and which one gets a lump of coal, which Susie deserves a doll and which one gets a boring sweater. If I can't figure that out, Christmas definitely won't be the most wonderful time of the year."

"Don't you keep a photocopy?" Robin asked. "Or an online backup?"

Santa was horrified. "And break Christmas tradition? Millions of children believe in me and the way I do things, just so. They have dreams about Christmas, and it's my responsibility to safeguard those dreams." He shook his head again. "If I modernized, there'd be an uproar—not to mention countless bugs in the system—and then you can bet the Easter Bunny would hack into my database and start grabbing my market share. No, everything's done by hand on a very long roll of parchment, the names of every single boy and girl written with a goose quill."

That must have been the world's largest two-column spreadsheet. "And how exactly was it stolen?"

"Someone broke into the offices of my North Pole headquarters. It's our busy season, all of my helpers doing double shifts, decking the halls, dashing through the snow. Our packaging department is a madhouse, full of complete sets of lords a-leaping, partridges, pear trees—and everybody wants five golden rings. We still have an overstock of last year's fruitcakes, and I don't know what to do with the figgy puddings. I was sure there'd be a demand for those again." He wiped a gloved hand across his forehead.

"It's very hectic. I was taking a break with Mrs. Claus. She had made a fresh batch of eggnog, and this time of year she spikes it rather heavily. I slept like a baby…and when I went back to the office the list was gone!" He tugged on his beard. "It had to be an inside job." He paced back and forth, scuffing his black boots on our all-weather carpet. "I checked with all the line-supervisor elves and every single one of the toy builders. This time of year they work around the clock without even restroom or cigarette breaks. But everyone had an alibi."

"Could you have been targeted by Homeland Security?" Robin asked. "Or some other law-enforcement organization monitoring your research as to who might be on a Most Naughty list?"

"I can see why they might want that," I said.

"Not at all, I have a close cooperative relationship with government agencies, considering all that airspace I fly over—and my work has to be done in a single night, so I have no time to mess with clearances. I even let NORAD track me every year. No, that list is in the hands of someone who means no good, mark my words…and no human could have gotten through my security. It had to be an unnatural."

He hung his head and seemed so sad that I wanted to sit on Santa's lap and give him a hug. He continued, "That's why I came to you, Mr. Chambeaux. If I don't get that Naughty and Nice list in time, I can't stop thinking about all those poor children who'll be disappointed, all those broken dreams, all those undelivered presents. It'll destroy their faith in Christmas…and they just might turn out to be naughty next year."

I was determined to solve the problem. It's not every day you get a chance to save Christmas—and not just because Christmas only comes once a year. "Don't underestimate how relentless a zombie can be, Santa. I'll find your list. If I have any questions or developments, how will I get hold of you? Do you have a business card?"

"Much better than that." Santa reached into a pocket of his red jacket and pulled out a bright green ribbon with a jingle bell attached. "Just ring this, and I'll be there. Even if I'm otherwise occupied, I have an answering service that can get hold of me."

The pink had come back to his cheeks, and a droll smile lifted his lips. "Oh-ho-ho, if you solve this case, there'll be something very special under the tree—for all of you."

Relieved and encouraged, Santa slung his empty sack over one shoulder and prepared to go. He closed his eyes and touched a finger to the side of his nose.

When nothing happened, he looked around our offices. Finding no chimney, he chuckled. "Sorry, I've been so worried about Christmas being ruined, I forgot how I arrived!" He left through the front door instead.

2

Although I knew I might have to go to Santa's North Pole seasonal offices to see the crime scene, I decided to search in the Unnatural Quarter first, which was much more convenient. (Riding up to the Arctic for hours in a freezing open sleigh sounded worse than flying in a middle seat in coach.)

I started with someone who kept a similar list—primarily a Naughty list.

Officer Toby McGoohan is a dedicated beat cop, but his penchant for telling off-color jokes to the wrong people had gotten him transferred to the Quarter. McGoo is also my BHF, my best human friend. We help each other on cases. We commiserate about life and unlife over beers at the Goblin Tavern.

I found him outside one of the Talbot & Knowles blood bars, which are frequented by vampires who need their daily caffeine and hemoglobin fix. Some fanged customers drink straight blood, while others go for berry-flavored blood frappés or, now that the weather had turned colder, steaming cinnamon-spice hot clotties.

"Hey, Shamble," McGoo said, tipping his blue cap. "What do you get when you cross a snowman with a vampire?"

"What?" I groaned in advance.

"Frostbite." He persists in telling me jokes. I haven't been able to convince him they're not funny, and he hasn't been able to convince me that they are. As a special favor, I did promise I would try to laugh at some of them. But only some. "What's new and exciting in your world?"

"I just picked up Santa Claus as a client. Somebody stole his list of Naughty and Nice kids."

McGoo's eyes widened. "Well, that's a miracle on…" he glanced up, looking for a street corner, "Thirty-second Street. If even Santa isn't safe from criminal activity, we are living in troubled times indeed. What does the list look like?"

"Long roll of parchment, millions of handwritten names. Two columns labeled N and N."

McGoo shook his head. "I'll keep an eye out, but we've got real problems of our own in the Quarter." He lowered his voice. "Kids are going missing, Shamble—a lot of them. We've received a rash of reports."

A vampire couple came out of the blood bar, chatting away. One held a to-go carrier with four cups of blood drinks marked with Type A (extra hot), Type O negative, and two with Type B positive (and a hand-drawn smiley face).

McGoo called, "Excuse me, can I see those for a second?"

The vampires turned, surprised. "What is it, Officer?"

"Your blood drinks. I want to show my friend something."

McGoo indicated the to-go cups, the first of which showed the printed picture of a young vampire boy who had been turned when he was maybe twelve years old. Big letters said, "Have You Seen Me?" Printed below the photo were the vampire kid's name, pre-turned age, and last-seen data.

The second cup showed a zombie boy with an incongruous smile beneath his sunken eyes. The third was a scruffy-looking full-furred werewolf, and the fourth showed a human girl in Goth makeup wearing an off-the-shelf gloomy expression.

After he thanked the vampire couple, they left. I shook my head. "That's troubling, McGoo. I think I recognize the werewolf kid. He was part of the gang at the rumble a few months ago, Hairballs versus the Monthlies."

"Yeah, he's not the only rough one. Some of the missing children are straight off the Wikipedia page for Juvenile Delinquent. Not all of those photos were in a family album—a few are from mug-shot files."

"Some of the disappearances could just be runaways," I suggested. "Visiting some nice old lady's gingerbread house in the forest."

"For the record, Shamble, she wasn't a nice old lady—I worked on that case," McGoo said. "Not all of the missing kids have records. We've got grieving parents or foster parents who want to find their

missing little angels. I don't know if the cases are related, or just a coincidence."

"I don't believe in coincidence," I said, wondering if this might also have something to do with the stolen Naughty and Nice list. "But I didn't believe in Santa Claus either, and now he's my client. Let me know if you get a lead on my case. I'll do the same if I hear anything about the missing kids."

McGoo nodded. "The Quarter's getting nervous—put your mind to it, see what you come up with. You've got a lot of space in that big empty head of yours."

I tapped the bullet hole in the middle of my forehead. "A little extra space maybe, but it's not empty." I tipped my fedora at him and left.

My first order of business was to figure out who would *want* to steal the Naughty and Nice list, and what anybody would use it for. In order to brainstorm, I invited Sheyenne to lunch.

3

Being a ghost, Sheyenne doesn't eat, not even their special "ephemeral" plate, and I don't need much sustenance. (I've avoided brains, because I don't want to turn into one of *those* zombies who are an embarrassment to the rest of us.)

The Ghoul's Diner, though, was a place to hang out, and Sheyenne likes it when we go out on lunch dates. Strolling down the sidewalk toward the diner, we free associated. Sheyenne wore a bright smile as always, and those blue eyes could make a man's heart stop beating, or start beating, depending on which condition he started from.

I wondered aloud that maybe the Big Uneasy had made the Grinch manifest as well, but Sheyenne doubted he'd reached a worldwide cultural status similar to vampires or St. Nick. I disagreed, because I had grown up on the Grinch; still, I conceded that he seemed too obvious a cartoon villain.

I then postulated that the perpetrator could be a Lorax with self-esteem issues, upset that Arbor Day didn't have the stature of Christmas, Hanukkah, Thanksgiving, New Years…or even Kwanzaa, for that matter. I didn't know if Loraxes were real, either. I seemed to be in a Seussian rut.

A light dusting of snow came down, reminding me that I had to find Santa's list before Christmas

Eve, or he would suffer a worldwide toy-distribution crisis. Festive decorations were already strung up in the streets of the Quarter: barbed-wire tinsel looped along windowpanes and awnings, colorful wreaths hung from nooses on gallows lampposts.

Before we reached the diner, Sheyenne and I stopped on the street where crowds had gathered and traffic halted for an early holiday parade. And it sure wasn't the type hosted by Macy's.

Elves capered and danced at the front of the parade, diminutive creatures dressed in pointed floppy caps and bright red outfits trimmed with white flocking. The costumes resembled a traditional Santa's elf suit, but these were cheap knockoffs that fit poorly with seams showing and with some of the white trim missing.

These elves were not the cute, smiling, industrious workers who stocked Santa's shelves and made the North Pole a cheery, if formerly imaginary, place. No, these elves came from the G-side of the family, having more in common with gremlins, goblins, and gnomes—pointy, stretched-out features, gray skin, and long ears that looked as if they had gotten caught in industrial picking machinery. When they smiled like good elves should, they showed alarmingly pointed teeth.

Behind the prancing elves came a bizarre motorized sleigh crawling along at pedestrian speed so everyone on the sidewalk had an appropriate opportunity to wave. Palm trees adorned the back of the sleigh. On a big wicker chair sat an elf with all the usual elf features (from the G-side of the family), but he wore a white rhinestone-studded jacket, trimmed in Christmasy green and red. He had slicked-back black hair, sideburns that extended halfway down his pointed chin, big garish sunglasses, and oddly out-of-place blue suede shoes.

"You've got to be kidding me," I said to Sheyenne.

"He's for real, Beaux. That's Elfis—I've seen his ads. You know, 'Santa Claus is coming to town, but Elfis will get there faster?' He's a celebrity on the cable-access channels."

I'm a decent enough detective, but I can be clueless about pop culture.

Elfis waved at the crowd and picked up a handheld Vegas-style silver microphone. "Thank ya very much. Santa's got competition this year, boys and girls, naturals and unnatural. The holidays should be for everybody, not just kids who pass some arbitrary naughty-or-nice test. Even naughty kids deserve presents, don't they?"

From the sidewalk crowds, a smattering of natural and unnatural children cheered—kids who knew they were included in the Naughty column, no doubt.

"Santa Claus has had a monopoly on the Christmas season for far too long—but I intend to undercut his position. Elfis Industries has wider distribution, more fairness, and less discrimination. More transparency in holiday gift-giving! We're going to expose all those 'secret admirer' gifts for what they are. And no more bribery with milk and cookies. *Everyone* deserves a present, and I'm the one to give it to them. It's time to put the kitsch back into Christmas!"

His elves began handing out candy canes, traditional red-and-white striped ones, blood-red ones, and black ones. A witch dressed in a midnight-blue gown and pointy cap stood by her young son who looked as if he might grow up to be a powerful necromancer. The boy ran forward to take a black candy cane, but his mother scolded him. "I told you not to take candy from strangers!"

The boy pouted. "He's not a stranger, Mom— that's *Elfis*!"

"Oh," the witch said, and handed him back the cane.

The motorized sleigh rolled by, with Elfis in his sequins and sunglasses waving from under his palm trees. He called out, "Who needs the cold? I have nightmares about a white Christmas! Let it snow, let it snow, let it snow—but somewhere far away! Stick with me, and the holidays will have a warm and sunny glow."

After the parade passed, Sheyenne leaned close to me. "So that's why Santa is so worried. He's got competition this year. And if his rival does a better job satisfying the customers…"

"Then Santa Claus won't be coming to town anymore," I said. "We might have our first suspect. Elfis has a motive to sabotage Santa's work. I better go talk to him and find out if his intentions really are as pure as new fallen snow."

I could tell this case was going to spell T-R-O-U-B-L-E.

4

After Sheyenne and I had a quick lunch at the diner (pink slime was on special), I went off to continue my investigation.

The headquarters for the competitive holiday operation was an office building in front of a fenced compound of airplane-hangar-sized structures, no doubt where Elfis manufactured and stored all the toys he planned to distribute ahead of his business rival. According to Sheyenne, Elfis's ads promised delivery by Christmas Eve Eve.

The sign at the front entrance had giant letters painted like candy canes, surrounded by yellow suns: "North Pole South: We're Better Because We're Closer to the Equator." Around the doorway was strewn blue sand or fake snow, which seemed incongruous…until I remembered "Blue Christmas."

When I entered the front door of North Pole South, I heard many busybodies working in the back, but the reception counter was empty except for a fist-sized fake rock sitting on top of an index card that said "Ring bell for service." I picked up the stone and realized it was hollow. When I shook it, a tinkling chime rang out.

A female elf receptionist scurried out of the back, smiling sweetly with her pinched face. "I see you found our Jingle Bell Rock," she snickered. "Very clever, don't you think? Elfis came up with it himself." She shuffled papers and handed me a temporary-employment application. "Looking for part-time holiday work? Many positions available."

I shook snow from the brim of my fedora. "That would be a conflict of interest. I've been retained by Santa Claus."

The receptionist's eyebrows rose. "I'll let Elfis know you're here." She took back the Jingle-Bell Rock and punched an extension on her phone. "He told us to expect an overture from Mr. Claus."

"Overture?" I asked. "I can barely hum a tune."

Elfis agreed to see me, probably out of curiosity; at least it got me through the door.

The chief elf's back office was bright and stiflingly hot. A large tropical mural covered the far wall. Wearing only a towel around his waist, Elfis lay back on a chaise lounge under a pair of heat lamps that could have been used to keep food warm in a res-

taurant. Standing on either side, a pair of Egyptian mummies gently fanned him with palm fronds.

Elfis lifted his sunglasses and sat up to regard me. "Dan Chambeaux, Private Investigator…that seems an odd choice for Santa, but I knew he'd send a representative before long. He has no option but to open negotiations. I suppose he wants to suggest some kind of merger and keep a token title for himself? Frankly I'd rather just buy his operations outright."

He waved for the mummies to back away. "Would you like some refreshment? I can get one of my boys to make you a mai tai or piña colada. Or, if you want to be more traditional, I have chestnuts roasting on an open fire."

Chestnuts weren't the only things roasting. "I'm surprised you keep it so hot in here," I said, tugging at my collar—and zombies don't perspire.

Elfis explained, "I want to change the paradigm of the holiday season. It's too cold, too snowy, too wintry. You really think shepherds prefer to watch their flocks in the snow? They'd rather be skiing. And if I want something frozen, I order a frozen margarita." He laughed, but it sounded more like heh-heh-heh than ho-ho-ho.

"Now then, let's talk about sending old Saint Nick into retirement. Here's my offer: I take over all his operations, but I let him keep his North Pole annex. He and Mrs. Claus get a nice pension, run their bed-and-breakfast, maybe do a few public appearances for old times' sake, but I license his likeness and the brand. I'm dreaming of a profitable Christmas."

"There's been a misunderstanding, Mr. Elfis. That's not why I'm here."

The elf slicked back his hair, adjusted his position on the chaise lounge. The mummies came forward again to fan him vigorously with the palm fronds. "Well, then, I'm all ears."

"Santa Claus hired me as a detective because something very valuable was stolen from him."

Elfis seemed completely uninterested. "Really? And what would old St. Nick find valuable? Can't he just wiggle his nose and make another of whatever it was?"

"It's more of a matter of administrative records gone missing," I said. "I'm investigating the theft."

Elfis snickered. "You must mean his list. Anal-retentive, if you ask me." He slid his sunglasses back down on his face, scratched his sideburns. "And you think I had something to do with it? Why in the world would I need a list like that? I explicitly *don't* discriminate. I give presents to all kids, without scoring them on social behavior. What gives Santa the right to make a subjective decision about who's Naughty and Nice? Judgmental jerk, if you ask me." He sniffed. "I plan to take discrimination out of Christmas gift-giving, make it equal for all. What would be my motive for stealing the list?"

I did have a theory. "You'd hamstring Santa's activities, make him look incompetent, while gaining brownie points for yourself."

"I don't have brownies, Mr. Chambeaux. I have elves. There's a difference."

"That doesn't address my theory."

"Look around you, Mr. Chambeaux. I'm sabotaging Santa's work by perfectly traditional means—undercutting prices, faster distribution, more transparency in my operations. I don't need a list for that."

One of the mummies served him a cool drink in a hollowed pineapple, complete with a colorful umbrella. "Thank ya very much." Elfis took a long refreshing sip. "Tell Santa if he wants to come to terms, I'm having a holiday special. His decision. Either way, it's time he faced some competition."

Elfis reached down beside his chaise lounge and pulled out a baseball-sized knot of thorny leaves, like a wadded tumbleweed studded with berries. "Here, Mr. Chambeaux—have a free sample. Part of my effort to put the kitsch back into Christmas."

He tossed it to me, and I caught it. "What's this?"

"Our new McMistletoe. Cheaper to manufacture, no preservatives needed, non-poisonous, non-habit-forming." He spoke at such a fast pace that my ears could barely keep up. "It's not intended to diagnose, prevent, treat, or cure any disease. These claims have not been evaluated by the FDA." He grinned. "But our McMistletoe is just as effective as real mistletoe. Try it out, you'll see."

I pocketed the mistletoe in my jacket's other pocket, because it didn't seem right to tuck it beside the jingle bell that Santa Claus had given me. "I'll try it," I said, though I doubted Sheyenne would be impressed.

5

I was already disturbed about the missing children McGoo was investigating, but I didn't see the actual pain until the Tannenbaums came into our offices.

Mrs. Tannenbaum buried her face in her husband's broad chest. "Our baby boy!"

Both of them were werewolves—the Monthly variety, so they passed for normal except on full-moon nights. They seemed like a nice couple with modest lives, middle-income jobs, probably had a home that was not extravagant but one they were proud of.

Robin hurried forward to comfort them. "Tell us what happened."

Mr. Tannenbaum pulled a wallet from his pocket and showed us a snapshot. "This is our son Buddy." The kid was of the full-furred persuasion, the type of werewolf who maintained a long muzzle, sharp fangs, moist black nose, and facial fur throughout the month.

"That's his school portrait," Mrs. Tannenbaum said with a sniff. "He was just about to graduate sixth grade." Sheyenne flitted in with a tissue for the grieving woman.

I studied the snapshot. Buddy Tannenbaum's black lips were curled in what I assumed was a smile, but might have been a snarl. What kid didn't make a goofy face when sitting for a school portrait? "Not much family resemblance. Adopted?"

Mrs. Tannenbaum snuffled loudly. "He came from an abused home, and we took him in. Poor Buddy! We wanted to show him all the love and affection he deserved. But one day after school, he didn't come home to do his chores."

Her husband continued, "He often gets preoccupied with friends—he has a strong social life. And what's a chore or two around the house? No need to bother the boy with them. I can do the vacuuming and take out the garbage while my wife cooks dinner."

"On the night he disappeared, I made a flesh-loaf with tomato sauce and onions. Buddy's favorite!" Mrs. Tannenbaum wailed, which came out as a trailing howl. "We had to eat it ourselves. We had leftovers for two days."

"Two days? Your son vanished and you didn't report it for two days?" Robin shot me a look, and I saw that furrow of concern on her brow.

"We thought he might be staying at a friend's house," said Mr. Tannenbaum. "He sometimes does that. We try not to be overprotective. A boy needs his space and…a wolf has to run free."

"Can you find him?" Mrs. Tannenbaum said. "We didn't want to go to the police because…because we want to keep his record clean. He's going to go to college someday, and it's really a private matter."

"You can count on our discretion, Mr. and Mrs. Tannenbaum." I doubted Buddy's disappearance was unrelated to the other children who had vanished.

"Can you give us the names of his friends, or places where he liked to spend time?" Robin asked.

Mrs. Tannenbaum considered. "He likes to hang out at the comic-book shop. Just Dug Up Collectibles, I think it's called."

"I know the place," I said. "I've been there."

In a fit of nostalgia, I had gone in to browse some of the old comics I'd bought and guarded so lovingly when I was a kid. One day, while tidying up my room, my mom gave them all to a thrift shop, and they sold for a nickel apiece before I could run down there to save them. A few months ago, when I looked in Just Dug Up Collectibles and saw the outrageous prices those issues were now selling for, I left the shop in despair and never went back….

"Is there anything else I should know? Anything that might help?"

The Tannenbaums looked at each other, as if uncomfortable, hesitant, then both shook their heads.

Sheyenne whisked in and made several color photocopies of Buddy's photo before returning the snapshot to Mr. Tannenbaum, who lovingly tucked it back into his wallet. "I'll also submit this to the Talbot & Knowles blood bars," Sheyenne suggested. "They can include it with the other photos of missing children."

Mr. Tannenbaum looked uncomfortable. "I'd prefer to keep this out of the public eye."

"We already talked to the blood bars," snuffled Mrs. Tannenbaum. "They said they were overbooked for the next two months until…until…" She began sobbing.

Mr. Tannenbaum completed the sentence. "Until Christmas." He patted his wife on the shoulder. "Please find him soon, Mr. Chambeaux. We have very important Hanukkah traditions, and Winter Solstice too."

She sniffled again. "The holidays just won't be the same without our dear Buddy. Please find him, Mr. Chambeaux. Such a dear, dear sweet boy."

6

"That kid is an unholy terror!" said Adric the comic-shop owner. He barely glanced at the picture of Buddy Tannenbaum. "He and his friends are monsters—and I don't mean that in a good way."

The wall behind the counter was plastered with autographed eight-by-tens of Adric posing with D-list celebrities. He was a gray-skinned, pot-bellied zombie, not nearly as well-preserved as the special variant-cover issues he kept bagged-and-boarded on high shelves. His complexion showed some signs of putrescence as well as fresh acne, which made him doubly unfortunate; although the undead suffer from numerous physical maladies, few are afflicted by zits.

Adric wore a powder blue *Star Wars* T-shirt with R2-D2 and C-3PO on the front, and it was much too small for him. I deduced that he'd bought the shirt when he saw *Star Wars* first run in theaters; in the years since, his body had enlarged considerably, though he probably told himself that the shirt had shrunk.

Adric handed me back the photo. "That kid and his friends are always in here stealing things, vandalizing, harassing customers, and of course never buying anything. A bunch of deadbeats and undeadbeats."

I frowned. It seemed Buddy Tannenbaum was not the upstanding young werewolf his parents imagined him to be. "He's gone missing. When was the last time you saw him?"

He snorted. "I kicked out the whole wild bunch two weeks ago—caught them shoplifting one time too many."

I had another thought. "So, does that mean you keep a list of, say, who's naughty and who's nice?"

"Nah, this is a comic store. We get all kinds in here. That Buddy Tannenbaum and his friends, though—they'd definitely go in the Naughty column."

As he talked, Adric used a box-cutter to slice open a cardboard case of new arrivals like an eager coroner working on his favorite autopsy. He opened the flaps and began pulling out shrink-wrapped

Christmas ornaments, clumsy-looking figurines of werewolves, vampires, scaly demons.

Frowning in disgust, he held up a crudely painted vampire with red marks smeared across his face. "Look at these! My customers want quality. The catalog said they're hand-painted, but this looks like it was finger-painted, or *claw*-painted." He shook his head. "Maybe even *flipper*-painted."

Adric dug into the box, pulled out a larger figure, a well-muscled werewolf in a cop uniform, holding an enormous Magnum pistol. "Does this look like Hairy Harry to you?" The rogue lycanthropic cop from the UQPD was something of a folk hero, even though he'd retired from the force.

"I wouldn't pay a premium for it," I said. I noticed the figures were labeled *Elfis Originals! Collect Them All!*

Adric kept pulling figurines out of the packaging then rolled his eyes as he lifted out six genuine Elfis figurines, each wearing a white sequin jacket, brushed-back black hair and sideburns, and big sunglasses. "What? I only ordered one of these."

Next, he removed a larger box showing a scaled aquatic gill-man labeled "Special Limited Edition Creature! (Comes with free lagoon!)". With his stiff zombie fingers, Adric pried open the package, removed the scaly figurine along with a tiny black plastic basin. Apparently, the user was supposed to fill it with water.

"Special Edition? Ridiculous! Look at this: 'Limited to 1,000,000 Units.' How the hell does that make it *collectible*? I'll be lucky to sell six…well, five, because I'll keep one for myself."

I tried to get back to the reason I'd come there. "Have you seen any of Buddy's buddies? Anyone I could talk to? His parents are distraught."

"No, and good riddance. Maybe they all ran off to join the vampire circus." Adric continued setting out the Elfis Originals holiday ornaments. "Mark my words, his parents will have a lot more silent nights this way. Just imagine what a handful that werewolf kid is gonna be when he hits his teenage years and hormones kick in."

He looked up at where two young zombies were pawing over back issues of *The Crypt-Keeper's Funniest Capers*. The zombie teens had their mouths open and they moaned in laughter at the panels.

Adric yelled, "Hey, you! Be careful with those—you get decaying flesh on any of the pages, you bought it."

The zombies looked up at him, moaned, then went back to the comics, noticeably exercising greater care.

I picked up a fine-print catalog listing of the Elfis Originals ornaments and collectibles and pocketed it for future reference. I thanked Adric and left.

7

When Santa Claus returned to our offices, he looked even more anxious than before. His face was sallow, almost jaundiced; his flowing white beard looked scraggly, with a thin brownish stain from where he'd been hitting the pipe a little too often. He had lost enough weight that his red jacket was gathered in folds around his waist with his wide black belt cinched tighter. I saw that he'd even punched a new hole.

"Usually when I visit, people set out milk and cookies for me." He sounded disappointed, beaten down. "I'll be glad to get back to running the bed-and-breakfast, but I have my duties first. I can't do my rounds without that list of Naughty and Nice." He slumped into a chair beside Sheyenne's desk and let out a sigh. "I tried to write a new one from memory, but my mind isn't what it used to be—too many bitter cold nights out in a reindeer-powered sleigh. I won't kid you, Christmas Eve is a hard night—a real nutcracker. After it's over, I crawl into bed and sleep for a week."

"My accountant says the same thing about Tax Day," I told him.

Santa adjusted his floppy red cap. "I haven't heard you jingle my bell, and time is running out. It's beginning to look a lot like a screwed-up Christmas."

"I've been investigating," I reassured him. "Particularly your rival Elfis. He makes no secret of the fact that he wants to take you out, but he insists he doesn't need your list to do it. What can you tell me about him?"

Santa's face fell, as if his heart had shrunk three sizes that day. "That elf deserves a lump of coal in his stocking on Christmas morning. Unfair business practices, inferior materials—do you know that his silver bells are made of cheap aluminum?" He frowned again, let out another sigh. "I try not to think ill of people, but I'd like to take a thick candy cane and go thumpety-thump-thump on his head. He's ruining traditions by taking away the incentive for children to be Nice. Just look at the rude manners in chat rooms on the Internet."

My heart went out to him. "I'm looking into his North Pole South operations, and Robin is studying his business practices. I haven't found any evidence that he arranged to steal your Naughty and Nice list, but I'll keep digging."

After rummaging around in the kitchen, Sheyenne flitted into the main room, carrying a plate with three stale chocolate-chip cookies and a glass of milk. "Look what I found for you, Santa!"

He brightened. "'Tis the season to be jolly—so I'll try my best." He pulled a paper ticket from the pocket of his red jacket. "Could you validate this for me? I've got my reindeer and sleigh parked on the roof."

"Of course," Sheyenne said, and stamped his parking ticket.

Santa took the rest of the cookies "for the reindeer" and slipped through the door just as Mr. and Mrs. Tannenbaum hurried in. They looked anxious, and my heart sank, wondering how I was going to tell them that their darling Buddy wasn't the sugarplum they believed him to be. If the young werewolf was getting into so much trouble, how could the parents not know? Were they willfully oblivious to the fact that their angel came straight from the dark side?

"We weren't entirely honest with you," Mrs. Tannenbaum said, then looked away shyly. "We have something else that might help."

Her husband said, "I convinced my wife that we needed to give you every detail if we want our Buddy back. Our son is more important than our shame and embarrassment."

"We thought you might be able to solve the case without it, and then we wouldn't have to admit…admit—" Mrs. Tannenbaum's lower lip quivered. Her eyes flashed golden, and I could see a hint of werewolf coming to the fore.

"Buddy's given us difficulties before," Mr. Tannenbaum admitted. "He's an unruly kid. I think it comes from his full-fur blood. Trouble in school, trouble with vandalism. He's even run away from home a few times."

"But he always comes back," Mrs. Tannenbaum interjected. "He's a good boy at heart."

I asked, "Do you think there's any possibility that he's just run off again?"

Both Tannenbaums shook their heads. "Not so close to Christmas. He would have waited to get his toys first. He's a troublemaker, but he's a greedy troublemaker."

I didn't know if that was the best kind or the worst kind. "The information doesn't help a great deal at the moment, but I'll keep asking around."

The Tannenbaums looked at each other. "Oh, that's not what we meant to tell you, Mr. Chambeaux. We were reluctant to say anything about what we did because…because, well, it's not exactly legal."

That's never a good phrase to include in a sentence. I braced myself.

"We had to do something because Buddy ran away so often. So, the last time we took him in to the vet…" Mrs. Tannenbaum swallowed hard, then lowered her voice. "We had a tracking chip implanted in the base of his skull. Nothing anyone would notice, mind you, but…just in case."

I perked up. "A tracking device? Then we can pinpoint his location right away!"

"Yes," said Mrs. Tannenbaum. "Do you think that might help you find him?"

I slapped my forehead, and it made a hollow popping sound from the bullet hole there. "The cases don't solve themselves," I said, "but I do need all the information."

"The tracking signal has a very limited range," Mr. Tannenbaum said. "Quite discreet, but not terribly useful. Still, if you get close enough…"

The Tannenbaums looked sheepish after they gave me the secret frequency and serial number of the tracker. "Just bring our little boy home, please? That would be the best present we ever had."

8

When we began our search, I decided to take police backup—McGoo—just so I could say I was being sensible. I didn't want to go overboard, though, because there was a better-than-even chance Buddy had just run away with his juvenile delinquent unnatural pals. Still, if Buddy's disappearance was connected with the other missing kids, McGoo would want to be along.

Then Robin insisted on joining us. With such a three-pronged approach, how could we not be prepared to solve any problem?

She had frowned in disapproval when she heard about the implanted tracker chip, claiming that it violated the civil rights of an underage werewolf. But McGoo had seen enough troublemakers in his work, and he was more inclined to try the "terrified straight" approach. Robin finally conceded that if the tracker meant we could reunite the full-time fuzzy kid with his once-a-month fuzzy parents, then all was for the best.

With the tracker's frequency and serial number, Robin downloaded a free but highly rated Track Werewolf app for her smartphone. She bundled up in a wool coat, and we all set off into the snowy night to find Buddy, leaving Sheyenne in charge of the office.

We wandered around the Quarter for a frustrating hour, following false signals (a garage-door opener and a universal TV remote control). I was beginning to think that we might not pick up the tracker's limited-range signal until after we had already found the subject in question. We were lost and frustrated; what had seemed to be an easy solution was turning out to be a headache and a waste of time.

Then Sheyenne called us and saved the day. She had found an update for the Track Werewolf app, which dealt with certain bugs and user issues and increased sensitivity. Once Robin installed the update, we found a strong signal. We were closer than we thought.

The signal led us straight to the tall smokestacks and gigantic toy warehouses behind Elfis's North Pole South complex.

Holding her phone, Robin took the lead, guiding us along the chain-link fence to the back service entrance of the gigantic manufacturing warehouses. The temperature was dropping, and fluffy snowflakes drifted down. Not a creature was stirring, not even the ones that usually stirred at that time of night.

Approaching the back guard gate, we found two burly golems wearing security guard uniforms. Their clay bodies were stiff and hardening in the cold, but one perked up. "Do you hear what I hear?"

The other said, "Do you see what I see?"

Now alert, the golems prepared to block our way, both of them focusing on McGoo's uniform, the dark blue police shirt, trousers, and cap. "That looks good on you," said one of the golems.

"We both wanted to be cops, but couldn't pass the tests," the other explained.

I knew why, but I didn't embarrass them by pointing out the reason.

McGoo said, "We're searching for a missing child, and we have reason to believe he's inside one of the warehouses." He held out a copy of Buddy's picture.

"Kids just can't stay away from toys," said the first golem.

Robin held up her smartphone, showing the app. "And we have electronic evidence he's in there."

The golems were again intrigued. "Is that phone one of the new models?"

The other said, "Does it have Angry Vultures on it? Or Curses with Friends?"

I knew if the golems started playing games on Robin's phone we would never get past the gate. "We need to have a look, bring that boy back to his parents."

The first golem had a stony expression on his clay face. "Sorry. We can't let you inside. Elfis is very strict."

The other golem looked intimidated. "He sees you when you're sleeping, he knows when you're awake, he knows when you've been bad or good." In tandem, they shook their smooth clay heads and pointed upward. "Security cameras."

Time for Plan B. I removed a folded sheet of paper from the inside pocket of my jacket and showed it to the two golems. "We have a duly authorized search warrant to enter the premises, signed by Judge Hawkins herself. This grants us unfettered access to all parts of the North Pole South warehouses so we can find and rescue the young man."

The first golem guard took the sheet of paper and studied it intently, while Robin shot me a questioning glance. She craned her neck to see what the guards were looking at. McGoo could barely keep the smile off his face.

The other golem took the sheet from his partner; they both had frowns on their clay faces. "All right then. We're security guards, sworn to uphold the law." They opened the chain-link gate for us. "Go on inside. I hope you find what you're looking for."

Robin was perplexed, but she glanced down at the blinking light on her Track Werewolf app. Buddy was definitely close, inside the big factory building ahead of us. With his best I'm-an-authority-figure gait, McGoo marched away from the golem guards. Robin hurried alongside me. When we were out of earshot, she asked, "What was that all about? When did you get a search warrant?"

"It wasn't a search warrant," I said. "It's the fine-print listing of Elfis Originals I took from Just Dug Up Collectibles."

McGoo worked at the warehouse door; it was unlocked. "Golems can't read," he said. "At least most of them can't. That's why they couldn't pass their UQ Police Department exams. Good work, Shamble."

Robin was astonished. "Then we got in here under false pretenses, and I have real ethical problems with that. We're trespassing."

"We're rescuing a missing child," I said. My boundaries were a little more blurred than Robin's, but I did manage to get things done.

Robin was about to continue her objections when McGoo opened the loading dock door. The dark, noisy factory hangar was worse than the worst New Year's Day hangover. It was a true holiday of horrors.

9

I doubted children opening their gifts on the morning of Christmas Eve Eve (if Elfis and his minions delivered on time, as promised) would want to know where their presents really came from.

We were seeing the ugly side of holiday cheer: appalling labor conditions, thick smoke, clanging hammers, grinding gears, and jets of steam venting from pressure valves. Foul water trickled out of rusty pipes overhead. A labyrinth of rattling conveyor belts rolled toys along to packaging lines. Sparks flew and blazing fires roared out of open furnaces fed with black coal that poured from supply hoppers in the ceiling. A separate set of conveyors dumped defective metal toys into a smoldering furnace. It was as if the Island of Misfit Toys had an active volcano.

Robin looked around in horror, shocked by what she saw. McGoo's face was stormy with anger.

Most appalling of all, though, were the kids shackled to the assembly line, hunched over the conveyor belts, red-eyed, dirt-smeared, waifish. They toiled at assembling dolls, painting action figures, stuffing collectibles into boxes. There were werewolves, zombies, ghouls, even human children, all looking dejected and haggard.

As I scanned the faces, I recognized many of the kids featured on the Have You Seen Me? pictures from the Talbot & Knowles blood bars. I saw one gray-furred werewolf boy, mangy and yet somehow still cute, chained to a station where he was applying black button eyes onto Raggedy Ann dolls. Either he was confused by the instructions, or the dolls catered to an entirely different type of unnatural, because he sewed three eyes on each doll.

"That's Buddy Tannenbaum!" I said.

The boy heard me even over the factory din. He turned, his tongue lolling out of his mouth, and his eyes lit up upon seeing us. He dropped the doll onto the dirty factory floor and leaped toward us, but was brought up short by silver shackles that bound his wrist and ankle.

"I'll be good! I promise!" he yelped. "I won't be naughty anymore. I don't want to be on the list!"

Robin was ahead of us, grim and determined. "We'll get you out of here, Buddy. Your parents hired us to find you."

"My mom and dad? But Elfis said they didn't love me anymore."

"Of course they love you," Robin said. "Parents love even naughty kids."

A steam whistle blew. More coal dumped out of the feeding hoppers, and the furnace burned brighter.

Then the elves came—evil elves, and ugly enough that they might have been disowned by even the G-side of the family. They carried cattle prods painted like cheery candy canes; others brandished icicle spears that dripped in the intense heat of the factory floor.

McGoo and I drew our guns and stood next to Robin. The ten elves closing in didn't look afraid of us at all. Too late, I realized that they were just a distraction.

Two other hench-elves stood up from behind the conveyor belt and hurled snowballs at us—icy snowballs with rocks in the middle. Cheater snowballs. (I did say they were evil elves.) Their aim was supernaturally true, and with one hail of hard snowballs, they knocked the guns out of our hands.

Then the hench-elves closed in, wielding icicle spears and candy-cane cattle prods. They overpowered us, shoved us to the factory floor, and used tough strands of satin ribbon to bind our wrists. We were going to have a black-and-blue Christmas. An evil elf even slapped a coordinating stick-on bow on each of us before they herded us toward the back of the factory.

"Elfis is going to want to see you," said one of the guards.

"Oh, by gosh, by golly, that was on my Christmas wish list," I said, which earned me a jab from one of the cattle prods. Since I'm a zombie, it takes a lot to shock me, but the experience was still unpleasant. I was more worried about McGoo and Robin, who could indeed be permanently damaged.

Elfis was at a raised supervisor's station near the warmth of the big furnace, sitting on a high director's chair with a small worktable beside him. Black dust from the coal hoppers left a gritty film on everything, but somehow it didn't affect his white sequined jacket or his blue suede shoes. He was perusing a rolled parchment filled with names—countless names, sorted into two columns, one marked N and the other one marked N. He muttered to himself as he used a large goose quill pen to check off names.

"Naughty…yes, got that one. Naughty…yes. Naughty…we have a very high success rate." Then he sneered at a line, crossed it out vigorously with the nib of his quill pen. "Somebody slipped up—this kid's in the Nice column! People tend to notice when *nice* kids go missing." A supervisor hench-elf scurried off to rectify the error.

Elfis picked up a bullhorn and began shouting toward the factory floor. "Listen up, kiddies! I have plenty more applicants to choose from, so if you want to be promoted in my criminal organization, you've got to produce, produce, *produce*! Only the best can survive this boot camp—also known as the Holiday Season! If you work hard, you'll be real henchmen by Easter." Elfis then started to laugh. "We're going to put that damned bunny out of business, too!"

He slid his sunglasses up on the bridge of his narrow nose as his fiendish hench-elves pushed us

forward. He seemed surprised to see us. "Mr. Chambeaux and friends—have you come to negotiate on Santa's behalf again? Well, it's too late. I've already got the holidays sewn up in a body bag, and now you'll never stop me."

When all else fails, when things look grimmest, I like to state the obvious. It puts villains off guard and usually gets them talking—too much. "You said you didn't have Santa's list of Naughty and Nice. That was dishonest."

He held up a long finger. "No, that was *misleading*. I said I didn't steal the list in order to earn brownie points or to make Santa look incompetent. I stole it strictly for my own purposes." Elfis waved the parchment, showing us the long list of names. "It's a recruitment tool, like a screening folder for job applicants. Santa already identified the *naughty* children for me, the ones suitable to become part of my operation."

"But you put them to work as slave labor," Robin said.

Elfis shrugged. "Well, they are naughty. Even criminals need to know the consequences of their actions. You do the crime, you pay the time. Community service for *my* community."

I struggled against the satin ribbons binding my wrists. It reminded me of my childhood, trying to snap the ribbons so I could open my presents. Now, as then, the ribbon had supernatural strength.

Elfis leaned forward, opening both of his hands to warm them at the nearby furnace. The conveyor belt continued to clatter, dumping defective toys into it, plastic ones as well as metal. "It's so nice to be warm for a change. And you three will be all toasty too. I'm afraid I can't allow my plans to be foiled—or tinseled. Into the furnace with them!"

The hench-elves swept forward like a blizzard of evil. Even though I'm a zombie, I had no desire to be cremated. And speaking for my two human friends, I knew that neither Robin nor McGoo wanted to tour the interior of the furnace either. I had to get us out of there.

Zombies, for all of our fragile bodies and flesh that's prone to decay, have very strong teeth. Some zombies use them for ripping into flesh and bone; now I discovered that my teeth were excellent at cutting Christmas ribbon. I tore into my colorful satin bindings, snapped the ribbon—and I was free.

But I couldn't fight all those armed hench-elves. Thinking of only one thing that might save us, I jammed my hand into my jacket pocket and grabbed the loop attached to the emergency jingle bell.

It wasn't much of a jing-jing-jingle—but it was enough to summon Old Kris Kringle.

The flames in the furnace brightened, then made a coughing sound. Black smoke swirled out, and with a whoosh of hot air Santa Claus slipped down the smokestack and made his dramatic entrance. The conveyor belt came to a screeching halt as the jolly guy in the magic red suit (which also proved to be non-flammable) emerged from the furnace like something out of *The Lord of the Rings*. He planted his gloved hands on his hips and bellowed, "Ho-ho-ho! Who's been a naughty boy?"

Elfis nearly jumped out of his skin and scrambled down from the director's chair so rapidly that his sunglasses clattered on the floor. With the empty cloth sack over his shoulder, Santa stalked forward like an avenging angel—and not the type that goes on top of a Christmas tree. He spotted his lengthy rolled-up list on the worktable and seized it, holding it up like a baton. "You have gone too far, Elfis. And now you'd better cry, because Santa Claus is coming to get you."

The hench-elves were panicked. They dropped their candy-cane cattle prods and icicle spears and cowered. Their teeth chattered as if they had gone caroling naked on a cold winter's night and no one was offering wassail, or even hot cocoa.

Elfis tried to run, but Santa quickly caught up with him. I couldn't believe how fast the old bearded guy could move, but he had to have a secret power if he could hit millions of households around the world in a single night.

McGoo held up his bound wrists for me to bite the ribbons. Now *that* was showing a measure of trust! "Good plan, Shamble."

"I call it Santa ex-Machina." I picked bright green satin out of my teeth, then turned to free Robin as well.

Santa had cornered Elfis by the big coal hoppers, and the evil elf had no place to go. Santa didn't need any help, but I was part of this, too—and I had a bone to pick with anybody who wanted to throw me and my friends into a furnace.

Next to me, one of the cowering hench-elves still had a sack filled with the icy rock-filled snowballs. I grabbed one and hurled it with perfect aim, proving that not all zombies are disoriented and uncoordinated. My snowball shot struck the release latch on the coal hopper just above Elfis's head. The trap dropped open, and Elfis looked up just in time to see a black avalanche dump down on him. He was buried under lumps of coal.

Robin, McGoo, and I rushed over to Santa, who gazed with satisfaction at the mound in front of him. "Coal is what Elfis deserved…although I'd hoped he would turn his life around if given the chance. Such a disappointment."

"You knew Elfis beforehand?" I asked.

Santa nodded. "He was one of my toy laborers, assigned to my workshop for community service, but he escaped, broke the rules of his North Pole parole. I was going to report him, but not until after the holiday season was over. It's a busy time of the year, you know."

We heard a groan, then a stirring. We moved the coal blocks away to reveal an Elfis now entirely covered in black dust. He plucked in dismay at his ruined jacket. "I guess I won't be having a *white* Christmas."

Santa unslung the sack from his shoulder, tugged it open, and strode forward. "Here comes Santa Claus."

Elfis scrambled backward when he saw the yawning sack. "No, Santa! Please! No!"

"Naughty children get what they deserve." Santa snatched Elfis, stuffed him into the sack, and cinched the opening shut. The captive kept squirming, but could not get out. Santa tucked his rolled up Naughty and Nice list under one arm. "Thank you all. I'll start checking these names, see who deserves to be sentenced to the North Pole for a few years."

"*Sentenced* to the North Pole?" Robin said.

"Oh-ho-ho, this list doesn't just show me who gets presents and who doesn't. The naughtiest of the naughty have to help me spread holiday cheer. Parents write me, too, you know. 'Dear Santa, please help me with my child who keeps acting out.' We have a community-service program up at the Pole, where naughty children can learn good behavior by doing good works." He had a twinkle in his eye.

"There's a long waiting list, but our success rate is remarkable."

"Except for Elfis," I said.

"Some nuts are harder to crack than others, but a few days of shoveling out the reindeer stables usually makes them a little more cooperative."

Moving with supernaturally swift footsteps, Santa stalked around the factory floor, grabbing the cowering hench-elves one by one and stuffing them into his sack, which was obviously much larger inside than it was on the outside. It needed to be. How else could it hold a world's worth of toys?

With the bulging, squirming load over his shoulder, he turned to Robin, McGoo, and me. "I'll let you free the children." He turned to the shackled waifs on the now-still production lines. "Ho-ho-ho! Have you all learned to be nice instead of naughty?"

A chorus of the enslaved kids affirmed that they had indeed learned their lessons. Some, including Buddy, even volunteered to do community-service work up at the North Pole—after they recovered back home with their loving families.

Santa went to the coal furnace, shifted his heavy sack. "I won't forget you on Christmas morning, Mr. Chambeaux. Or you either, Ms. Deyer, or Officer McGoohan. And now, Merry Christmas to all, and to all a good"—he pushed down his black glove so he could double-check the time on his wristwatch—"a good night." He tossed the squirming bag ahead of him into the mouth of the furnace, touched the side of his nose, and vanished up the smokestack.

"Elfis has left the building," I said. "But the kids are still here."

The three of us spent the better part of an hour freeing the natural and unnatural children from their shackles. When Robin unlocked his chains, Buddy Tannenbaum threw himself into her arms. "Thank you, thank you! Can you take me back to my mom and dad now?"

"You'll be home for Christmas," I promised.

For a lot of families, it would be a happy holiday season, except perhaps for those who had ordered their gifts from Elfis Industries and were expecting delivery by Christmas Eve Eve.…

While McGoo called for backup to shut down the factory and secure the crime scene, Robin took down names and developed a plan to reunite the kids with their parents. I called the Tannenbaums directly, and Buddy's parents rushed right down. It was a wonderful reunion, with the werewolf kid nuzzling his parents and promising he would be good.

10

It was Christmas morning in the Chambeaux & Deyer offices—and we found surprise gifts waiting for us, brightly wrapped in colorful paper with holly leaves and berries, wreaths, and little snowmen. Since we didn't have a chimney, Santa could only have delivered the presents by breaking-and-entering, but I wasn't going to press charges.

"Looks like Santa was true to his promise," I said.

Grinning, Sheyenne brought the gifts into the conference room. "If you can't trust Santa to keep a promise, who can you trust?"

I hadn't put anything on my wish list, but Santa Claus was supposed to know exactly what a person wanted or needed. I had to admit I was curious.

"You first, Robin." I nudged the thin, rectangular box with her name on it. As a lawyer, Robin tried to remain cool and businesslike, but I could see the sparkle in her brown eyes as she tugged the ribbon aside, and politely worked at the tape. When she couldn't get it unwrapped, she used a letter opener to slash the paper with all the finesse of a well-practiced serial killer.

Inside was a single yellow legal pad and a sharpened No. 2 pencil. Her excitement dimmed, though she remained smiling. "I can certainly use these. And not every lawyer gets to use a pencil and legal pad from Santa himself."

"There's a note," I pointed out.

Robin pulled a slip of holly-fringed stationery from behind the second yellow sheet, skimmed the handwritten note, then read aloud as her smile grew. "'I don't normally give magical gifts—I don't want to establish a present precedent, but I am so grateful for your efforts. After checking my list and the footnotes I made throughout the year, Robin, I know that your work delights you more than anything else. This special legal pad will never run out of paper, and the enchanted pencil will take notes for you so you can have your hands and mind free to concentrate on your client. Ho-ho-ho, best, S.C.'"

Robin's smile was wide. "I can't wait to try it out!"

Excited, Sheyenne picked up the box with her name on it. She used her poltergeist abilities to undo the bow, pull the ribbon aside, and then, giggling, ripped the wrapping paper to shreds. She opened the box to find an envelope inside—with both our names written on it.

"It's something the two of us can use, Beaux!" With luminous fingers, she opened the flap of the envelope to find an embossed, official-looking certificate inside. "Oh! An all-expense-paid romantic weekend for us at the cozy North Pole Winter Wonderland Bed and Breakfast! Off-season only, it says."

"Now that has definite possibilities," I said, imagining a wonderful time away with my girlfriend. We would have to be creative to overcome the supernatural difficulties that precluded us from touching, but I was up to the challenge.

"Open yours, Dan." Robin handed me the very small box with my name on it.

Judging by the size, I thought it might be a new pair of cufflinks or a tie clip, but who was I to doubt Santa's wisdom or imagination? Zombie fingers are not the most adept at unwrapping small gift boxes, and Santa's elves had used way too much tape, but I managed.

I opened a hinged, velvet-covered box to reveal a small plastic cylinder labeled "Magic Lip Gloss. Use Sparingly." I wasn't disappointed so much as confused, not sure what Santa had been thinking. "Lip gloss?"

Sheyenne made a delighted sound and snatched the tube out of the box. "I think it's for me, Beaux—and that means it's for you." She popped off the cap, extended the lip gloss, and applied it to her widening smile. "A special film for my ghostly lips that might just allow a kiss.…"

She leaned closer, but I told her to wait. "Just a minute, let's do this right." I slipped a hand into my jacket pocket and withdrew the wadded and prickly tumbleweed ball of the McMistletoe artificial substitute that Elfis had been trying to bring to market. I raised it up over my head. "This is supposed to be as good as mistletoe."

Robin was skeptical. "With all the quality that we've come to expect from Elfis Industries?"

Sheyenne's lips glistened invitingly from the magic lip gloss. Under the McMistletoe, she came very close, and her ectoplasmic lips brushed against mine. Yes, I definitely felt a warm tingle.

"I think it works just fine," she said.

Copyright © 2013 WordFire, Inc.

Eric Leif Davin is the author of two books about science fiction—Pioneers of Wonder: Conversations With the Founders of Science Fiction, *and* Partners in Wonder: Women and the Birth of Science Fiction, 1926-1965. *This is his fourth appearance in* Galaxy's Edge. *Two of his previous stories were reprinted in Baen Books' "Year's Best" anthologies.*

GHOST DANCE

by Eric Leif Davin

Buffalo Bill Cody was magnificent in profile. He stood erect, head up, his goatee pointed outward and his long hair flowing from under his wide-brimmed flop hat down to his shoulders. He wore spurred knee-high boots with one foot before the other in order to fully display his manly image. He was the very picture of the intrepid frontiersman, a brave and competent man who feared nothing, neither wild beast nor bloodthirsty savage. The Great Scout knew this, as he took much care in cultivating his legend. The legend, however, was founded on fact. He was, after all, one of the youngest riders in the famed Pony Express. A Civil War veteran, he'd scouted for Custer and was friends with Wild Bill Hickok. One year he slaughtered over five thousand buffalo to feed the workers on the Union Pacific Railroad as it crawled its way across the Great Plains. All together it was said he slaughtered forty thousand buffalo in his career, thus earning his name.

The fringe strips of rawhide along the edge of the sleeves of his colorfully decorated buckskin shirt shimmied in synchronized waves as he lifted his Winchester '73. He nestled its butt in his right shoulder. He levered a bullet into the chamber and took careful aim at something in the distance, out of sight to the viewer. He fired, and smoke roiled around him. Without changing his stance, the famed buffalo hunter and Indian fighter levered another round into his Winchester and fired again. Then he did it again, and yet again.

"Stop!" Thomas Edison yelled from where he stood beside the bulky camera. "That should do it."

"I can keep firing," Buffalo Bill said. "As long as you need."

"I think we have enough," Edison replied. "Time is precious, Bill. It's the only capital any man has, and the one thing he can't afford to lose. Let's move on to your Little Miss Sure Shot." Edison lifted his ever-present stogie, held between his forefingers, and took a big draft. He exhaled a cloud of cigar smoke that mixed with the lingering smoke from Buffalo Bill's Winchester. He turned to his cameraman, William Kennedy Dickson, who had filmed Buffalo Bill firing his rifle. "How does it look, Dickson?"

Dickson patted the one-ton behemoth he'd used to film the plainsman. "Looking good, Mr. Edison. We got him."

"Very well," Edison replied, eyeing the huge wooden object beside Dickson. He nodded toward the Indian fighter still standing before the camera, rifle in hand. "Bill, could you ask Miss Oakley to come in while we get ready?" Buffalo Bill relaxed from his pose. "I'll bring in Annie," he said, and walked out. Edison and Dickson busied themselves with the camera, which looked like a large upright piano, getting it ready to film Annie Oakley, the surest shot in the world.

In 1877, when Edison developed his phonograph, which recorded sound onto wax cylinders, it had proven instantly popular. Opera stars and musicians of international fame hurried from Manhattan across the Hudson River to his barn-like heavily draped studio in West Orange, New Jersey, to immortalize their voices on his cylinders. Edison's phonograph business became quickly profitable. However, Edison felt he could make it even more profitable if customers could actually see the singers whose ghostly voices emerged from the tin horns to which they cocked their ears.

So Thomas Alva Edison, the greatest inventor of the age, set to work with his assistants in his West Orange invention factory to somehow couple sound and moving image. At first they tried to imitate the phonographic cylinder, and in 1888 came up with a cylinder with half-inch high photographic images that revolved in a groove behind a peephole. The next year, however, George Eastman began to produce a photographic emulsion on a nitro-cellulose base. "That's it!" Edison cried, and immediately purchased a fifty-foot strip of film from Eastman's Rochester, New York, plant.

Edison then devised a rapid-fire lens shutter and Dickson, his principal assistant, came up with the idea of rolling the film through the camera by punching holes along the edges of the celluloid strip so that a sprocket could synchronize each frame with the lens shutter. By 1892 Edison and his men were mass-producing peephole machines he called Kinetoscopes. These ran fifty-foot films over a series of small rollers driven by a battery operated motor. One spectator at a time bent over the peepshow boxes to watch the films through a viewing lens.

Then Edison and his men began to mass-produce the films the customers would see through the peepholes. They began filming jugglers, dancers, acrobats, prizefighters, wrestlers, anyone who moved in an interesting way. They also began filming celebrities, well-known people that common people would want to see. Sandow, the world-famous bodybuilder, ferried across the Hudson to flex his mighty arms for Edison's camera. And so did Buffalo Bill Cody and Annie Oakley, the stars of Buffalo Bill's Wild West Show, just returned from their 1892 tour of Europe, where the show had performed on the grounds of Buckingham Palace in a command performance for Queen Victoria.

Buffalo Bill ushered Annie Oakley into Edison's studio. Like Buffalo Bill she was attired in fringed buckskin. The hem of her skirt sported rawhide fringe, and more fringe crawled up each side of the skirt. She wore fringed leather gauntlets and a cowboy hat from which flowed her long brown hair. Like Buffalo Bill she also carried a lever-action Winchester '73. She levered a round into it and raised it to her shoulder. "Ready when you are, Mr. Edison," she said.

"Ready, Dickson?" Thomas Edison asked his assistant. Seated behind the behemoth camera, Dickson nodded and said, "Rolling." Then Edison gestured with his forefingers, still holding his stogie, toward another assistant holding a basket of clay balls. The assistant nodded back and then tossed one of the clay balls into the air with an underhand pitch. Annie Oakley fired, scarcely seeming to aim, shattering the ball. In quick succession the assistant tossed up

ball after ball and, just as quickly, Annie Oakley shattered each of them with sure shots, rapidly levering new rounds into her rifle as she did so. The small studio boomed with the enclosed sound of her shots and rifle smoke filled the air, but only the smoke and Annie Oakley's deadly aim were recorded on Edison's film. In short order the assistant's basket of clay balls was empty. Annie Oakley lowered her rifle. She turned and looked directly into the camera. She smiled and bowed.

"Stop!" Edison yelled, and Dickson stopped filming. "How was that?" Annie Oakley asked. Edison looked at Dickson, who nodded back. "Very good, Miss Oakley," Edison said. "We have now captured your true aim for all the world to see, and for all time." Annie Oakley smiled at the wizard inventor who had thus immortalized her and left the studio, her rifle cradled in her arms.

Then Buffalo Bill, who had been waiting patiently to the side, spoke up. "Now, how about the Injuns? They're waiting outside, made up and ready to go."

Thomas Edison removed his stogie from his mouth and exhaled another billowing cloud of smoke. "Is it safe?" he asked the Indian fighter.

"They're friendly savages, not hostiles," Buffalo Bill reassured him. "I handpicked them and we've just returned from a performance before Queen Victoria with no problems."

"I don't mean that," Edison replied. "I'm not afraid of them. But is it legal? Hasn't the government banned the Ghost Dance?"

The frontiersman smiled at the inventor. "It's true the government banned the dance out West on the reservations. They were afraid Sitting Bull was using it to stir up his followers into some kind of uprising. But Sitting Bull is dead and, besides, I know these Injuns and their rituals. It was never some kind of war dance. It was a religious dance, honoring their ancestors. In any case, these Injuns are under my protection, and I've obtained a dispensation from the government for the dance. They can dance for you without any fear of repercussions.

"Besides, everyone wants to see Injuns dance. They're a vanishing race. Soon they'll just be a few wandering gypsy bands of blanket beggars. After that, they'll be gone forever. This is an unparalleled opportunity to immortalize the last of the Injuns performing a dance that few white men have ever seen, and soon will see no more."

Thomas Edison took another deep draft from his stogie and contemplated the frontiersman as he exhaled another gray cloud of cigar smoke. "Are they picturesque? Are they interesting?"

"These are real Injuns, Sioux, from Sitting Bull's own tribe. In fact, Sitting Bull's nephew, Kicking Bear, the Injun who started the Ghost Dance, is the lead dancer. You can't find a more picturesque band of Injuns than these. They're the last of the real thing."

"Very well, bring them in." Edison gestured to Dickson, letting him know to prepare the camera for the dancing Indians.

Buffalo Bill opened the door to the studio and gestured for those waiting to come inside. A dozen silent Indian warriors, stripped to the waist, entered. They wore moccasins, fringed buckskin leggings, and their naked torsos were painted with white stripes, circles, crosses and stars. Eagle feathers dangled from their braided hair. It seemed to Edison that a band of brute barbarians from some antediluvian past had just stepped into his New Jersey studio. Despite his claim that he was not afraid of Buffalo Bill's Indians, a cold fist briefly clenched his stomach.

At the head of the group was a large brave who stood silently and stared at the white man. A large red cross was painted on his dark chest. His face glowed with painted symbols. Rainbows extended from his outer eyebrows and a white crescent moon decorated one cheek, while a large white star blazed on the other. A leather medicine bag, adorned with eagle feathers, dangled from his right hand. The Indians behind him were painted in similar barbaric fashion, with eagle feathers dangling from them. Some of them carried small drums covered with rawhide and small sticks with which to beat them. Edison grunted in satisfaction. They looked exotic enough to justify filming them.

Buffalo Bill clapped his hand on the shoulder of the large warrior in front. "This is the Injun I told you about," he said. "He's Kicking Bear, Sitting Bull's nephew. He's the one who brought the Ghost Dance to Sitting Bull's Standing Rock Reservation. No one knows the Ghost Dance better than Kicking Bear."

Kicking Bear had learned the white man's language and understood what Buffalo Bill said about him. He nodded at the white man who stood smoking the cigar in front of him, acknowledging that what Buffalo Bill said was true. Although he was a Miniconjou Lakota from Cheyenne River, Sitting Bull, the Hunkpapa Lakota chief at Standing Rock, was his uncle. And no one knew the Ghost Dance better than he, for he had learned the Ghost Dance from Wovoka himself. The Great Spirit had sent his visions first to the Paiute Messiah, Wovoka, and instructed him in the Ghost Dance. Thereafter Wovoka began dancing, singing, and spreading the good news sent by the Great Spirit: If all Indians everywhere left the white man's path and danced the Ghost Dance and sang the ghost songs, salvation would be theirs and the buffalo would return. The message spread like a prairie fire among all the western tribes, agitating and inspiring them. Could it be true? Could the buffalo return, as in days of old?

So Kicking Bear set out with a band of Lakota from the Pine Ridge Reservation and journeyed far to the West, to Nevada, to visit the Paiute Messiah to learn if this was true. Wovoka told them of his vision quest and the promises of the Great Spirit, and Kicking Bear and the others came to believe that it was true. They learned the Ghost Dance from him and then they returned to the Dakotas and told of what they learned. Sitting Bull listened in silence, not sure if what they said was true.

But others who heard, believed. They began dancing the Ghost Dance that Kicking Bear taught them. The dancing spread among the tribes on the various reservations, with Kicking Bear teaching them of the meaning of the Ghost Dance, and leading them in the dancing. If they believed, and danced long enough to show their devotion to the Great Spirit, the buffalo would return, and the ghosts would come. Soon, all were dancing in all the tribes, dancing through the day, dancing through the night, dancing until exhaustion felled them and visions then came to them as they writhed in semi-conscious spasms on the ground.

Then Sitting Bull donned his ghost shirt, with the eagle feathers dangling from it, and also began dancing the Ghost Dance. The people ceased going to the white man's churches and his schools, and those charged with overseeing the reservations became nervous and fearful. The army came to stop the dancing and force the people back to the churches and the schools.

It was then that Kicking Bear fled the reservations, taking his followers into the rugged badlands northwest of Pine Ridge, a place they called "the stronghold." There, they continued to dance the Ghost Dance, hour after hour, day after day, to bring back the buffalo and the ghosts. Sitting Bull said that he would join his nephew in the stronghold, and bring his people with him, and they would all dance the Ghost Dance. Before he could do so, however, the white man's Indian police came for Sitting Bull at Standing Rock, seized him, and killed him in a short fight. After that, the army seized the reservations and forced the people back into the schools and the churches. Then Custer's Seventh Cavalry killed Big Foot and his people, who also danced the Ghost Dance, at Wounded Knee, and then the dancing stopped.

Except in the stronghold of the badlands northwest of Pine Ridge, where Kicking Bear and those few who followed him continued to believe and continued to dance. If they continued to believe, they said, and danced long enough, the vision of the Paiute Messiah would come to pass, the buffalo would return, and the ghosts would come. Sitting Bull was gone, but Kicking Bear danced on.

Until finally, General Nelson Miles surrounded Kicking Bear and his dancers in the stronghold and starved them out, forcing them to surrender. General Miles took them to Fort Sheridan, where he imprisoned them, fearful that they would start dancing again if they were released.

General Miles had no reason for such fear. As Kicking Bear and his few followers sat in their cells at Fort Sheridan, they came to realize that the Paiute Messiah had, after all, been a false prophet. Kicking Bear had gone to see him and hear with his own ears of his visions. It was Kicking Bear who had believed him and returned to bring the Ghost Dance to the Lakota. And it was Kicking Bear who had been the last dancer, dancing alone with his few followers in the badlands to bring back the buffalo and the ghosts of their people, long after the Lakota elsewhere had ceased to dance and had returned to the white man's path.

But the buffalo had not returned, and the ghosts had not come. Kicking Bear, finally, sitting in his dark and filthy cell at Fort Sheridan, realized that it was all a lie, and that there was no hope. He vowed that he would dance no more. He bowed his head and waited for the day his uncle would come for him and take him to another life in the life beyond this one.

But Sitting Bull did not come for Kicking Bear at Fort Sheridan. Instead, it was Buffalo Bill who came for Kicking Bear. The Wild West was dead or dying, but it still lived on in legend and Buffalo Bill, who'd done so much to tame the Wild West, was part of that legend. Even more, Buffalo Bill was the major promoter of that legend. With his Wild West Show Buffalo Bill brought the Wild West to the East, and to the world. Featuring the sharp shooting Annie Oakley, hard-riding cowboys, stagecoach robberies, and, of course, wild Indians, his Wild West Show toured the big cities of the white man's world.

In the past, Buffalo Bill had recruited Sitting Bull, the man who'd killed Custer at the Little Big Horn, as his main Indian attraction. Sitting Bull was now dead, but the Wild West Show still needed Indians, so he'd come to Fort Sheridan to recruit Kicking Bear and the braves imprisoned with him. Not only was Kicking Bear related to Sitting Bull, but he was also the last of the Ghost Dancers. Given the recent fear of an Indian uprising that had swept the Eastern cities as the Ghost Dance had swept the prairies, Kicking Bear had become somewhat of a minor legend in his own right. Would Kicking Bear join the Wild West Show, as had his uncle before him, and come with Buffalo Bill to see the white man's world?

Kicking Bear thought about this. Perhaps this was a sign from the Great Sprit. So Kicking Bear and those few with him decided to go with Buffalo Bill. It was better than languishing in the darkness and filth of their Fort Sheridan cells. Besides, their world was dead and gone. Nothing could bring it back. Only the white man's world remained. Why not see that world?

So General Nelson Miles released Kicking Bear and his followers from their Fort Sheridan imprisonment. Buffalo Bill then took them to the white man's cities, where the people crawled in their endless multitudes like ants in anthills, more people than Kicking Bear ever imagined existed in the world. And the world was far larger, and stranger, than anything Kicking Bear ever conceived. Beyond the cities was boundless water, so much water that the land disappeared and water extended to the edge of the world. And on the other side of the endless water were even more white men, speaking strange languages and wearing strange clothes and walking in strange lands. The cowboys and Indians of the Wild West Show traveled through lands with names like Alsace-Lorraine and Bavaria and the Germanic tribes came to see them and marvel at them.

And Kicking Bear and his fellow Lakota warriors, vanishing people of a vanishing past, rode their ponies and played their parts in Buffalo Bill's pageant of the vanishing Wild West. They whooped their war cries and waved their rifles until Buffalo Bill rode in at the head of a posse of hard-riding cowboys and drove them off, drove them into the past, drove them into oblivion. Kicking Bear came to accept it. It was the way of the world. His own world was dead; the world now belonged to the white man. He wondered at his own ignorance that he had once thought it could ever have been any different.

Then they crossed the great water again to return to the land that the white men called "America," and the great place they called "New York City." Kicking Bear wore the white man's clothes and walked the streets of the place called "Manhattan," jostled by the seething crowds and lost in the dark shadows cast by the topless towers. He walked for endless hours, knowing not where he went, his mind reeling from the limitless hordes, the numberless streets, the vast vistas. In the end, his own world, the world of the Lakota and the prairies, of Sitting Bull and his own Cheyenne River, almost became a dream, a misty fever dream he struggled to recall. It was as if it had never existed. All that was, or could be, was the world of the invincible white man, vast beyond imagination, stretching on into eternity, forever and ever.

Then one day Buffalo Bill came to Kicking Bear and his fellow Sioux at their Wild West encampment. He told them he wanted them to bring their "costumes," as he called their native clothes, and their feathers and their paints and their drums and go with him to see a "wizard," who wanted to see them dance the Ghost Dance once more.

"No one wants to see the Ghost Dance," Kicking Bear told him. "It is forbidden. No one remembers it any longer."

"All the more reason you should dance it one more time," Buffalo Bill said. "Dance it while you still remember it, before it is forgotten forever. Besides, the White Father has given you permission to dance the Ghost Dance one more time, for the wizard, so that it will be remembered for all time."

"Tell me of this wizard, and why he wants to see us dance."

"He is a wizard who has created many new things that never existed before. He created light in a glass ball that glows without fire. He captured sound from the very air, so that a song may be heard again and again, endlessly. And now he has created a way to capture motion for all time, so that those far away, or even those yet to come in the far future, may see people walk and move, even dance, again and again, for all time."

"Can this be true? He can capture a dance so that the dancer will dance for all time?"

"He is a wizard and what I tell you is true. And he wants you to dance for him and he will make you dance for all time, so that people yet unborn may yet see you dance."

Kicking Bear thought about this. He frowned as he thought, perhaps in doubt. Finally, he nodded and said, "Yes, we will come and dance the Ghost Dance the last time, for your wizard."

And so now Kicking Bear and his fellow Sioux warriors, the last of their kind, the last of the Ghost Dancers, stood in the studio of the great wizard who promised to make them dance for all time to come.

"Are you ready?" Edison asked him. Kicking Bear nodded. Edison turned to Dickson and gestured with his stogie. "Are you ready, Dickson?" Dickson, standing beside his camera, nodded. "Rolling," he said.

"Time is short," Edison said to Kicking Bear. "Start dancing."

And Kicking Bear and the last of the Ghost Dancers began dancing, once more, the forbidden Ghost Dance, so that the white man might see it, so that those in the far future might see it, so that his people would not be forever forgotten. They beat their drums, they chanted their incantations, and they danced, around and around in a circle, endlessly circling, dancing, chanting. "You shall live again," Kicking Bear chanted, "you shall live again, all of you shall live again. My father, you shall live again. My mother, you shall live again. Grandfather, you shall live again. Grandmother, you shall live again. Sitting Bull, my uncle, you shall live again. You are not forgotten. You shall live again, forever and ever, as long as I dance, you shall live again, I will rescue you from the grave and you shall live again, and the buffalo will come again."

And so the last of the Ghost Dancers danced and danced, chanting their chants. But their chants were not only that the ghosts would come again and the dead would return and live once more. There was also that other part of the Ghost Dance, the part that frightened the white men the most when the Lakota danced the Ghost Dance at Standing Rock and Pine Ridge and Cheyenne River and their last stronghold in the badlands. For Wovoka had promised them that if they believed and danced long enough, not only would all their dead, their children and their parents and grandparents, return once more, but the white man also would disappear. The white men would all go away, and the land would be as it once was before the coming of the white man, wide and open and thundering with buffalo. All this would come to pass, if only they danced and danced and danced long enough.

And so Kicking Bear and the last of the Lakota dancers danced the Ghost Dance for Buffalo Bill and for Thomas Edison and for those yet to come, and it went on and on into the night, and into the next day, and into the day after that, and the day after that. Never had Kicking Bear and the Lakota dancers danced for so long, even in the badlands. They danced into exhaustion, and then they continued to dance, beyond exhaustion, longer than any dancer could possibly dance, past all human endurance. They danced for the lost buffalo, they danced for their lost world, and they danced for their lost people. They lost all sense of time and place, for all that existed was the Ghost Dance, and the Ghost Dance, the wizard had said, because of his machine, would go on forever and ever, until the end of time, long after even the dancers themselves were dead and their names forgotten.

And the walls of the studio dissolved and melted away and Thomas Edison and William Kennedy Dickson, and even Buffalo Bill Cody, faded away into the mists from which they'd come, as if they never were.

Then Kicking Bear and the Ghost Dancers stopped, at last, at long last, and looked around them. There was nothing but wilderness, green grass, and tall dark forests, as far as their eyes could see. Grazing deer in lush meadows stopped and lifted their heads to peer at them in curious wonder. The only sound was the trill of myriad birds, flickering here and there among the branches of the endless trees.

And then Kicking Bear saw the lone figure walking toward him across the meadow. Tears poured from his eyes and ran down his painted cheeks. He raised his arms wide in greeting, shouted in joy, and ran toward the figure to embrace him, for he knew the man well. It was his uncle, Sitting Bull, coming back to him, just as Wovoka had said that he would, if only Kicking Bear believed, and if only he danced the Ghost Dance long enough.

Copyright © 2017 by Eric Leif Davin

*Steve Pantazis is a Writers of the Future winner.
This is his third appearance in* Galaxy's Edge.

IT'S ONLY SKIN DEEP, DARLING

by Steve Pantazis

"Are you sure about becoming a human?"

"Of course, darling. I've been talking about it for months, haven't I?"

"I know, it's just that…"

"That we're here, doing this, and it's real."

"Yes. Plus, I didn't think we would be in an actual dressing room. It's so…claustrophobic."

"Lorexa, there's nothing to worry about. The curator ensured me total privacy, so we can take our time looking at this assortment of fabulous skins."

"Yes, but…"

"Darling, how long have you known me—three, four-hundred sun cycles? I hired you as my personal assistant right after your pupal stage. I've never steered you wrong, have I?"

"Well, there was that one time when you devoured our guests. Granted, they were rude to you."

"Besides that."

"Never."

"Then trust me, darling, I'm making the right decision. Now which skin shade do you like the best?"

"These are all light beige to dark brown. I think teal would look good on you."

"This is human skin, darling, not Andorellian hide. Humans aren't teal."

"Then I think the shade with the tan skin tone is the best choice. It's the most you."

"Oh, darling, I think you nailed it! Here, help me try it on."

"I'm surprised you can fit all your tentacles in this. It seems so…small."

"Don't worry, I can squeeze in just fine. There. How's that?"

"Not bad. Don't forget about your eye stalks. Humans don't have those."

"Ah, yes, wouldn't want those swaying out there, would we? I'll just retract them, like this. The other stalks can be tucked away behind the ears. See? This is coming along quite nicely, I have to admit."

"Zarrissa, I still don't get why you want to be human. I mean, what about your singing career?"

"Transhuman, darling. I'm not electing for surgery, at least not yet."

"Okay, transhuman. You're a famous singer across the entire spiral arm of the galaxy. Why would you risk that?"

"Sweetheart, I've explained it a thousand times: I'm a human in a Vendufu body. Ever since I visited Earth, I knew I was born in the wrong body. Can't you understand that?"

"Not really."

"Let me put it this way. Remember that song I wrote decades ago about the fifty-eyed anasaka beast who couldn't take his eyes off his true love?"

"Of course. It was number one in the Kaan and Benu Systems for like forty weeks."

"Stolen from a Frankie Valli album on Earth."

"You're kidding me."

"Nope. And the one about all the single tetrahedrons?"

"It stayed on the top-ten list twice as long."

"Beyoncé."

"Oh, my goodness!"

"Now do you understand? Being human is a calling. I can't pretend that I want to keep singing about devouring my offspring or feasting on the brains of Jonkian slaves. I don't want to secrete acid to sign the tentacles of my fans anymore. It's not me."

"I'm sure your mate will be furious when he finds out."

"Which one? I have four mates, darling."

"Four? I thought you had just Cxinku left, and ate the rest."

"No, no, sweets. They're all alive. But don't you see what I mean? I'm not like other Vendufu women. I can't eat my mates, even after they fertilize my hatchlings. I want to cuddle in their arms after mating and talk about the future, like buying a house for our brood and growing old together and sailing the methane seas of Gargoros when we retire. Doesn't that sound wonderful?"

"I think I get it. You don't want to keep living a lie. It's not the true you."

"Exactly!"

"But the public backlash could kill your singing career. It's not like Vendufu have openly accepted the whole trans-species movement."

"I know, but there are many among us. Most are too scared to show their tentacles and speak out, but I want to be their voice. I want to change the way Vendufu see us. I want to take that risk. You can understand, darling, can't you? You wouldn't leave me, would you?"

"Of course not. I'm yours, always and forever. Well, until you decide to eat me, of course."

"Oh, Lorexa, that's the sweetest thing I've ever heard. So…what do you think of the new me?"

"Your tail is still sticking out. Other than that, I think you look fabulous in your new skinsuit."

"Wonderful! I feel so much better that we talked. You're the best friend a gal could ask for."

"So…what do we do now?"

"Now, darling, it's time for the most human of human activities: reality TV."

Copyright © 2017 by Steve Pantazis

Barry N. Malzberg, former Galaxy's Edge *columnist for our first twenty-six issues, is the winner of the first Campbell Memorial Award, a multiple Hugo nominee, and the author of close to one hundred novels and collections.*

A QUESTION OF SLANT

by Barry N. Malzberg

Midway into the central confrontation of his science-fiction novelette, the baby screaming in the next room, his wife muttering pointless comforts as she rattles furniture, midway into the *Encounter of the Aliens*, Constantine finds himself seized with an idea more genuine than he has ever known and rolls the story out of the typewriter, throws the seven accumulated pages of the script cursing into the corner and embarks instead upon a portion-and-outline for a sex novel. "It doesn't pay," he says, referring to science-fiction, "two cents a word, three cents a word, markets, requirements, editors, slants, concepts, the hell with the whole thing, I'm going to make some of that easy money instead." Forty-five-years old, the winner three years ago of a convention "old-timers" award for services to the field above and beyond the cause, he types the title I'M COMING, SWEETHEART below his name and address and begins with some facility to write an extended sex scene between a middle-aged college professor and a coed who is trying to persuade him to give her a passing grade. "This is more like it," Constantine sings as the first conjoinment of genitals takes place before him in the clean second paragraph. "Simple, simple, basic forms, no question of ideation, just hustle and scurry in the dark. Fifteen hundred dollars cash on the line. Should have done it years ago."

Constantine, forty-five-years old, blazes through the first four pages of his sex novel in a high dream-like state, now unconscious of the moans of his first-born, the sniffles and curses of his wife, the sound of plastering two floors below in his West Side tenement. Never a sex writer (one of the citations of the old-timers award had noted his "integrity"), he is surprised by the easy skill of his writing, the quick, twitching lurches from scatology to moans of which he is capable, the energy of his two characters which more than any he has ever created seem to be above and beyond him. "Now I've got it," he says in falsetto as he double spaces and begins a long transition into the impotent past of the professor, "now I'm swinging, now I'm getting into some kind of decent bag, now I know what it's all about." He feels ennobled, sanctified. It is hard for him to know exactly how long this impulse, these talents have been generating. In any event it seems to be worth it.

Pulp, pulp, it is all interchangeable, all of it on the same level. With sanctified ease he converts rocket boosters to breasts, engine pumps to surging genitals, alien dialectic to the cracked screams of love. He is so deep into it that he is barely aware of his wife's presence in the room until she strikes him sharply on the shoulder with a plank of wood left over from the baby's hastily-constructed crib and says, "I can't stand this anymore. He cries and cries all the time. We had no business getting into this, I'm too old for it. What do you think I am, fourteen years old?"

"I'm busy, dear," Constantine says and tries to get back to his scene (the professor was unable to make it with a whore on his seventeenth birthday and this failure has polluted all of his life) but his wife is insistent, the baby is hysterical in the background and even as he types he begins to feel it all go away from him, the motions of generation now only fervid twitches as his fingers slow on the keyboard and then he is at a dead stop. "Don't you understand!" he screams, "I'm just trying to make us a living! You've got to have some goddamned respect for what I'm trying to do."

"I can't stand science-fiction," his wife says. It seems that some kind of confrontation is on the way on this of all afternoons. "I can't stand anything about it: I don't even understand what you're writing and all of the people in it are crazy and it pays about six thousand dollars a year. How can a grown man your age devote himself to—"

"You don't understand," Constantine says with what he hopes is a winning smile but he suspects that it is only a stricken grin, the same stricken grin, perhaps, with which he greeted his wife's pregnancy or the announcement from the Association of Science Fiction Writers that one of his major markets was now being blackballed, "you don't understand, I'm not writing science fiction just now. I'm doing a sex novel. Now if you'll just leave me alone and let me be, I'll be able to knock down an easy couple of thousand—"

"Sex novel!" his wife says, "sex novel, you're not going to publish *that* stuff under my name," and before Constantine can explain that the sex market is invariably composed of pseudonyms, that none of the writers of sex paperbacks ever puts his real name to his work, that the question of identities in sex novels is completely interchangeable, his wife takes the manuscript from his desk, original and carbons, and tears it in half, dumps it triumphantly into the wastebasket and before Constantine can say anything whatsoever leaves the room, leaving the door open behind her. "I would think," she says, "that you had had quite enough of sex by now. Wouldn't you?" He hears a series of high-pitched shrieks which can only indicate that the child, being raised abruptly from its crib, has noticed the absence of a bottle.

"Oh, God," Constantine says, "oh, God, I really can't take this any more," but there is no time for any of that, of course, so he only allows himself to sigh heavily once or twice more (and that is a question of gesture rather than otherwise) and then he picks up the last page of the manuscript of *Survey Starlight* and locates himself, puts it back into the typewriter and begins where he left off, right in the middle of the alien captain's speech. *You Earthers do not understand, this is a colonial investiture,* the Captain says, *we are linked to the Galactic Mindlords by a cosmic and complex chain.*

Constantine feels the cosmic and complex chain. It seems to be about three feet long and is bound around his chest. Nevertheless, as he works into the expository sections a slow smile works itself unconsciously around the thin corridor of his mouth; one would think (if one did not know better) that he has the aspect now, typing, of a Man Who Has Had His Fling.

Copyright © 1970 by Barry N. Malzberg

Dan Koboldt has appeared in Clarkesworld *and* Apex *magazines. His* Gateways to Alissia *series about a Las Vegas magician who infiltrates a medieval world is published by HarperCollins. This is his first appearance in* Galaxy's Edge.

THE COMING OF DARKNESS

by Dan Koboldt

I'll never forget the sound of the grid failing for the last time, the moment that our world's steady electric hum faded to silence. It was March 17, Olivia's birthday. I'd spent most of the month's electricity quota baking a lopsided cake in the toaster oven. She insisted on covering her eyes while I iced it. Looked just like her mother when she did that. Same fine, tawny hair. Same sharp little nose. It tugged at me to notice that, but I forced a smile and slid the cake in front of her.

"Happy birthday, Livvy."

She dropped her hands. "Aw, Dad, it's cute!"

She had the prettiest eyes. Not the color of desert sage like her mother's, but hazel like mine. They were the only thing she'd inherited from me. I prayed that didn't mean what I thought it did.

"Can't believe you're fourteen already," I said. "Go ahead, try some."

"Want to split it?"

"No, it's your birthday."

"Oh, come on. You know you—"

She cut off because the lights went out. A numb and unsettling silence filled the condo. Sunlight streamed through the UV-filtered windows, but not enough to see by. For me, at least. I had the Turner family legacy to thank for that. The doctors had some fancy name for it, retinitis pigmentosa or some such, but we Turners called it what it was.

Night blindness.

"Uh, Dad?"

"I'm right here. Must be a brownout."

"Damn."

"Livvy!"

"Sorry, I mean, *dang.*"

I frowned at her, though I doubted she could see it. I stood and skirted the table's sharp corner on my way to the window. Light or no light, I got by just

fine in the condo. As long as Olivia didn't move the furniture on me.

I found the cord and lifted the UV shade. "Make that a blackout. Everything's dark."

"It's always dark with you," Olivia teased. She joined me at the window and looked out. "Oh."

"Do you see anything lit up?"

"The high rises are dark. Wait, I see some lights."

I started to relax a little. "Where are they?"

"On the street."

"What color?"

"Um, orange. I think."

The tension returned to my shoulders. "Those are emergency backups. Battery powered."

"What should we do?"

"Pack up your stuff. We'll make for the hideaway in the morning."

"But I have school!"

"No, Livvy, you don't." I stared out at the fading cityscape. I could almost feel the rising sense of panic in the air. "Nobody has school."

It always surprised me how many people didn't plan for the gridfail. We'd had plenty of warnings: the shrinking electric quotas, the rate hikes, the brownouts. I worked in mechanical engineering for fifteen years before they laid me off; planning was in my blood. So I'd stashed a trailer out in a desert canyon with everything we'd need to rough it long term. Tools, first aid supplies, non-perishable food, the works. I'd spent my last paycheck putting gas in the truck.

That was six months ago now. I still had seven-eights of a tank.

I woke Olivia a little after sunrise, as soon as it was bright enough to see. For me to see, that is. A normal guy, without the night blindness, could have started an hour earlier.

"Do we really have to go?" she asked.

"Yes. But if they get the power fixed, we'll come back."

"Promise?"

"I promise." I kept the hard truth from my face. I'd stayed up all night, watching the darkness for signs that the grid might come back. I'd not seen any.

She sighed, and somehow made it sound like she'd conceded Poland to Germany. "Fine."

We threw everything worth taking into the back of the truck. Granted, that wasn't much. Our condo was tiny and I'd been out of work for months. No need for any electronics, that was for damn sure. We had good reason to hate anything with a screen.

I said a little prayer, and turned the key. The engine sputtered, whined, and fell quiet. *Damn.* I tried it again, no dice. I counted to ten, and then hit the gas while I turned the key. The engine rumbled to life. I let out a long breath. "Buckle up, baby girl."

Driving made me nervous as hell. Technically, I'd lost my license about six months ago. The eye doc let me go on as long as he could, but I'd lost too much peripheral vision. I figured it didn't matter today. The cops would have their hands full as it was.

I turned on the headlights to get out of the parking garage, with Olivia helping me check the corners. Didn't even have to ask her; she'd been doing it since she was twelve, and she realized I had almost no peripheral vision.

We pulled out on the street, turned up toward the highway, and hit a goddamn wall of traffic.

"Son of a—" I started, then caught myself. "Gun."

Livvy fiddled with the radio and found only static. "Guess we're not the only ones trying to get out of town. Can I go back to bed now?"

"No." The fact that so many others were fleeing only told me my instincts were right. This wasn't a brown-out or even a blackout. This was total grid failure.

We fought our way into the logjam. The only advantage to our crappy condo was its location on the outskirts. But the traffic was worse than I'd imagined. We moved at a crawl for five hours while the needle on the fuel gauge marched ever downward.

We reached the desert at last. Traffic thinned out a bit then, with people going whatever direction felt right for them. Some only wanted a country road while others fled north or west toward the bigger metropolises. A few probably headed out to raid the equipment on the solar and wind farms that powered the city. Which was fine by me. No point in keeping them operational now that the grid had failed.

We had ninety miles of deep desert country to cross to reach the trailer. Mostly no-name, two-lane roads to get there. I'd modeled the traffic a hundred different ways, figuring on a mass exodus

when the shit hit the fan. The trick was to get off the arterial highways as soon as possible. To rely on rough unpaved thoroughfares weak-ass electric cars couldn't handle.

The desert roads wouldn't be a problem, as long as we had enough gas. What worried me was the lamprey town.

During the energy crisis, the city built big solar/wind farms out in the desert to try to keep up with demand. When the quotas hit, everybody had to cut back to bare essentials: climate control, lighting, and utilities. Devices and flat-screens were prohibited. That was an issue for a lot of people who'd grown dependent on them. Once they got kicked off the city grid, they moved out to the desert in big groups. Set up along the power supply lines from the energy farms and tapped into them illegally, like lampreys sucking blood from a salmon.

That's where Olivia's mother had gone when she left us. To be with the other juice-suckers who couldn't live without screens. The towns were lawless places, too. No real infrastructure, no hygiene, just a bunch of addicts getting their electronic fix. With the gridfail, they'd be in withdrawal, and that made them more dangerous than ever.

A mile or two out, I started to ease off the gas. It was mid-afternoon by then; a shaky mirage danced over the road as it heated up.

Olivia glanced up from her paperback. "Why are we slowing down?"

"Coming up on the lamprey town."

She winced. I hated myself a little for it. Hated her mother, too, for ever causing that pain in the first place. For picking her goddamn screens over her family. Should have seen it coming, I guess. The things she'd done for juice even before our daughter came along…well, I tried not to think about them.

Olivia tucked a strand of hair behind her ear. "Is this the town that—"

"No. That was another one."

I'd gone out to find her mother a couple of times. Tried to talk her into coming home. But she wouldn't even take off her headphones or look at me. Hadn't been eating, as far as I could tell. The third time I went looking, she was just gone. Some other juice-sucking punk had moved into her shack, and after a few minutes of me beating the shit out of him, he told me she was dead. Which shouldn't have surprised me.

I never went back again. Never told our daughter about it either.

Olivia gasped. "Dad, hit the brakes!"

I slammed on them by instinct; I'd trusted her eyes for years. The truck's axles groaned in protest. "What is it?"

"Something in the road."

I saw it then, a tangle of burned-out car frames piled up against a battered tractor-trailer. Blocked most of the road and shoulder. There was gap about big enough for the truck to squeeze through, but a few people loitered there. Two men and a woman, all of them wearing soiled clothes that hung limp from their too-thin frames. All of them had their eyes down on the glowing smartphones or tablets in their hands.

I should have floored it. Should have just run them down. But I didn't want Olivia to see that.

The closest one looked like a hippie with an unkempt beard. He lounged in the shade against the side of the trailer, just kind of twitching. When we got close, I saw the interior was stuffed with cables, electronics, and stacks of blocky shapes. Shoeboxes, maybe. I couldn't make them out in the trailer's semidarkness. I rolled down my window as Skinny Beard sauntered over.

"Where you headed?" he asked. The other two lampreys stood behind him, still glued to their screens.

"Out west," I said. I wasn't about to give any specifics. "Is there any way through?"

"This here's a toll road now."

I felt a spike of irritation, and let him see it. "Since when?"

"Since we lost the juice."

I sighed. "How much?"

He leaned against my windowsill to look at the dashboard. His scraggly beard brushed against my arm. I resisted the urge to shove him away. Lampreys hated being touched.

"About a quarter tank," he said.

"That's nearly all I have!"

He shrugged. "Gotta feed the generators."

So that's how they were keeping up with their electronic addiction. What a waste. I gripped the steering wheel and did the math. If I gave them a quarter tank, I'd have about an eighth left. That would get us there, but barely. Made it a one-way trip, that was for damn sure. "Can I pay with something else?"

"Whatcha got?"

"Not much," I admitted. We'd already moved the crucial stuff to the trailer. It was just me and Livvy and some basic supplies. I'd have gone around, but there wasn't enough gas to look for another route. The lamprey toll road was the only way. "Just the gas."

"You're lucky, bud. Some folks wanted through with electric cars." His eyes had a shine to them, that fever-glow I'd come to recognize from a lamprey with nothing to lose. That's when I recognized the rectangular blocks piled in the trailer. They were car batteries.

It was all I could do not to glance at the burned-out hulks that blocked the road. "Fine. Take the gas."

"Dad—" Olivia started.

I held up my palm at her. "It's fine, Livvy."

Skinny Beard had to shout at his two lackeys to get their attention. "Hey!"

They glanced up, irritation and stupor written in their screen-glowed faces.

"Siphon."

That got them moving. The woman, who had dirty blonde hair tied up in rags, ducked into a trailer for a gas canister and a piece of tube. She moved with quick, jerky movements, but started the siphon by mouth like she'd done it a hundred times before. I didn't shut off the motor. Skinny Beard leaned on my windowsill again so that he could watch the fuel gauge. His nearness made my skin itch.

The needle was below half and slipped further away from it as the lampreys took their toll. I ground my teeth as it slid past one-fourth.

"All right, that's it," I said.

Skinny Beard ignored me. He stared at the gauge like a starving man looking at a side of beef. The gas kept flowing out of my gas tank and into theirs. If they took much more, we wouldn't even have enough to roll past their barricade. That would leave us in the desert heat with a bunch of lampreys.

Not gonna happen.

I wrapped my fingers in the scratchy beard. He grunted in surprise as I yanked him down over the windowsill. With my other hand, I lifted my jacket so he could see the Smith & Wesson holstered in my armpit. "I said we're done."

He blinked into reality for a second. The whites showed around his eyes. He snapped his fingers twice, and they stopped siphoning.

I held on to him. "Tell them we're allowed through."

"Gah! Jesus! They're…good to go."

I tweaked his beard a little. "Louder."

"They're good to go!" he shouted.

In the mirror, I saw the two lampreys back off, clutching the tube and the now-heavy tank of gas. I released Skinny Beard and wiped the grime from his beard on my pant leg. I nudged the truck around their barricade, hit the gas, and shot us onto the open road beyond.

Cold sweat gave my skin a chill. The char of the burned-out cars lingered.

"Do we have enough gas left?" Olivia asked.

"I think so," I lied. We'd probably get within walking distance, but not enough to drive down into the canyon. We'd have to abandon the truck. But the real concern was the length of the shadows the saguaros cast across the road.

If the gas didn't run out, the daylight would.

The gas ran out first. Once the needle dropped past E, the engine started sputtering right on cue. "Dry already," I muttered. "God—" and I caught myself again, because Olivia took her headphones off. "Bless America."

"Is that it?" she asked.

"Just about."

"Why'd you let them take so much gas?"

"No choice, Livvy. We had to get through, and that was their price."

She pouted. "You could've offered money."

"They don't want money. Be glad we had some gas to give them." I remembered those burned-out car frames and shuddered.

"What if we didn't?"

"Let's not talk about it." I eased off the gas pedal and started looking for a decent place to pull over while the engine choked on fumes. It stalled a minute later. I coasted to the shoulder and off of it, down into a drainage ditch. If we couldn't carry everything, I didn't want the truck looted before I got back.

"Jeez, Dad!" Olivia squeaked. "Are we going to be able to get out of here?"

"We won't need to." Fuel prices had already been outrageous before the gridfail. Now they'd go through the roof. I doubted I could afford half a gallon. "We'll have to hike a bit. I think it's around two miles."

"Uphill or downhill?"

"Both."

She rolled her eyes and wrenched open her door. "God, it's hot."

That didn't surprise me. With the grid down, the government's weather modulation programs would probably be out too. I loaded backpacks for both of us—with mine about four times as heavy as hers—and we shouldered them.

"Ugh. What did you put in this, bricks?" Olivia asked.

"Water." Good, clean water to stock the trailer. We had some canned food and clothes but they'd have to stay in the truck until I could make another trip.

We set out from the road, hiking cross-country for the little pocket canyon. About two hours' walk, give or take. I set a good pace and tried to ignore how long the shadows had gotten. How the sun was dropping lower in the sky. We'd spent a lot of weekends out here getting acclimated while I retrofitted the trailer. My damn tunnel vision still made me stumble on a few rocks, but we made good time.

I'd just begun allowing a hint of optimism when Olivia stopped short.

"Dad."

"What?" I couldn't keep all of the irritation from my voice.

We still had about half an hour to go, and I hadn't told her about the worst part. About the hardest part. But I saw her now and she was pointing at the western sky. The sun had gone from yellow to bronze, and where it kissed the horizon the sharp, clear orange light was fuzzy. As if we were looking at it through a glass of water. I saw it and my guts went cold. Words failed me, but I'm sure she saw the terror on my face.

"What is it?" she asked.

"Sandstorm."

"Shit!"

For once, I didn't bother chiding her.

We hustled for the canyon, scrambling over rocks and around saguaros as safely as we could. Rushing like this was foolish, but I didn't want us caught in the open when the sandstorm came. The thin blur on the western horizon rose like a tidal wave. Started to block out the already-setting sun. By the time we got to the rim of the pocket canyon, I could barely see at all. A hundred feet below us, on the canyon floor, I could just make out the metallic blur of the trailer. But the rock face getting down there was steep, practically vertical.

"How do we get down?" Livvy asked.

I eased out of my pack, set it down, and fumbled it open. Felt around for the coil of thick paracord inside. "By rope."

She looked around us, frantic. "There's nothing to tie it to!"

"I'll hold it and lower you."

"Why don't we climb down?"

In full daylight we probably could. Both of us had done some rock climbing. But climbing down was hard enough. Doing it when you couldn't look for handholds was just asking for it. It didn't matter that she was still young. The night blindness knew no age once it came on you. I remembered being fourteen. I remembered the sheer darkness that twilight had meant for me. And with the sandstorm blocking out most of the sun, that's exactly what we were in.

I sighed. "I can't see, Livvy."

"So? I'll go first."

"You're just as blind as I am, once we lose the light."

"No, I'm not," she said.

She's lying. "Livvy," I said, in that *Dad-doesn't-believe-you tone.*

She hugged me suddenly, startling me. Squeezing me tight. She pressed her face up against my neck, shedding warm tears.

"What's wrong?" I asked.

"I was pretending," she whispered.

"Huh?"

"I—" she sobbed, took a breath. "I don't have the night blindness."

I hadn't seen her cry in years. She'd always been so grown-up for her age. The sound of it shattered me inside. "Wh-why?" I managed.

"I didn't want you to feel alone."

God, what a sweet girl she is. Her mother didn't deserve her. Neither did I, really. But she was all I had, and I'd try my best to get her through this. I settled myself. "All right, then. Show me the way down."

We tied up with the paracord, a figure eight double-loop for her belt, and a slipknot for mine. That way if she fell, I could clamp down on it. If I did I wouldn't pull her down with me.

"Be careful," I said.

"Dad, it's fine." She slid her belly over the edge and found footholds. I quietly changed the knot on my belt so I could release it if I started to fall. Then maybe she'd still make it. The area beyond the cliff's edge was like a black hole to my eyes. I focused on the sound of her breathing and tried to follow, fumbling around with my boots to find purchase.

"Here." She put her hand on my foot and guided it to a flat spot. I tested it and put my weight on it while she worked her way farther down. Then I slid to make it my handhold, working by feel. Trying not to think about falling. *Sweet Jesus.*

That's how we went. Slow, painful team climbing down the slope, with her finding the safe spots for my feet, while the roar of the approaching storm got louder. Sand started raining down on us. My next foothold grated off the edge and I flailed for purchase.

I almost couldn't believe it when my feet found the bottom. We stumbled to the trailer and threw ourselves inside. I slammed the door behind us, barred it, and fumbled for the panel. Light bloomed. Sweet, merciful white light that brought the world and my Livvy into view for me. And revealed just how grubby and sand-coated she was.

"You're a mess," I said.

"So are you!"

I smiled. "I can't believe you were pretending all that time."

"It was easy."

"Psh!" But I knew she was right. I was so fearful I'd passed along my affliction to her. I guess I didn't need much convincing. "You beat the odds, baby girl. A fifty-fifty shot, and we're so alike I guess I just assumed."

A cloud passed over her face. "I don't think it was fifty-fifty."

"Why not?"

"I'm not—" she paused. "I'm not yours."

My heart broke a little. My tongue felt thick in my mouth, but I forced a smile. "Of course you're mine."

"But mom said—"

"I don't care what she said." I'd shared every moment of Olivia's life since birth. I still remembered that too. She came out pink-skinned, bright-eyed, and with a set of lungs that could wake the dead. "You'll always be my little girl."

She looked down and away from me. "Do you mean that?"

"Course I do." I put two fingers under her chin, and tilted her face up so I could look at it. So I could stare at those big, beautiful eyes that weren't mine at all. "It's you and me, just like always."

"Do you think she'll ever come back to us?"

Maybe I should tell her. It killed me to think she still hoped for something that would never happen. Letting go of that dark secret might take some of the knots out of my shoulders.

Then again, she'd spent four years bumbling around in the darkness. Hitting her shins on furniture and never going anywhere at night, even with friends. She'd done all of that so I wouldn't feel alone. A glimmer of hope was the least I could offer.

I hugged her tight against me so she couldn't read the lie from my face. "Maybe someday she will."

Copyright © 2017 by Dan Koboldt

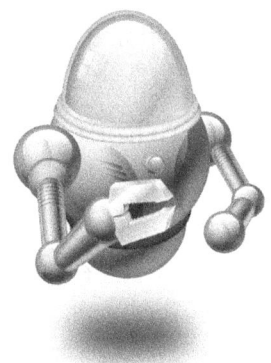

Sandra M. Odell's work has appeared in such venues as Jim Baen's Universe, Crossed Genres, Daily Science Fiction, Pseudopod, *and* Deep Cuts. *She is a Clarion West graduate. We are happy to have her back in* Galaxy's Edge.

GREEN

by Sandra M. Odell

At the sound of hoof beats, I came around the corner with my courage and my ax. The last white riders didn't like no free black man working his own land. An ax couldn't do much against a gun, but I'd cut down as many as I could before I let them set a hand on my skin, and God have mercy on their souls if they put an eye on my baby girl.

A single rider came in fast, his horse foaming and streaked with sweat and west Texas dust. Not a thing came behind him. I put myself between him and the house, ready to call him out, when I caught sight of the horse's horns. Two of them, long, sharp, jutting out front of its head and made pretty with silver rings dangling from the tips. In all my years, I'd never seen a horse with horns.

The rider pulled to rein. I thought about taking a step toward the animal, thought twice about not. "Howdy," I said when I could.

The horse tossed its head. Them rings sounded like far off church bells on a cool spring morning. The rider turned to me, head bowed beneath the wide brim of his dusty hat so as I couldn't see his face, but I could see his long, white hands that never worked a day. He wore a long trench over dark britches, and a shirt stained fresh red across the belly. I looked from the stain, to the horse, to the wide-brimmed hat. That's when the rider fell out of the saddle and onto his face.

I dropped the ax and run to him. The horse whinnied and scampered back when I called out, "Ruth, come quick!"

My girl come running onto the porch. She stopped cold at the sight of the horse. "Da?"

She sounded scared; couldn't say that I blamed her. "Get the bucket and bring water from the creek."

As I talked, my hands worked up the rider all on their own. His hat came off, showing hair bright as the sun, and a wicked gash over his right eye. He smelled like fresh cut hay and the hot copper of new blood. I looked up at the horse, those horns. The rider was white, but he weren't from around here.

Ruth stood stone still on the porch.

"Get on now!"

She done moved at that. I shouldered the rider up the front steps and into the house. I expected to work under him, but he weighed next to nothing for a fellow his size. The Devil's voice weighed me down more, saying I should leave him in the dust, what did I owe some man who would sell me and my kin soon as look at us? For all my fear, I kept hold of the truth of the Good Samaritan and put the Devil and his wicked tongue behind me.

I stretched the fellow out on my rickety bed; his feet hung over the end. He groaned and opened eyes the swirling green of leaves in a stream, called out something I didn't understand in a voice like the preacher for his horse's church bells.

"You're gonna be just fine, mister," I said, working his arms out of his coat.

I can't say as he heard a word I said, but he closed his eyes and went limp. A hand on his chest made sure he was still breathing.

Ruth come back in with the water, and I had her put it on the fire to boil the way Delilah would have done before the Lord called her and baby Matthew home.

Ruth twisted the bottom of her blue sack dress in her hands. "I can give the horse water, too, can't I, Da? A little water won't give it no colic, right?"

By then I had the rider's shirt pulled up and his belt undone. "You're straight-on smart, baby girl. A sip or two won't hurt none. Just set the bucket in front of it. Wake up the fire and set the dish rags in the water pot to boil before you go."

A smart girl, my Ruth, smart and pretty like her momma. I sure could have used Delilah's hands beside mine. She'd always had a way of nursing body and soul back to health, but she was in Heaven not quite a year now and I had to make do on my own.

The gash on his forehead bled some yet weren't so bad as the cut in his side, all jagged like someone took to sawing him in half and stopped after a stroke or two. A few bruises, some scratches, the backs of his hands ragged sliced. I plastered his head and hands with brown paper and a few drops of witch hazel, and cleaned up his belly with the dishrags after they boiled a time. Then I got my sewing kit and set to stitching his side with thread soaked in a little Sunday sipping whiskey. He grunted with the push of the needle, but didn't make no other complaint.

I took my time, did my best, all I could do. There weren't much light except for what came through the door and the chinks in the mud daub between the logs. I studied his skin, pale as moonlight on milk. And his ears. I brushed that sunlight hair back over those strange double points on top, and the fine gold hoops and chains on the bottoms.

I took the water off the fire, set the soup pot back over the edge of the coals.

Ruth kept her eyes to the stranger like she was curious but too afraid to get near. "He gonna die, Da?"

"That's for the Lord to say. Get on out now."

Sitting at bedside all day only ate up sunlight, so I headed out after her to see about the rider's horse. That strange beast nosed the red dirt near the water bucket like it was looking for grass that just weren't there, like it were a real horse and didn't have no horns. Ruth watched from the porch as I come down the steps slow and easy. The horse looked up with swirling eyes like the rider's, bright silver instead of green.

"What you gonna do?" she said, tugging on her dress.

"Don't rightly know. Hey, there." I kept my voice low. I figured if horses liked such talk, chances was a horse with horns would too. "You're a big fella, ain't you?"

The horse shook its head, pranced, twitched its tail. Were that some kind of horned horse talk? Did it understand me?

The horse let me set a hand on its neck. It had a strong pulse under the chestnut hair, not so fast at all. It smelled musky like a horse, but of growing things, too, like the rider. Close up, I eyed the sleek lump of the saddle, the two small saddlebags on the rump, how the bridle weren't that much different than ones I'd seen before though the beast's teeth were coyote sharp.

The horse sighed, shifted a might. "Good boy," I kept up softly. "Good boy. Come on, now."

A bucket of water hadn't done it no harm, so I told Ruth to sit tight and led the horse to the creek south of the house. Right away, it dipped its head and began to drink. When I tried to lead it away, the horse stayed solid put until it had its fill of the muddy water. Seemed the beast knew what it needed. Besides, with no rains for well on three months, it was a wonder the creek run at all.

The drought set me thinking again of packing up, selling off the acreage to the railroad men. Rumor had it they was coming through and paid good money for land, maybe even to a black man like me. I could take the money and move to San Francisco, get on with a good job, maybe find my baby girl a new momma. After the war, Delilah and me headed west before anyone could tell us otherwise. Our own land, freedom, a family. Now her memory and two graves were all that kept us here, and memories didn't feed hungry bellies come another winter.

More of the Devil's tricks. I tore up handfuls of dried grass and brushed the horse down. When it were finished drinking, I lead it round back to the lean-to where I used to keep Julius before I traded him for eggs and flour.

The saddle didn't look heavy, but I couldn't let the horse suffer under the weight in the heat. I had the kit-and-caboodle on the ground when I caught eye of a green glow coming from the nearest saddlebag. Had it been glowing before and I just now noticed it? I looked around. The horse stood quiet, and Ruth weren't nowhere to be seen, so I eased open the flap thinking I'd close up whatever were open then head on back to chopping wood.

Inside the bag were some dried fruit and a small box like some sort of woman's keepsake with that green glow seeping from under the lid. Knowing it were a sin, but too curious to tell the Devil to mind his own matters, I lifted the lid to peek inside. Out shot every color of spring like a rainbow of birds. Reds, yellows, greens, blues, all of them come together smelling of tart green apples and cool water. The light spilled up over my face and onto the uneven lean-to planks. A peace so profound come over me, I lost myself in its ease.

I stayed like that, on my hands and knees, until the horse nuzzled my shoulder with its cool damp nose.

I closed the box, and the glow went away though the ease lingered, and with it a touch of fear because. . .I wanted to open the box again with a powerful wanting. Maybe the Devil knew something I didn't.

I checked in on the rider before midday, sleeping fitful, calling out words I didn't know in his dreams. I wiped his face and chest with a wet rag. Those swirling eyes, they drifted open without seeing much, then settled closed. I set the rag on his neck with a prayer for his health and peace in the Lord. I didn't have no idea if my Lord were the same as his, but I figured a prayer couldn't hurt.

Come afternoon, I was shucking a pitiful few ears of corn from my withered garden and thinking about that wanting feeling when a rider came in from the north, riding easy. He looked a sight, a small, sun-dark man on a thick-bodied dun, a bedroll behind him, no gun that I could see. He looked road lonesome, but I could tell from his squint his whiteness was still better than my blackness.

He stopped a neighborly distance away. "Howdy, boy."

Made my neck prickle, the way he said it. I didn't look away or wring my hat. This were my land. "Howdy yerself."

Odd to have two riders on the same day. And I wondered at how he looked at everything but me like looking for something that weren't found.

He tipped his head to see around the back of the house. "Name's Jed Bothell. Looking for work. I'm handy with an ax and saw. I can put up fences or push a barrow."

"Strong working man is always a good thing, but I got no work for you nor money to pay if I did."

His eyes told me he didn't like straight talk from colored folk. I kept shucking my corn.

"Not for pay," he said after a while. "A good meal and a place to rest my head is enough for me."

Those words didn't sit well with me. Maybe how he said them, or the way he hitched his lips when he did. "Can't help you there none, neither. Widow Carson a mile or so west of here," I pointed that way, "she can always use an eager hand, and she's a right good cook."

He squinted his eyes at me in deep and sour thought. Then he smiled, kind of tight-lipped. "Thanks kindly, boy."

Weren't nothing kind about him. "My name is Solomon Hatchett and this is my land."

"Apologies. Solomon." He put a finger to the brim of his hat. "Nice to know folk are looking out for their neighbors."

"Yup."

He watched me for some little time. "That corn there lookin' kind of puny."

I picked up another cob, tearing open the husk with a green sound and smell that brought on thoughts of the rider. "Yup. Eats puny, too."

He shifted in the saddle. "Been a while since I had me corn so fresh I seen it shucked."

"Widow Carson put up some fine corn relish last summer. Ask her for some with her biscuits."

"Oh." Jed looked again toward the back of the house. Two fingers of his right hand fiddled with a thing in his vest pocket. "It's sure on hot. You got a place I could set Martha out of the sun, bo—Solomon? Maybe I could step inside the house for a sip of cool water?"

I had a sudden longing for my shotgun, and not only cause I'd seen his kind before. "Didn't need the lean-to so I cut it up for kindling, and there's cooler water in the crick if you can find it through the mud."

I saw it again, that sour look. It cleared as quickly as it come. "No matter. I'll ask on with the widow."

Jed turned his mare around and headed off a few steps, then stopped and fumbled at his chest. He held out his hand, slowly moving it this way and that, stopping finally in the direction of the woodshed and lean-to.

"Problem there, Jed?"

He moved his hand to his chest, like to put something back in his pocket. "Just getting light enough to check the time. Eyes ain't what they used to be and all." Jed looked over his shoulder, tipped his hat. "Have a good evening."

Would have been easier to believe him if his shadow weren't long toward the woodshed.

I stayed put until Jed Bothell was mostly out of sight, then brought the corn inside and put it on the table. The rider lay eyes closed and quiet on the bed. I went over to check the plaster on his head, and he grabbed my hand in one of his. He opened them eyes, stared up at me hard as flint, then croaked out something I didn't understand. He made the same sounds again. I tried to pull my hand away, but his grip kept me to him like a shackle.

A terrible rage come on me then. I weren't no animal for him to grab. I earned my freedom from President Abraham Lincoln! Lord help me, I raised my fist against that strange rider and the Devil laughed in my face, laughed and called me out as a coward if I didn't name myself a man and strike that rider down.

It were God Hisself stopped me. God said, son, look at him, give him all your eyes. Look at him, see him, see the man hurt and alone in a strange place. Fixing to get beat because he different. Because he talked best he could and it sounded all gibberish to me.

Lord above, Lord above. That's all I could think for the longest time. Lord above.

I uncurled my fingers, drew a hard breath, and set that hand on top the rider's trembling fingers. "I don't know what you're sayin'. You speak good American, maybe? Or Mexican? _Habla español?_"

He pulled me down and hisself up until we were close enough that I could feel his breath warm against my cheek. He said whatever it were more slow without much breath, his eyes tight on my face.

"I'm sorry, mister, I don't ken to what you're telling me."

He sagged and let go my hand.

I made him comfortable, fetched a wet rag to mop his face. A sip of water dribbled more down his chin than in his mouth. He lay his head back.

"A stranger come and went. Is that it? He wanted to look around, but I called him off. Lord only knows what he were after, but I made sure he didn't see nothing about you or your horse."

Should I say something about the glowing box? Best not. "I need to check my stitch work. Can I do that?"

The rider turned his head away and closed his eyes.

The stitches looked healthy, smelled like fresh grass with no hint of blood at all. The rider didn't say nothing else, didn't take no water when I offered, and in time he fell back to sleep.

That night after a supper of soup and the last of the cheese, Ruth asked, "Why you cleanin' your gun?"

My little girl played with her rag doll. The rider slept sound on my bed.

"I thought I saw a rattlesnake." I kissed the top of her curly head. "You go on and wash your face, and get on to bed."

The Lord helps those that help themselves. I figured it were better to be ready for help and not need it than need it and be waiting for the Lord in vain.

✧

Dark shapes eyed me from the trees. Leeches with great, heavy chains and swirling gray eyes dragged me under murky water, bidding on my last breath, watching, waiting…

I gave a little scream and sat bolt upright from my pallet by the fire. Ruth stirred beside me, and I peeked under her blanket to make sure there weren't no leeches or chains. Nothing but her rag doll. I let out a shaking breath, covered her back up, and looked to the rider.

In the faint red light of burned down coals, I saw him at the end of the bed, head bent over cupped hands. Sounded to me like he whispered a prayer, but that might could have been the wind. Maybe he had the box? I eased forward, hoping to have another peek inside. "You all right?" I said real soft.

He poured whatever were in his hands into a bag. The mess of things sounded heavy and a bit like metal. He stood real slow, then staggered with his bag of something over to my shotgun by the door. Lord help me, I had some un-Christianly thoughts.

He brought the sack and gun to me, and offered them up. For a minute, I didn't know how to think of it, but I finally took them with my held breath. The sack was filled with shotgun shells. I breathed out. "What am I gonna do with these?"

He didn't bother talking this time, just pointed to the bag, the gun, then me.

I looked at him standing there, a milk pale magic man, eyes all aglow. "These ain't for normal men, is they? You did somethin' to them because there's, there's somethin' else comin'. Lord above, what kind of man are you?"

The rider all but fell back on the bed. He drew a deep breath and let it free as a sigh, pulled his blanket around him, and turned on his side away from me.

I fished a handful of shells out of the bag. They glowed like some faint star high in the sky, so soft the light barely brushed my palm. Most went into the pockets of my dungarees, but for two I cracked the breech, slipped them in, and closed it up with a snap.

I stirred the coals, and went to fetch me my Sunday whiskey, in need of a sip for all it were Wednesday. The box didn't feel so needful anymore when all I could think on were leeches and chains and dark night fears.

✧

I hadn't meant to sleep, but the next thing I know my head came up at the sound of hoof beats in the early morning light steaming through the walls.

Ruth raised her sleepy head. "Someone comin', Da?"

Lots of someone by the sound of it. The rider weren't nowhere to be found. Righteous fear wiped away any sleep in me, fear for what might come for the rider and find me and my baby girl in his place. "Ain't nothin' but a dream. Close your eyes and go back to sleep."

Strange drowsy like, she laid her head down. I took up my gun and made for the door. Outside rode up four horses from the direction the rider come yesterday morning, three riders on chestnuts with long, slender horns, and Jed Bothell on his dun.

I come down the stairs easy like, the gun down but ready. "How you come on with Widow Carson, Jed?"

He hitched his shoulders in a sort of shrug. "Wouldn't know," he said, not bothering to hide his white hate for me. "My friends here are looking for someone and think he might be here. They aim to have a look around."

He didn't have no sidearm that I could see, but the other three had jagged swords under their long coats. My fingers tightened on the gun. "You tell them there ain't no one here that has business with them."

The other three riders looked me up and down. Their eyes swirled dark gray beneath wide-brimmed hats. They had that same milk pale skin like the green-eyed rider before them, the same smooth, long hands. Could have been brothers for all I knew, but the wind made little dust devils behind them, and brought me the smell of rotting leaves and dead things.

One of them urged his horse forward a few steps, and talked at me in those different words. I somehow expected he'd sound like a rattler's tail, but his words had preacherful grace. He touched a hand to the grip of his sword. That weren't grace.

They could have been a righteous gathering, those gray-eyed riders, but something of their smell and their eyes said they wasn't to be trusted. Jed Bothell, he didn't look shamed or scared or nothing, just sat there like a cat waiting for Lucifer hisself to pour a bowl of cream. And they was looking for a man I doctored up in good faith. I pulled back the hammers. "I don't right know what he said, and don't much care to, so it's best if you all turn around and—"

From behind the house come a scream that curled my toes and brought my gun to bear. Faster that spit, the first rider come around the back corner, dug his heels into his horse's flanks, and jumped the beast right over the one closest to me. An unshod hoof caught the gray-eyed rider in the face, tumbling him into the Texas dirt. That quick, the first rider came down on the other side and wheeled around, hair wild and green eyes full of burn.

One of the gray-eyed riders gestured. Black vines erupted from the ground and twined around the legs of the first rider's horse. The horse screamed, and the sound knocked the surprise right out of me. I opened up with both barrels at that same gray-eyed rider, and caught him high in the chest. He flew back off his horse, and the vines turned to dust.

The gray-eyed rider on the ground near me come up on his knees, sword in hand, and hissed words at me through his bloody mask.

My heart clenched tight and I screamed. I couldn't breathe, couldn't think, dropped the gun and to my knees as pain fired my whole body. I felt my heart take its last beat. Sweet Delilah said my name.

The world turned black all around, hoof beats came at me hard. Jed Bothell yelled something. I heard another scream—mine?—and my chest swelled with light. The Lord stood me right up and pushed me out of the way as the first rider, off his horse now, pulled one of them swords out of the chest of the gray-eyed rider on the ground.

I took up the shotgun and slapped two shells home. Fast as that, I fired at the last gray-eyed rider, catching his horse in the neck with both rounds.

The beast went up on its back legs and fell over. He twisted out of the saddle quicker than I've ever seen a man move until the first rider leapt even faster and drove him to the ground with the sword between them.

Another reload. I pinned Jed Bothell in my sights. "Don't move."

Jed held his hands out wide and empty, his face pasty white and afraid of a black man like he'd never been before. "I-I ain't raised a hand against you. Don't go doin' nothin' rash."

Both hammers came back. The Devil whispered temptation, *shoot him, shoot him,* but I kept God in my heart. "That's right, so you get offa my land before I decide you need a good scratchin'."

He wasted no time riding back the way he came.

It was done. The first rider scrambled off the last gray-eyed rider, leaving the sword sticking out of the sumbitch's chest. Fresh blood slicked the first rider's shirt beneath his coat, and a scorch mark covered where a man would have a heart.

He staggered to his horse, tore open his saddlebag, and pulled out the keepsake box. I thought to feel that strong need again, but it never came. I'm ashamed to say I felt a might sad at that.

The rider opened the lid a bare bit. A rainbow lit over his face, and he let out a sigh more like a sob. He closed the box and set it real gentle back in the saddlebag, whispering grace-filled words. That's when he turned to me and smiled, and we understood one another just fine.

☼

Ruth slept right through. I don't know why I woke up, maybe on account of being responsible for my land.

The rider gathered up the horses on a lead behind his own. They didn't mind none, nor when he spoke words over the gray-eyed riders and they turned brown and crumbly at the touch of his hands. This he stared at for a time, writing green fire letters with a long finger through the piles. The fire faded, leaving dark mounds reminiscent of good earth. He swept the piles into his hat with the side of his hand, favoring his left side as he went.

"Let me have a look at them stitches," I said. I wasn't sure what could be done about the burn.

He ignored me until every bit of brown was scooped into the hat, then stood and gestured me follow him to the paltry garden beyond the house. I did, and stood by as he scattered a fistful of remains over the rows. "We got to be eatin' that," I said.

He smiled at me, and threw out another bunch into the creek. That smile said whole books worth, but I'd no idea what it meant beyond good will.

The sun was full over the horizon and promising Texas heat by the time we walked back to the horses. He didn't speak against me when I gave him a hand into the saddle. I pointed to the saddlebag. "You take care of that, you hear?"

He smiled again, pointed toward the garden, and I liked to think said the same. I looked over my shoulder and shook my head to clear what I saw. Couldn't be. New green spread over the cornstalks, plumped the beans. Clean, fresh water had broken through the creek mud and filled the bed true as far as the eye could see in both directions.

I turned back around. The rider and horses were dust on the other side of the creek.

Copyright © 2017 by Sandra M. Odell

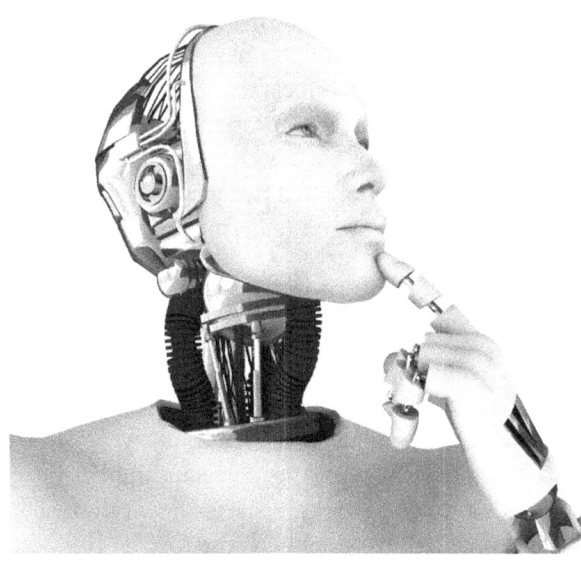

Nancy Kress is a multiple Hugo and Nebula winner, and one of the pre-eminent writing workshop leaders in the field. We're thrilled, as always, to welcome her back to Galaxy's Edge.

BY FOOLS LIKE ME

by Nancy Kress

Hope creeps quietly into my bedroom without knocking, peering around the corner of the rough doorjamb. I'm awake; sleep eludes me so easily now. I know from the awful smell that she has been to the beach.

"Come in, child, I'm not asleep."

"Grandma, where's Mama and Papa?"

"Aren't they in the field?" The rains are late this year and water for the crops must be carried in ancient buckets from the spring in the dell.

"Maybe. I didn't see them. Grandma, I found something."

"What, child?"

She gazes at me and bites her lip. I see that this mysterious find bothers her. Such a sensitive child, though sturdy and healthy enough, God knows how.

"I went to the beach," she confesses in a rush. "Don't tell Mama! I wanted to dig you some trunter roots because you like them so much, but my shovel went clunk on something hard and I…I dug it up."

"Hope," I reprimand, because the beach is full of dangerous bits of metal and plastic, washed up through the miles of dead algae on the dead water. And if a soot cloud blows in from the west, it will hit the beach first.

"I'm sorry," she says, clearly lying, "but Grandma, it was a metal box and the lock was all rusted and there was something inside and I brought it here."

"The box?"

"No, that was too heavy. The…just wait!"

No one can recognize most of the bits of rusted metal and twisted plastic from before the Crash. Anything found in a broken metal box should be decayed beyond recognition. I call, "Hope! Don't touch anything slimy—" but she is already out of earshot, running from my tiny bedroom with its narrow cot, which is just blankets and pallet on a rope frame to keep me off the hard floor. It doesn't; the old ropes sag too much, just as the thick clay walls don't keep out the heat. But that's my fault. I close the window shutters only when I absolutely have to. Insects and heat are preferable to dark. But I have a door made of precious and rotting wood, which is more than Hope or her parents have on their sleeping alcoves off the house's only other room. I expect to die in this room.

Hope returns, carrying a bubble of sleek white plastic that fills her bare arms. The bubble has no seams. No mold sticks to it, no sand. Carefully she lays the thing on my cot.

Despite myself, I say, "Bring me the big knife and be very careful, it's sharp."

She gets the knife, carrying it as gingerly as an offering for the altar. The plastic slits more readily than I expected. I peel it back, and we both gasp.

I am the oldest person on Island by two decades, and I have seen much. Not of the world my father told me about, from before the Crash, but in our world now. I have buried two husbands and five children, survived three great sandstorms and two years where the rains didn't come at all, planted and first-nursed a sacred tree, served six times at the altar. I have seen much, but I have never seen so much preserved sin in one place.

"What…Grandma…what is that?"

"A book, child. They're all books."

"Books?" Her voice holds titillated horror. "You mean…like they made before the Crash? Like they cut down *trees* to make?"

"Yes."

"Trees? Real *trees*?"

"Yes." I lift the top one from the white plastic bubble. Firm thick red cover, like…dear God, it's made from the skin of some animal. My gorge rises. Hope mustn't know that. The edges of the sin are gold. My father told me about books, but not that they could look like this. I open it.

"Oh!" Hope cries. "Oh, Grandma!"

The first slate—no, first *page*, the word floating up from some childhood conversation—is a picture of trees, but nothing like the pictures children draw on their slates. This picture shows dozens of richly colored trees, crowded together, each with *hundreds* of healthy, beautifully detailed green leaves. The trees shade a path bordered with glorious flowers. Along

the path runs a child wearing far too many wraps following a large white animal dressed in a wrap and hat and carrying a small metal machine. At the top of the picture, words float on golden clouds: ALICE IN WONDERLAND.

"Grandma! Look at the—Mama's coming!"

Before I can say anything, Hope grabs the book, shoves it into the white bubble, and thrusts the whole thing under my cot. I feel it slide under my bony ass, past the sag that is my body, and hit the wall. Hope is standing up by the time Gloria crowds into my tiny room.

"Hope, have you fed the chickens yet?"

"No, Mama, I—"

Gloria reaches out and slaps her daughter. "Can't I trust you to do anything?"

"Please, Gloria, it's my fault. I sent her to see if there's anymore mint growing in the dell."

Gloria scowls. My daughter-in-law is perpetually angry, perpetually exhausted. Before my legs gave out and I could still do a full day's work, I used to fight back. The Island is no more arid, the see-oh-too no higher, for Gloria than for anyone else. She has borne no more stillborn children than have other women, has endured no fewer soot clouds. But now that she and my son must feed my nearly useless body, I try to not anger her too much, to not be a burden. I weave all day. I twist rope when there are enough vines to spare for rope. I pretend to be healthier than I am.

Gloria says, "We don't need mint, we need fed chickens. Go, Hope." She turns.

"Gloria—"

"What?" Her tone is unbearable. I wonder, for the thousandth time, why Bill married her, and for the thousandth time I answer my own question.

"Nothing," I say. I don't tell her about the sin under the bed. I could have, and ended it right there. But I do not.

God forgive me.

☼

Gloria stands behind the altar, dressed in the tattered green robe we all wear during our year of service. I sit on a chair in front of the standing villagers; no one may miss services no matter how old or sick or in need of help to hobble to the Grove. Bill half carried me here, afraid no doubt of being late and further angering his wife. It's hard to have so little respect for my son.

It is the brief time between the dying of the unholy wind that blows all day and the fall of night. Today the clouds are light gray, not too sooty, but not bearing rain either.

The altar stands at the bottom of the dell, beside the spring that makes our village possible. A large flat slab of slate, it is supported by boulders painstakingly chiseled with the words of God. It took four generations to carve that tiny writing, and three generations of children have learned to read by copying the sacred texts onto their slates. I was among the first. The altar is shaded by the six trees of the Grove, and from my uncomfortable seat I can gaze up at their branches against the pale sky.

How beautiful they are! Ours are the tallest, straightest, healthiest trees of any village on Island. I planted and first-nursed one of them myself, the honor of my life. Even now I feel a thickness in my shriveled chest as I gaze up at the green leaves, each one wiped free of dust every day by those in service. Next year, Hope will be one of them. There is nothing on Earth lovelier than the shifting pattern of trees against the sky. Nothing.

Gloria raises her arms and intones, "Then God said, 'I give you every plant and every tree on the whole Earth. They will be food for you.'"

"Amen," call out two or three people.

"'Wail, oh pine tree,'" Gloria cries, "'for the cedar has fallen, the stately trees are ruined! Wail, oaks—'"

"Wail! Wail!"

I have never understood why people can't just worship in silence. This lot is sometimes as bad as a flock of starlings.

"'—oaks of Bashan, the—'"

Hope whispers, "Who's Bashan?"

Bill whispers back, "A person at the Crash."

"'—dense forest has been cut down! And they were told—told!—not to harm the grass of Earth or any plant or tree.'"

Revelation 9:4, I think automatically, although I never did find out what the words or numbers mean.

"'The vine is dried up!'" Gloria cries, "'the fig tree is withered! The pomegranate and the palm and the apple tree, all the trees of the field, are dried up! Surely the joy of mankind is withered away!'"

"Withered! Oh, amen, withered!"

Joel 1:12.

"'Offer sacrifices and burn incense on the high places, under any spreading tree!'"

Amy Martin, one of the wailers, comes forward with the first sacrifice, an unrecognizable piece of rusted metal dug up from the soil or washed up on the beach. She lays it on the altar. Beside me Hope leans forward, her mouth open and her eyes wide. I can read her young thoughts as easily as if they, too, are chiseled in stone: *That metal might have been part of a "car" that threw see-oh-two and soot into the air, might have been part of a "factory" that poisoned the air, might have even been part of a "saw" that cut down the forests!* Hope shudders, but I glance away from the intensity on her face. Sometimes she looks too much like Gloria.

Two more sacrifices are offered. Gloria takes an ember from the banked fire under the altar—the only fire allowed in the village—and touches it briefly to the sacrifices. "Instead of the thornbush will grow the pine tree, and instead of briars the myrtle will grow. This will be for the Lord's glory, for an everlasting sign which—"

I stop listening. Instead I watch the leaves move against the sky. What is "myrtle"—what did it look like, why was it such a desirable plant? The leaves blur. I have dozed off, but I realize this only when the whole Village shouts together, "We will never forget!" and services are over.

Bill carries me back through the quickening darkness without stars or moon. Without the longed-for rain. Without the candles I remember from my childhood on Island, or the dimly remembered (dreamed?) fireless lights from before that. There are no lights after dark on Island, nothing that might release soot into the air.

We will never forget.

It's just too bad that services are so boring.

✿

ALICE IN WONDERLAND
PRIDE AND PREJUDICE
BIRDS OF INDIA AND ASIA
MOBY DICK

MORNING LIGHT
JANE EYRE
THE SUN ALSO RISES

I sit on my cot, slowly sounding out the strange words. Of course the sun rises—what else could it do? It's rising now outside my window, which lets in pale light, insects, and the everlasting hot wind.

"Can I see, Grandma?" Hope asks, naked in the doorway. I didn't hear the door open. She could have been Gloria. And is it right for a child to see this much sin?

But already she's snuggled beside me, smelling of sweat and grime and young life. Even her slight body makes the room hotter. All at once a memory comes to me, a voice from early childhood: *Here, Anna, put ice on that bruise. Listen, that's a—*

What bruise? What was I to listen to? The memory is gone.

"M—m—m—oh—bee—Grandma, what's a 'moby'?"

"I don't know, child."

She picks up a different one. "J—j—aye—n… Jane! That's Miss Anderson's name! Is this book about her?"

"No. Another Jane, I think." I open MOBY DICK. Tiny, dense writing, pages and pages of it, whole burned forests of it.

"Read the sin with the picture of trees!" She roots among the books until she finds ALICE IN WONDERLAND and opens it to that impossible vision of tens, maybe hundreds, of glorious trees. Hope studies the child blessed enough to walk that flower-bordered path.

"What's her name, Grandma?"

"Alice." I don't really know.

"Why is she wearing so many wraps? Isn't she *hot*? And how many days did her poor mother have to work to weave so many?"

I recognize Gloria's scolding tone. The pages of the book are crisp, bright and clear, as if the white plastic bubble had some magic to keep sin fresh. Turning the page, I begin to read aloud. "Alice was beginning to get very tired of sitting by her sister on the bank—"

"She has a *sister*," Hope breathes. Nearly no one does now; so few children are carried to term and born whole.

"'—and tired of having nothing to do: once—'"

"How could she have nothing to do? Why doesn't she carry water or weed crops or hunt trunter roots or—"

"Hope, are you going to let me read this to you or not?"

"Yes, Grandma. I'm sorry."

I shouldn't be reading to her at all. *Trees* were cut down to make this book; my father told me so. As a young man, not long after the Crash, he himself was in service as a book sacrificer, proudly. Unlike many of his generation, my father was a moral man.

"'—or twice she had peeped into the book her sister was reading, but it had no pictures or conversation in it, "and what is the use of a book," thought Alice, "without pictures or conversation?" So she was considering—'"

We read while the sun clears the horizon, a burning merciless ball, and our sweat drips onto the gold-edged page. Then Gloria and Bill stir in the next room and Hope is on the floor in a flash, shoving the books under my sagging cot, running out the door to feed the chickens and hunt for their rare, precious eggs.

✿

The rains are very late this year. Every day Gloria, scowling, scans the sky. Every day at sunset she and Bill drag themselves home, bone-weary and smeared with dust after carrying water from the spring to the crops. The spring is in the dell, and water will not flow uphill. Gloria is also in service this year and must nurse one of the trees, wiping the poisonous dust from her share of the leaves, checking for dangerous insects. More work, more time. Some places on Earth, I was told once, have too much water, too many plants from the see-oh-too. I can't imagine it. Island has heard from no other place since I was a young woman and the last radio failed. Now a radio would be sin.

I sit at the loom, weaving. I'm even clumsier than usual, my fingers stiff and eyes stinging. From too much secret reading, or from a high see-oh-too day? Oh, let it be from the reading!

"Grandma," Hope says, coming in from tending the chickens. "My throat hurts." Her voice is small; she knows.

Dear God, not *now*, not when the rains are already so late…. But I look out the window and yes, I can see it on the western horizon, thick and brown.

"Bring in the chickens, Hope. Quick!"

She runs back outside while I hobble to the heavy shutters and wrestle them closed. Hope brings in the first protesting chicken, dumps it in her sleeping alcove, and fastens the rope fence. She races back for the next chicken as Bill and Gloria run over the fields toward the house.

Not *now*, when everything is so dry…

They get the chickens in, the food covered, as much water inside as can be carried. At the last moment Bill swings closed the final shutter, and we're plunged into darkness and even greater heat. We huddle against the west wall. The dust storm hits.

Despite the shutters, the holy protection of wood, dust drifts through cracks, under the door, maybe even through chinks in the walls. The dust clogs our throats, noses, eyes. The wind rages: *oooeeeeeeeooooeeeee*. Shrinking beside me, Hope gasps, "It's trying to get in!"

Gloria snaps, "Don't talk!" and slaps Hope. Gloria is right, of course; the soot carries poisons that Island can't name and doesn't remember. Only I remember my father saying, "Methane and bio-weapons…"

Here, Anna, put ice on that bruise. Listen, that's a—
A what? What was that memory?

Then Gloria, despite her slap, begins to talk. She has no choice; it's her service year and she must pray aloud. "'Wail, oh pine tree, for the cedar has fallen, the stately trees are ruined! Wail, oaks of Bashan, the dense forest has been cut down!'"

I want Gloria to recite a different scripture. I want, God forgive me, Gloria to shut up. Her anger burns worse than the dust, worse than the heat.

"'The vine is dried up and the fig is withered; the pomegranate—'"

I stop listening.
Listen, that's a—
Hope trembles beside me, a sweaty mass of fear.

☼

The dust storm proves mercifully brief, but the see-oh-too cloud pulled behind it lasts for days. Everyone's breathing grows harsh. Gloria and Bill, carrying water, get fierce headaches. Gloria makes

Hope stay inside, telling her to sit still. I see in Gloria's eyes the concern for her only living child, a concern that Hope is too young to see. Hope sees only her mother's anger.

Left alone, Hope and I sin.

All the long day, while her parents work frantically to keep us alive, we sit by the light of a cracked shutter and follow Alice down the rabbit hole, through the pool of tears, inside the White Rabbit's house, to the Duchess's peppery kitchen. Hope stops asking questions, since I know none of the answers. What is pepper, a crocodile, a caucus race, marmalade? We just read steadily on, wishing there were more pictures, until the book is done and Alice has woken. We begin JANE EYRE: "'There was no possibility of taking a walk that day….'"

BIRDS OF INDIA AND ASIA has gorgeous pictures, but the writing is so small and difficult that I can't read most of it. Nonetheless, this is the book I turn to when Hope is asleep. So many birds! And so many colors on wings and backs and breasts and rising from the tops of heads like fantastic feathered trees. I wish I knew if these birds were ever real, or if they are as imaginary as Alice, as the White Rabbit, as marmalade. I wish—

"Grandma!" Hope cries, suddenly awake. "It's raining outside!"

☼

Joy, laughter, dancing. The whole village gathers at the altar under the trees. Bill carries me there, half running, and I smell his strong male sweat mingled with the sweet rain. Hope dances in her drenched wrap like some wild thing and chases after the other children.

Then Gloria strides into the Grove, grabs Hope, and throws her onto the altar. "You've sinned! My own daughter!"

Immediately everyone falls silent. The village, shocked, looks from Gloria to Hope, back to Gloria. Gloria's face is twisted with fury. From a fold of her wrap she pulls out ALICE IN WONDERLAND.

"This was in the chicken coop! This! A sin, trees *destroyed*…you had this in our very house!" Gloria's voice rises to a shriek.

Hope shrinks against the wide flat stone and she puts her hands over her face. Rain streams down on her, flattening her hair against her small skull. The book in Gloria's hand sheds droplets off its skin cover. Gloria tears out pages and throws them to the ground, where they go sodden and pulpy as maggots.

"Because of you, God might not have sent any rains at all this year! We're just lucky that in His infinite mercy—you risked—you—"

Gloria drops the mutilated book, pulls back her arm, and with all her force strikes Hope on the shoulder. Hope screams and draws into a ball, covering her head and neck. Gloria lashes out again, a sickening thud of hand on tender flesh. I cry, "Stop! No, Gloria, stop—Bill—let me go!"

He doesn't. No one else moves to help Hope, either. I can feel Bill's anguish, but he chokes out, "It's right, Mama." And then, invoking the most sacred scripture of all, he whispers, "We will never forget."

I cry out again, but nothing can keep Hope from justice, not even when I scream that it is my fault, my book, my sin. They know I couldn't have found this pre-Crash sin alone. They know that, but no one except me knows when Gloria passes beyond beating Hope for justice, for Godly retribution, into beating her from Gloria's own fury, her withered fig tree, her sin. No one sees but me. And I, an old woman, can do nothing.

☼

Hope lies on her cot, moaning. I crouch beside her in her alcove, its small window unshuttered to the rain. Bill bound her broken arm with the unfinished cloth off my loom, then went into the storm in search of his wife.

"Hope…dear heart…"

She moans again.

If I could, I would kill Gloria with my own hands.

A sudden lone crack of lightening brightens the alcove. Already the skin on Hope's wet arms and swollen face has started to darken. One eye swells.

Here, Anna, put ice on that bruise. Listen, that's a—
"Grandma…"

"Don't talk, Hope."

"Water," Hope gasps and I hold the glass for her. Another flash of lightening and for a moment Gloria stands framed in the window. We stare at each other. With a kind of horror I feel my lips slide back,

baring my teeth. Gloria sees, and cold slides down my spine.

Then the lightening is gone, and I lay my hand on Hope's battered body.

☼

The rain lasts no more than a few hours. It's replaced by day after day of black clouds that thunder and roil but shed no water. Day after day. Gloria and Bill let half the field die in their attempt to save the other half. The rest of the village does much the same.

Hope heals quickly; the young are resilient. I sit beside her, weaving, until she can work again. Her bruises turn all the colors of the angry earth: black and dun and dead-algae green. Gloria never looks at or speaks to her daughter. My son smiles weakly at us all, and brings Hope her meal, and follows Gloria out the door to the fields.

"Grandma, we sinned."

Did we? I don't know any more. To cut down *trees* in order to make a book…my gorge rises at just the thought. Yes, that's wrong, as wrong as anything could ever be. Trees are the life of the Earth, are God's gift to us. Even my father's generation, still so selfish and sinful, said so. Trees absorb the see-oh-too, clean the air, hold the soil, cool the world. Yes.

But, against that, the look of rapture on Hope's face as Alice chased the White Rabbit, the pictures of BIRDS OF INDIA AND ASIA, Jane Eyre battling Mrs. Reed…Hope and I destroyed nothing ourselves. Is it so wrong, then, to enjoy another's sin?

"We sinned," Hope repeats, mourning, and it is her tone that hardens my heart.

"No, child. We didn't."

"We didn't?" Her eyes, one still swollen, grow wide.

"We didn't make the books. They already *were*. We just read them. Reading isn't sinful."

"Nooooo," she says reluctantly. "Not reading the altar scriptures. But Alice is—"

Gloria enters the house. She says to me, "Services tonight."

I say, "I'm not going."

Gloria stops dead halfway to the wash bucket, her field hat suspended in her hand. For the briefest moment I see something like panic on her face, before it vanishes into her usual anger. "Not going? To services?"

"No."

Hope, frightened, looks from her mother to me. Bill comes in.

Gloria snaps, with distinct emphasis, "*Your* mother says she's not going to services tonight."

Bill says, "Mama?"

"No," I say, and watch his face go from puzzlement to the dread of a weak man who will do anything to avoid argument. I hobble to my alcove and close the door. Later, from my window, I watch them leave for the Grove, Hope holding her father's hand.

Gloria must have given him silent permission to do that.

My son.

Painfully I lower myself to the floor, reach under my cot, and pull out the white plastic bubble. For a while I gaze at the pictures of the gorgeous birds of India and Asia. Then I read JANE EYRE. When my family returns at dusk, I keep reading as long as the light holds, not bothering to hide any of the books, knowing that no one will come in.

One heavy afternoon, when the clouds steadily darken and I can no longer see enough to make out words, a huge bolt of lightening shrieks through the sky—*crack*! For a long moment my head vibrates. Then silence, followed by a shout: "Fire!"

I haul myself to my knees and grasp the bottom of the window. The lightening hit one of the trees in the Grove. As I watch, numb, the fire leaps on the ceaseless wind to a second tree.

People scream and run, throwing buckets of muddy water from the spring. I can see that it will do no good—too much dry timber, too much wind. A third tree catches, a fourth, and then the grass too is on fire. Smoke and ash rise into the sky.

I sink back onto my cot. I planted one of those trees, nursed it as I'd once nursed Bill. But there is nothing I can do. Nothing.

By the light of the terrible flames I pick up JANE EYRE and, desperately, I read.

And then Hope bursts in, smeared with ash, sweat and tears on her face.

"Hope—no! Don't!"

"Give it to me!"

"No!"

We struggle, but she is stronger. Hope yanks JANE EYRE out of my hands and hurls it to the floor. She drops on top of it and crawls under my cot. Frantically I try to press down the sagging ropes so that she can't get past them, but I don't weigh enough. Hope backs out with the other books in their plastic bubble. She scrambles to her feet.

"We did this! You and me! Our sin made God burn the trees!"

"No! Hope—"

"Yes! We did this, just like the people before the Crash!"

We will never forget.

I reach for her, for the books, for everything I've lost or am about to lose. But Hope is already gone. From my window I see her silhouetted against the flames, running toward the grass. The village beats the grass with water-soaked cloths. I let go of the sill and fall back onto the cot before I can see Hope throw the books onto the fire.

Gloria beats Hope again, harder and longer this time. She and Bill might have put me out of the house, except that I have no place to go. So they settle for keeping me away from Hope, so that I cannot lead her further into sin.

Bill speaks to me only once about what happened. Bringing me my meal—meager, so meager—he averts his eyes from my face and says haltingly, "Mama…I…"

"Don't," I say.

"I have to…you…Gloria…" All at once he finds words. "A little bit of sin is just as bad a big sin. That's what *you* taught me. What all those people thought before the Crash—that their cars and machines and books each only destroyed a little air so it didn't matter. And look what happened! The Crash was—"

"Do you really think you're telling me something I don't know? Telling *me*?"

Bill turns away. But as he closes the door behind him, he mumbles over his shoulder, "A little bit of sin is as bad as a big sin."

I sit in my room, alone.

Bill is not right. Nor is Gloria, who told him what to say. Nor is Hope, who is after all a child, with a child's uncompromising, black-and-white faith. They are all wrong, but I can't find the arguments to tell them so. I'm too ignorant. The arguments must exist, they *must*—but I can't find them. And my family wouldn't listen anyway.

Listen, Anna, that's a—

A nightingale.

The whole memory flashes like lightening in my head: my father, bending over me in a walled garden, laughing, trying to distract me from some childish fall. *Here, Anna, put ice on that bruise. Listen, that's a nightingale!* A cube of frozen water pulled with strong fingers from his amber drink. Flowers everywhere, flowers of scarcely believable colors, crimson and gold and blue and emerald. And a burst of glorious unseen music, high and sweet. A bird, maybe one from BIRDS OF INDIA AND ASIA.

But I don't know, can't remember, what a nightingale looks like. And now I never will.

Copyright © 2007 by Nancy Kress

Jody Lynn Nye is the author of forty novels and more than one hundred stories, and has at various times collaborated with Anne McCaffrey and Robert Asprin. Her husband, Bill Fawcett, is a prolific author, editor and packager, and is also active in the gaming field.

RECOMMENDED BOOKS

by Bill Fawcett and Jody Lynn Nye

On Labor Day weekend in Atlanta, the Dragon Awards were presented for the second time at DragonCon. These awards are unique in several ways. With between eight- and ten-thousand fans voting and the voting open to anyone who registers, they are by far the closest science fiction has to a true people's choice honor. Of the seventeen awards covering everything from comics, games to movies and TV, seven go to novels. (There are no short form awards. For more on the Dragon Awards go to http://awards.dragoncon.org/.) This month, along with some other outstanding novels, we will take a look at the winners.

Best Fantasy Novel
Monster Hunter Memoirs: Grunge
by Larry Correia and John Ringo
Baen Books
June, 2017
ISBN-13: 978-1481482622

Set in Larry Correia's bestselling Monster Hunter's International universe, this novel is a collaboration between two of military science fiction's most popular authors. Here, monsters and even old gods are painfully real. Dedicated, often hard-bitten and cynical, monster hunters protect a generally unaware public. The government pays a bounty based on the threat to their nation. World-ending old gods pay really well. Therefore, there is a lot of troll versus machine guns action in these books. The MHI novels range in time from the thirties to today.

Set during the Reagan era, Grunge follows the training and development of Oliver Gardenier, destined to become one of MHI's most flamboyant and effective agents. And he really is destined in the biblical sense of the term. The marine was killed in the bombing of their barracks in Beirut, but when he reaches the pearly gates, Saint Peter gives him a choice: heaven or take on a mission for the boss back on Earth. The marine takes the mission, and soon finds himself a new member of Monster Hunters International. Written with humor and amazing action, this book combines the strengths of both authors. Grunge also provides a chance to take a good look at the Monster Hunters International as a company, as a group of determined and brave fighters, and to see how a MHI agent is trained. If you like great combat scenes, contemporary fantasy with a touch of humor and a story that is written with an appealing lack of reverence, Grunge is for you.

✧

Best Science Fiction Novel
Babylon's Ashes
by James S.A. Corey
Orbit USA
October, 2017 (reprint edition)
ISBN-13: 978-0316217644

This is the sixth book in The *Expanse* series co-written by Daniel Abraham and Ty Franck, a sweeping epic of a time when a gateway opened the stars to humanity and everything changed. The series begins with the story of how the Belters, who have been repressed by both the UN and Martian government, rebel. Next, a mysterious biological attack devastates humankind. This sixth book is set after the Belter's Free Navy has almost destroyed the Earth, but has gained them a tenuous freedom. The problem for the newly liberated force is building an independent and sustainable ecology now that they no longer have access to Earth's food supply. Free navy ships are stopping and pillaging colony shops sent out from the crippled Earth and commandeering their cargoes. Complications follow, and old grudges return in force, but humanity is not its own greatest foe. Just beyond mankind's new interstellar gate, an alien enemy is waiting. We recommend you begin this well-written series with its first novel, *Leviathan Wakes*.

✧

Best Young Adult/Middle Grade Novel
The Hammer of Thor—Book 2 of the Magnus Chase and the Gods of Asgard series
by Rick Riordan
Hyperion (Disney)
October, 2016
ISBN-13: 978-1423160922

This is the second Magnus Chase novel and is set in the same world as Rick Riordan's Percy Jackson novels and movies. While Percy Jackson (son of Poseidon) lives in New York City, which is dominated by the Greek/Roman gods, Magnus Chase lives in Boston, the new home of the Norse gods. Magnus is the half-divine son of Frey. In the first book (*The Sword of Summer*) Magnus dies heroically, and is taken by a Valkyrie to Valhalla. Odin's Feasting Hall is now a modern hotel complex full of amenities with a big park in the center where the immortal warriors can fight and die in a glorious but hopeless battle each afternoon. This prepares them to fight well in Ragnarok, the final glorious but hopeless battle that will end the world. Then, they all resurrect and have an evening feast.

Magnus, having penned the Fenris Wolf, finds himself unwillingly involved in a recovery effort. Thor, as he has done several times, has lost Mjolnir, his hammer. Without it, the realms, including our Earth of today, are vulnerable to a giant invasion. An invasion that will trigger Ragnarok. The hammer is hidden eight miles deep by an Earth Giant. To get it, Magnus has to deal with challenges, ranging from defeating a giant dragon to transporting a bowling ball and bag the size of a small mountain.

Enough about the plot; there is one important thing to know about this series: It is beautifully written, irreverent and tremendous fun to read. The story flows, the situations are both logical and just short of absurd. Magnus and his friends are modern teenagers, questioning it all even as they fight. The chapter headings alone are worth reading. If you ever enjoyed Robert Asprin's *Myth Adventures*, Piers Anthony's Xanth, or Terry Pratchett's Discworld, you must read Rick Riordan's books next. These are very suitable for young adults, but certainly a laugh-out-loud read for any grown up as well. Witty, well phrased, and full of an amazing blend of the modern world with classic mythology.

✿

Best Military Science Fiction or Fantasy Novel
Iron Dragoons
by Richard Fox
Triplane Press
March, 2017
ISBN-13: 978-1545210307

This is a unique and yet still almost classic tale of soldiers in powered armor. The action follows a recruit from his enlistment when his parents are killed to when he becomes one of a corps of elite soldiers whose victory or death attitude would do a Spartan or French Foreign Legionnaire proud. Richard Fox is a West Point graduate and decorated ten-year veteran. You don't just wear the suit; it is wired into you. Not only does it become part of you, but you part of it as well.

Written by a soldier who has seen the elephant himself in Iraq, the feel and taste of war rings true, even in the far future. This book has a lot going for it—great feel, fascinating technology, plenty of explosive action, and well-drawn main characters. The second novel in the series has been released, *Ibarra Sanction*. Anyone who reads military science fiction should consider these two a must-read.

✿

Best Alternate History Novel
Fallout: The Hot War
by Harry Turtledove
Del Rey Books
May, 2017 (reissue edition)
ISBN-13: 978-0553390759

This is not a comfortable book to read. It is certainly as well written as any other novels by this master of alternate history. *Fallout*, with its tight plotting and characters you care about, is a story that strikes too close to today, and really brings up goose bumps on those of us old enough to remember when we were taught to "duck and cover".

The premise is simple, and even likely: when the Chinese pour over the border during the Korean War, General Douglas MacArthur demands to be allowed to drop atom bombs on the advancing armies. He argues that this will save tens of thousands of American lives and put the world on notice. President Harry Truman, who in reality denied the politically powerful general's demand, agrees. The bombs drop, but Russian Premier Joseph Stalin reacts, turning major European cities into nuclear wastelands. From there, things quite logically, and much too understandably, escalate.

We see the world destroy itself through the eyes of characters ranging from Truman and Stalin to displaced families and a pub owner in Britain. Each step, once the cascade has begun, seems reasonable and necessary, but the result is a Hot War, not the Cold War we all survived.

If we were preachy, we would observe that everyone should read this novel as a warning tale. With North Korea and Iran preparing nukes and politicians sabre rattling, the parallels are uncomfortably similar. As a book of fiction, it will prove an amazing read for any and everyone who likes alternate histories, anyone interested in the Cold War or post World War II conflicts, and those who find human struggle in a world gone mad intriguing.

Best Apocalyptic Novel
Walkaway
by Cory Doctorow
Tor Books
April, 2017
ISBN-13: 978-0765392763

A review of *Walkaway* was published in a previous issue of *Galaxy's Edge*. It was gratifying to see so many fans agreed with our recommendation. Here's an excerpt from that review: "Doctorow paints an amazing, detailed world that seems half steampunk, half psychedelic overload, but his characters are sympathetic and so very human.

"In most dystopian novels, the narrative concentrates on the breakdown of society. Doctorow pictures just the opposite: a future in which people are kind to one another, and support each other's needs and dreams. From the rave that begins the book to the satisfying conclusion, *Walkaway* is a fascinating read. Recommended for anyone who is weary of end-of-the-world scenarios in which people devolve to their worst."

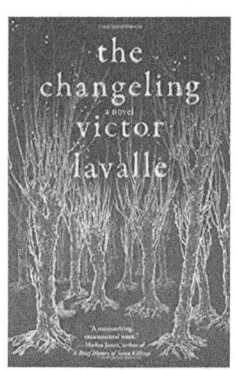

Best Horror Novel
The Changeling
by Victor LaValle
Spiegel & Grau, Penguin Random House
June, 2017
ISBN-13: 978-0812995947

Even if you normally do not read "horror" this is a novel you might want to consider. It is as much an urban dark fantasy as a classic horror novel. Victor LaValle has found that voice that Stephen King made famous, where the world seems almost, sort of, just about normal and everyday things go on as they do every day. Then, things begin to change and nothing is normal, but you are trapped into that feeling of your normal somehow being part of LaValle's horrible. The book itself is a modern, and much wider, telling of the classic myth *The Changeling*.

Dark when told hundreds of years ago, it remains wonderfully dark in a modern setting. It begins when young teenager Apollo Kagwa's father simply disappears. All that he leaves is a box of books, including one titled "Improbabilia." Apollo begins selling magazines and then books, until he is one of Manhattan's prominent rare and used book dealers. All goes normally, even well and happily, until his wife and child mysteriously disappear. Later, a stranger appears who claims he can help him locate his wife, but that there is some danger involved. Then his journey from what was left of his reality to a world of graveyards and mysterious forests begins.

Each section of this novel offers gems to the reader. The parts about Apollo as a bookseller are themselves fascinating and will entrance bibliophiles. The study of obsession and love is masterfully told, and the ending is not what you will expect. LaValle's writing is at times just short of poetic, bringing a world that is not ours, *maybe*, into sharp focus. More than highly recommended not only for horror fans, but also for anyone who likes any form of dark fantasy or urban fantasy.

Other novels we reviewed this issue:

Mars Girls
by Mary Turzillo
Apex Book Company
June, 2017
ISBN-13: 978-1937009526

From a talented writer and poet, *Mars Girls* makes brilliant use of language in a tale of two girls fighting against the many systems on near-future Mars. Nanoannie Centime is a bit of a drama queen, not quite ten mears (Martian years) old. Stuck far out on her parents' Pharm in the middle of Martian nowhere, she fantasizes much of her life. Her best friend, a Kiafrican girl named Kapera Smythe, one of the few people she has seen in the flesh, pleads for help when her own Pharm is invaded and her parents killed or kidnapped. Partly out of loyalty to her friend, partly out of desperation for something interesting to do, and partly because she has concocted a crush on Kapera's brother Sekou (a boy she has never met), Nanoannie sets out to rescue her friend and find the truth of what happened to her parents. Along the way, they run into Renegade Nuns, a pyramid cult, agents from the Corporations that run Mars, all told from the point of view of the two girls in a fun and futuristic lingo.

Mars Girls moves like a rocket, drawing the reader along for the ride. While one might be exasperated by Nanoannie's endless reveries on the romance she craves, she's resourceful and loyal. Kapera, whose point of view is expressed through diary entries as letters to that long-lost brother, is sweet and brave despite a life-threatening illness. The setting is well considered, introducing the reader to the complicated structure of a chaotic Martian society. It's a lot of fun to read, with mysteries and excitement unfolding in every chapter. This book is recommended for young adults, but all readers will find it a rewarding romp.

Terminal Alliance (Janitors of the Post-Apocalypse)
by Jim C. Hines
DAW Books
November, 2017
ISBN-13: 978-0756412746

This book almost got passed by because the cover honestly states that the main character is the Repair Officer on a space warship. Who wants to read a space opera about a janitor? I should have known better as one of my own favorite characters is a quartermaster who could not shoot straight. Do not make the same mistake. If you see *Terminal Alliance*, get it. From a very original premise to the near constant action and tension, this book is a page-turner.

The initial premise is that a gene-modifying virus was set loose on the Earth and regressed every human (and ape) to a savage, unaware state. Picture the "ferals" as being like zombies in that they are totally unaware and constantly hungry, but ferals are also fast and very strong. Fifty years later the alien Krakau have recently begun a project to save the human race by restoring most of their original genetic make up. These restored humans are then used by the insectoids as military personnel, mostly shock troops. Even the restoreds still have an abnormally hardy constitution and a willingness to obey their saviors. The Krakau, and three other races they dominate, are in a battle for survival against the Prodryan. This is a paranoid race that is aware that their xenophobia and violent reaction to all other races is unreasonable, but just cannot help themselves.

A few tens of thousands of humans have been restored. One of these is a woman, Marion Adamopoulos is also known as "Mops". She was trained after her restoration to be the lieutenant in charge of cleaning and routine maintenance on a war cruiser mostly manned by humans, but commanded by the Krakau, The cruiser answers an emergency call and rescues an allied ship from attack by two Prodyan raiders. The five cleanup crew are in air-tight suits repairing a toxic spill after the battle when things get very complicated. Protected by suits they find they are the only sane humans left when all two hundred other crewmen suddenly revert to feral state. The ferals then kill and eat their alien officers. Just trying to survive and then restore their fellow crewmen leads Mops and her team deeper and deeper into an alien conspiracy.

Do not let the lighthearted janitorial premise fool you. This is a well-written space opera that revolves around a mystery and desperate journey. The plotting is tight and action exciting. Jim Hines' wicked sense of humor just adds to the realism and suspense. This will be a great read for all space opera fans, those who want a good and very readable book to just enjoy, and those who like to try to solve the mystery before the last chapter.

Copyright © 2017 by Bill Fawcett and Jody Lynn Nye

Gregory Benford is a Nebula winner and a former Worldcon Guest of Honor. He is the author of more than thirty novels, six books of non-fiction, and has edited ten anthologies.

A SCIENTIST'S NOTEBOOK

by Gregory Benford

EVIL AND ME

Russian poet Yevgeny Yevtushenko asked in his broken English: "You atheist?"
I replied, "It's more that I hate Him."
—Memoirs, Kingsley Amis

How can a scientist deal with the huge questions of religious thought?

It all started with experience, as most philosophical positions should. What's an idea worth if it cannot withstand the rub of the real?

My mother taught English and my father taught agriculture in Robertsdale High in southern Alabama. Except for his three years fighting in the war. My twin brother and I were born in 1941 and sensed that he was gone, and only when he returned in August 1945 did why he went dawn on us.

I recall a big party with much celebration and I asked my father in the 1980s what that had been about. I expected that he would say it was for his return. But he told me it was because the bomb had dropped on Hiroshima and everyone knew he wouldn't have to go to Japan for the invasion.

He was a forward observer in field artillery, fighting across France, the Bulge, and through Germany to Austria. I believe he was the only of the starting forward observers in his battalion to survive the war, and suspect that his farm boy field smarts made the difference. In 1945 he returned to teaching, developing an agriculture-training program for the whole state. Then in 1948 the Cold War called him with a regular army appointment, which he seized as a way up into a world he had glimpsed in the war. We went with him, first to his training in Oklahoma at Fort Sill (where in 1967 he retired as commandant), then to Japan for 1949–51. Into the world beyond blissful America.

My father served on MacArthur's general staff and we saw the range of Japanese life, hard and strange, with communists rioting in the streets and farmers working the rice paddies only miles away in a fashion unchanged by millennia. With my brother I lay in bed at night in our compound housing and listened to marines firing at communists trying to get inside, and realized that the world was a lot bigger and tougher and darker than sunny Alabama knew.

As the Cold War deepened and its chill winds blew the Benfords to Atlanta in 1952, then Germany in 1954, where I saw the colossal damage wrought by the Big One and the suffering that followed. That shocked me, coming out of my Episcopal upbringing. Both parents had firm religious faith. My brother and I were acolytes in the church and confirmed in formal ceremony in 1954. But my experience in devastated lands meant that more and more I thought about theodicy, or the problem of evil—if God is omniscient, omnipotent, and omni benevolent, then why do bad things happen to good people?

This is the "hellmouth" that can suddenly open before you, for no reason. There are three classical answers: we don't understand what God's justice is, and maybe it's a lesson; or maybe we sinned without knowing it, so are punished; or true mercy is beyond human conception. There's a crucial scene in Kingsley Amis's *The Green Man* that captures these issues. The devil appears to a man taking a bath and simply says humans don't understand the real issues at all. If God doesn't halt suffering, he is cruel, and if he can't he is weak. But maybe the game between God and evil is just more complex than we can fathom. Christ suffered on the cross to no end; maybe he, too, was deluded into thinking it would do any good to man.

Then there's the free will argument. To be free we must be able to commit error, and from that comes pain. The Bible is full of Godly interventions, though, mostly shielding Jews or murdering their enemies. But…why has that stopped in the face of the Holocaust, etc.? (A televangelist argued recently that the Holocaust was God's way of getting the Jews back to Israel.) Christianity needs heaven to explain evil and make up for it. Can anyone believe such pain will be made okay at the end time?

And what could heaven be like? Either it's a place where we cannot sin (no free will) or we don't want to sin.

But my teenage self couldn't buy that. If heaven makes up for suffering, why wait? Why not make us suitable Godly companions right now—angels, as it were? This idea bothered me a lot. If heaven allowed continuity between our mortal selves and our states in heaven, why was heaven free of sin? I read Dostoyevsky and found he had the same worry in "The Dream of a Ridiculous Man."

I came to the conclusion that either God is impotent or evil…or he's simply nonexistent.

There the issue rested until the 1990s. If nothing else, the reality of death and the experience of losing loved ones punctures even the most gratifying and well-ordered life. My wife, Joan, died in 2002 after a long struggle with kidney disease and cancer. She suffered greatly for years and when the cancer returned she felt it. She told me to tell no one and bore it out. I collapsed two days after her death and left many of the details of her memorial service to our children.

Days later, coming out from an errand onto the street in Laguna Beach around noon, I looked up at our house and mused vacantly about Joan's schedule, where she would be, calculating if we could meet for lunch—and suddenly saw that *she was nowhere now*, not in this universe anymore. In such moments the enormity of our lives hammers home. I realized the emotional conclusion of my loss of faith.

Life kept hammering. Three months later my father died. My mother's faith carried her through. A few months later, as I walked with her through Fairhope, Alabama, where I grew up, we met an old family friend who had not heard the news. He asked how my father was. "Oh, he's in heaven," my mother said in a lively voice. But I could hear something darker under it.

In two more years she was gone as well. Indeed, she deliberately ignored an infection, refusing to take the antibiotic her doctor prescribed, and died within a week of sepsis. I believe she wanted to join my father. So religion proved to have a downside I had not foreseen.

Every religion with an afterlife theory has something that survives death or is resurrected—and that gets interpreted as the essence of what it means to be human. Often the strength of faith seems shaky, so you believe you must have the One Truth Religion to which others must convert or go to hell.

But indifference, not doubt, is the greater adversary of faith. The Europeans are in that slow retreat of the Sea of Faith that Matthew Arnold lamented in "Dover Beach."

As I became a scientist I learned ways of accounting for how strong religion is among us. Through multilevel or group-level selection evolution has given us the many essential genes that benefit the group at the individual's expense. Some are essential to a social species—genes that underlie generosity, moral constraints, and plausibly, religious behavior. Such traits are difficult to account for, though not impossible, on the view that natural selection favors only behaviors that help the individual to survive and leave more children.

So I now believe that evil isn't a problem. It's just a feature of our world. Perhaps many people cannot live meaningful lives without God. But I'm happy to now.

Copyright © 2017 by Gregory Benford

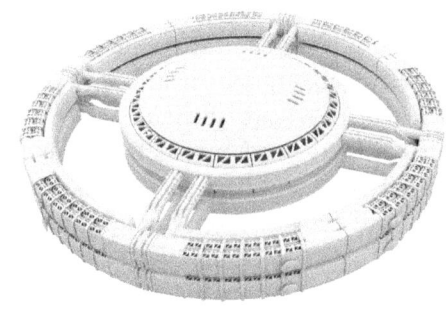

Robert J. Sawyer is the Hugo, Nebula, Campbell Memorial, Heinlein, Hal Clement, Skylark, Aurora, and Seiun Award-winning author of twenty-three bestselling science-fiction novels, most recently the #1 Locus *bestseller* Quantum Night. *A Member of the Order of Canada—the highest civilian honor bestowed by the Canadian government—his physical home is Toronto and online it's at sfwriter.com.*

DECOHERENCE

by Robert J. Sawyer

THE HOT NEW THING

I've been a published novelist twenty-seven years now. In any other field that much experience would make me highly valuable. But publishers don't want experience; they want the hot new thing—someone who doesn't have a track record, who doesn't have a sales history, someone who has had years—*decades!*—to shape their debut book.

The best my current publisher, or any other, can do for my next novel (or that of most of my colleagues), no matter what song-and-dance their sales force puts on, is to ship perhaps ten percent more copies than they did of my last book. Even if my editor and I agree that this one is my magnum opus, my best book yet, my crowning glory, there's no way in hell they can initially move out substantially more copies than they did the last time.

Why? Because booksellers don't care about *what* the new book is about, or *how good* the publisher claims it is. All they care about is *how well* your previous books sold—and woe betide you if your last one didn't sell as well as the one before it; if you're trending downward, your publishing days are numbered.

These thoughts were brought to mind by a recent flood in my storage locker. Suffering some water damage were my copies of *Locus*, the trade journal of the science fiction and fantasy fields, from 1990, 1991, and 1992, right around the beginning of my book-publishing career. I brought them back to my home to dry out (something writers occasionally have to do for other writers, anyway, so I

figured why not extend the same courtesy to those magazines?).

I thought it would be nostalgic fun to leaf through these old issues. But it wasn't. Not because so many of the big-name pros from back then have since passed on; that was to be expected. But rather because so many members of my own cohort, the new writers of the late eighties and early nineties featured in those pages, even though they are mostly still alive and well *are no longer being published*, and, indeed, many of them haven't been for a decade or two. It would be impolite to name these poor souls, but there were far more who had been dropped by their publishers than had been kept by them.

Of course, bookselling has changed a lot since my crowd was breaking in. Online retailer Amazon is now the largest bookseller in the world, and it controls to an almost monopolistic extent the e-book marketplace. As Amazon consolidated its power, I supported the merger of Penguin (my current publisher) and Random House, because they said they were doing it to form a megacorporation that could stand up to Jeff Bezos. But, even combined, they couldn't—and so they, and other publishers, instead find ways to keep money that should go to their authors.

In the almost three decades I've been a published novelist, there have been enormous cost-savings in the book-publishing business, ranging from cheap in-house computerized typesetting directly from the author's freely provided wordprocessing files to a vast reduction in the number of bookstore accounts that have to be serviced. Not one penny—not one—of those cost savings has been passed on to the authors by the publishers.

More: when I started, publishers paid authors their advances half on signing of the contract and half on acceptance of the manuscript. Later, it shifted to thirds: some on signing, more on acceptance, and part three on publication—a year or more after the author had finished his or her work. Now, the Penguin Random House standard is *four* installments: signing, acceptance, first-format (usually hardcover) publication, and second-format (paperback) publication, some *two years* or more after the author has finished writing the book.

I long ago observed that few authors get substantially better than their first sale: a mental switch is thrown that says, ah, okay, I'm publishable now, and for most writers, that's the end of their creative growth. Oh, sure, there are exceptions, but not as many as you'd think.

But now there's another reason for creative stagnation: a lack of monetary incentive. If you spend three years on a book (as I did on my last one), instead of the usual one (or, for some of my colleagues, if you spend nine months on a book instead of the usual three), there's simply no economic model by which the extra effort will be rewarded—because there's no way (short of starting over under a pseudonym) for you to be seen as the hot new thing.

Indeed, one of the big five SF publishers recently whispered to an agent I know that its *entire* strategy now in science fiction is looking for splashy debut novels, à la Andy Weir's *The Martian* (despite the fact that this very publisher, along with all the other New York SF houses, turned down *The Martian* when it was submitted to them).

Okay, so the Class of 1990, in those moldering pages of *Locus*, is mostly a lost cause. But how can you—a new writer—make a publisher think your first novel is going to be that coveted next big thing? Well, for starters, they'd like it best if you've got what's called a *platform*—a popular blog, or YouTube channel, or whatever, that demonstrates a pre-existing audience for your work because, as another long-serving New York editor once confided in me, publishers have no idea at all how to build an audience for a science-fiction author.

And, yeah, having a platform can work spectacularly. My friend John Scalzi is the gold standard, bursting on the scene as a bestselling author with *Old Man's War* (2005), thanks in large measure to the huge following of his blog "Whatever." But the platform notion fails more often than not; it would be impolitic for me to mention writers by name who have huge online presences but negligible actual sales—but they're far more common than the Scalzis of the world.

So, then, how *do* you raise the heat?

I was contemplating this question recently; a great friend of mine has made a bit of a name for herself with short stories in anthologies and major magazines (including this one), and she's looking to make the leap to novels.

The best advice I could give her was what I alluded to in the first paragraph of this column: take your time, write the best damn book you can, knock people's socks off, be that splashy debut author that publishers are salivating for—because you only get one chance at being *new*.

It's win-win: she got good advice and, if she follows it, we'll all get a great book to read, a standout in a field that, because of the lack of economic incentive I discussed above, has mostly stagnated into predictable mediocrity.

Copyright © 2017 by Robert J. Sawyer

Joy Ward is the author of one novel, has several stories in print, in magazines and in anthologies, and has also published a hundred non-fiction articles, including interviews, both in written and video form, for local and international publications.

Jack McDevitt is a Nebula winner, a multiple Hugo and Nebula nominee, and the author of numerous bestsellers

THE *GALAXY'S EDGE* INTERVIEW

Joy Ward Interviews
Jack McDevitt

Jack McDevitt is a writer who always makes us think. His heroes are women and men with hearts of gold and feet of clay, like many real people.

Jack McDevitt: I can't remember a time I didn't want to write. It might be that it had to do with when I first became enthusiastic about science fiction and I realized they were doing stories and stuff and I thought I would like to do that too. But I developed an absolute connection with science fiction when I was four years old and I never recovered.

I grew up in south Philadelphia and my father used to take me to the local theater called The Bell. They ran westerns. I remember the movies of pilots and war. It was World War I movies about pilots and I didn't really care about those. I didn't know what was going on, but they also ran serials and the serials I remember. There was Buck Rogers and Flash Gordon. Flash Gordon has this great rocket ship that Dr. Zarkov built it in his garage—this thing, it had no air. I didn't realize at the time it had no air lock. It went to Mars in this thing in one of the episodes, in one of the series. There were three serials actually. They went to Mars in this thing and it had no air lock and it had no washrooms I could make out.

I absolutely loved the serial. I remember, though, I got annoyed with it. I can remember telling my dad one time coming out of the theater why is he's got this great rocket ship and he can go anywhere he

wants and all he can do is pick fights with this guy who looked like one of my uncles?

It was really pathetic, but I loved the rocket ship and I never got past that. I remember one night we came out and there was a full moon up over the rooftops. I asked my dad if we were ever going to go to the moon, and he said he didn't see it was going to happen. The reason is, well, it was, unfortunately, it would never happen and the reason for that was that rockets need something to push against. You can't just take them out into a vacuum and expect to be able to steer the thing, which I understand later was a fairly common view back in the '30s. But anyway, I just loved that stuff and I never got over it.

I go, once in a while, to speak to groups. Not science fiction groups, the library group or something like that. Whenever I do there's always, at the end, there's some guy who will come up and say, "You know, I don't read the stuff myself, but I've got a nephew…" The tone is that the nephew does other idiot stuff as well, but he likes it. I usually stand there and I feel sorry for this guy because the train has missed the station.

He's stuck in south Philadelphia or wherever and he never really gets, gets out. He lives his life bound to the Earth. Those are the sort of science fiction enthusiasts we get clear. We don't do it physically, but we get clear all the same, and it counts for a lot.

Joy Ward: What's important about that, that we get clear?

Jack McDevitt: We're born with a natural curiosity. What's out there? What's going on? Look at this thing recently where they were talking about taking people on a one-way flight to Mars. They had all kinds of people volunteering to go. I'm not saying that's rational but there's something going on about what we, we look around us and we see this universe, this wide universe is out there and we know so little about it. Right now it's what science fiction does. What science fiction does, plays games with astronomy and other sciences. We get to look at, at what is, and as far as we can tell, what's possible.

It's an indicator of who we really are. We're something better than somebody who wants to kind of live at the end of the street and we got a place in the garage. We have our families and everybody grows up and after a while we die and, and go into the dust. I think most of us want more. We're curious. It's a reason. If we weren't curious we never would have made it to the Americas.

It makes me feel very happy. I, I feel honored when people come to me at places like this and say nice things. They talk about how their lives have been influenced by some of the stuff they read. That is true for me. My life with—without science fiction, it would be like…I've been a baseball nut all my life. I can't imagine my life without baseball, and the same thing with science fiction. There are certain things that make my life seem worthwhile other than the usual stuff. You know, having children, having a family, that's all great. You can't get along without that, but there's got to be more to life. There have to be other things to it. For a lot of us the other things are wondering about what's out there, what the possibilities are, where we're headed—and that's a big thing. Where are we headed?

The average human being pretty much ignores the possibilities of what's going on until we get surprised. It's not the way nature intended or God intended. We don't really know what God intended so much. But I think the future is coming on us very quickly. We are getting close to a point now, for example, where women are going to the doctor and the doctor's going to say to women who are going to conceive, and the doctor will say, "Well, something we can do for you if you like. We can arrange things so that your child will have a much higher IQ than the people around him. Do you want that? Or we can make him pretty handsome or we can, we can arrange things so that child is going to live an extraordinarily long life." We're not far from that kind of thing.

I think what we try to do is to get people accustomed to the fact that the world is changing and that it's a good idea to look not only for what happened yesterday and what's in the news today, but what the potential is in the future. What is the fu-

ture going to look like and what do we really want to do? For example, the question about global climate change. We've got a lot of people who absolutely refuse to accept the notion that there was global climate change even though the science seems to indicate that yes, in fact, something has changed. Look what's happening. We have people who refuse to accept that idea. That is very serious. From everything I've read we are past the point now where we could have moved in time to stop it. But at least we could slow it down. We could recognize that whether you won't admit that anything to do with automobiles running around or whether it's some kind of cyclical thing is irrelevant. The thing is we don't want to continue adding carbon to an atmosphere that's already got too much.

It should teach us to be a little bit smarter. I have a, a friend who's always talking about his grandchildren, but who refuses to accept the climate change. It's like, yeah, I love my grandchildren. Did I ever tell you about the story about my, you know? And, and you always get all this kind of stuff and his grandchildren will be facing a pretty dismal world if the scientists are right and he's wrong. But he doesn't, doesn't take that into his confidence, ignores it because it's inconvenient. It reflects ill on his political views for one thing.

JW: When did you sell your first writing?

JM: When I was in high school I was a columnist for the high school newspaper. That was South Catholic in Philadelphia, and I enjoyed that. I went to La Salle and they, they ran a short story contest every year, freshman short store contest and I won that. I wrote a science fiction story for it. One that they published in the school's literary magazine.

So I was off and running, and I thought well, maybe I do have a future at this stuff. I made a mistake. I read *David Copperfield* and I thought, my God, I'm never going to be able to write at this level. I can't compete with this guy. I did not realize that I didn't have to. I didn't have to compete with Charles Dickens, but I didn't know that. I did not attempt another piece of fiction for, I don't know, somewhere twenty-five to thirty years before I went back and tried again.

What eventually happened is I married Maureen McAdams. This is after I spent several years in the navy and I became an English teacher. I ran into Maureen while I was in my teaching years. I mentioned to her a few times about how I would love to be a science fiction writer. At one point after we'd been married for, oh boy, twenty-three years, something like that, a long time, and it was around 1980. I discovered I couldn't make enough money. I was the English Department chairman in a system in New Hampshire. My father died, Maureen's father died, and Maureen was about to have our first child and we just couldn't afford it. I was supporting both our parents, both our mothers and, and a child coming. Fuel bills in New Hampshire, you got a lot of snow and it gets cold. The newspaper was going on about how teachers were overpaid and I was making $10,000 a year. So I, I quit teaching and became a customs inspector. I looked at people's suitcases and I made twice as much money as a customs inspector as I did as the English Department chairman.

I was in Pembina, North Dakota, for a few years and then I worked there and they sent me to the academy in Brunswick, Georgia. I guess I had mentioned again to Maureen what I was missing with my life. And she said, "Well, don't you try it?" So I did.

To keep her happy I wrote a story about a guy who worked at a post office who falls in love with a young woman at the other counter down the way, but he's afraid to make a move because he's afraid of being rejected. I didn't get the connection at the time that I was doing this story of what my life had become. I wrote this story and we sent it to *Asimov's* and they said, "Thanks, but no thanks." I had a lot rejected it. That's it, I had enough. You know, I, I just don't need the rejection. Maureen brought it to her friend, by the way, before we sent it out again and I rewrote a little bit. She went down to the, down to the local store one day and came back with a copy of *The Twilight Zone Magazine*. This was about 1980 and, uh, she persuaded me to send it to *Twilight Zone*.

We were wrapping up our assignment here at the time. We closed everything out and drove back to North Dakota. I had a postcard waiting for me when I got back to North Dakota, which is now

framed and hangs over my desk in my office, saying in effect we can't pay you a lot of money, but you'll get a national audience. At that point, I had sold the story. It was a *Twilight Zone* and I was on my way.

Incidentally, I should tell you a little bit about the story that it is a little more irony in this than that I realized at the time. What the is story about, I mentioned the guy's a post office clerk. What really kicks the story off is a letter comes in that had been mailed by Ralph Waldo Emerson to a friend, I guess, eighty or ninety years before. Of course, the friend's long gone. There's nothing they can do with this ninety-year-old letter. So the, the clerk opens the letter and looks at it, and I used some lines that Emerson actually had written in his essays. One of the lines being that if you can learn to believe in yourself, you can do almost anything. I think that's what took hold of me. I didn't at the time. I didn't realize the point of that whole business, but that's exactly what happened.

Uh, there has been research done that almost all of us tend to be smarter than we realize. What happens to us is that authority figures in our lives spend a lot of time showing us what we do wrong, what we screw up, telling us just stay clear, leave it alone. You'll just mess it up. After a while we start to behave that way as if that's really the truth. I was a communication specialist when I was in the navy and during that period I attended a cousin's wedding. Afterwards, I was looking around the house while they're having a big party, and there was a new FM radio that they had. I was kind of toying with the radio. My father said, "Don't touch it, you'll break it." My father was a good dad, but that's the way we do things.

One of the things that is so good about writing science fiction, and I suppose about writing in general, particularly science fiction, is that you're not just sitting in a room, as I was in the beginning with a typewriter, an electric typewriter, and making this stuff happen. To a degree, you actually live the experience. I feel as if I've actually traveled to Mars and, and been to various stars. Priscilla Hutchins, who's a, who's a major character in seven or eight of my novels. I feel as if Priscilla is an actual person in my life. I love her.

You get a sense that the universe opens up and I can make things happen. It's particularly effective when—I don't do good guys versus bad guys and stuff like that. My interest in science fiction is in discovery. What's out there? What could be out there? What could happen? What does happen to the woman who goes to a doctor and when she's getting ready to have a child and the doctor says, "All right. I can arrange things so that your child will not grow old. Your child will hit about twenty-four, twenty-five and stay that way indefinitely, okay? But because of population problems, your child will not be able to reproduce."

What do you want to do, Mom? Which way do you want to have it? It just makes for a fascinating approach to the kind of world that we live in. The world is changing so quickly that it's becoming increasingly hard to keep up with. What really matters? When I sat down to write that story, I had no clue what the mother was going to, what the mother's decision was going to be. I think I created a problem for, for a close friend of mine. I went to lunch with a close friend in Philadelphia. He and his wife went along. I told them about the story I was working on and I asked Art, I said, "What would you do?" She didn't think that, uh, living a long life was good. She said, "Listen, I wouldn't want to go through this again for anything." That's what makes science fiction so much fun, really. If you are writing a western you know who the bad guys are. The little shootout at the end and that'll take care of them and that'll be it. But with science fiction you have to deal with stuff like this. The one that I'm working on right now is Beyond Centauri. Priscilla Hutchins lives in New York two hundred years from now. She's a star ship pilot and they're shutting everything down. A lot of scientists are saying right now, including Stephen Hawking, that we should not be sending out all these signals because we don't know what's out there, that somebody might come down here and have us for dinner.

In Priscilla's time, it's become a political issue. The president wants to shut it down. They've got interstellars, they've got star ships, and it's crazy. A lot of people think it's absolutely nuts to go out there and draw all this attention to ourselves. The way the storyline sets up, we detect a signal coming in from a place that's seven thousand light years away. It's a waterfall. Just a picture of a waterfall. It's a directed signal, and they want to go out and take a look. We go, we've got to. We've got really very fast ships. We're going to go out and take a look, see what it is. You just don't know. You don't know what you're getting into. So they do launch what everybody is saying is going to be the final mission and they almost get stopped. The orders come in to stop it before the whole takeoff. They go out there and they discover several things, but one of the things that they run into is a world which is mostly an ocean world and there are creatures on it that look like dolphins, except they walk around on the islands.

They go down and take a close look. The lander that they're operating in has a malfunction and crashes. Priscilla could've landed on the, on the beach. They could have probably made it to the beach, but there were a lot of these dolphins that were in the water and she would have killed some of them, probably, if she had tried. So she goes down in deeper water. They lose the land. They have no way of getting back to the star ship. And the dolphins do a rescue. The thing that sets the, the story line in motion is the waterfall that they saw from the seven-thousand-year-old signal had to do with, with black holes. There was a pair of black holes in the neighborhood, and those black holes are now approaching on this world where the dolphins are. The dolphins have very limited technology. And now your problem is, can you go home and persuade the people back home to put together some star ships, to build some star ships and come back out and do a rescue for people who think that it's deadly dangerous to do stuff like that.

JW: You are one of these people who can write about these issues, who can do it. You know you can do it now. How does this change your life?

JM: I have people who tell me how much my work has meant to them. That means a lot. I've had things like that happen before with some of my former students who are still in touch with me. I get emails on a pretty regular basis from people who thanked me for my books and tell me what it means to them. I hear periodically from scientists telling me that they got started in sciences because of science fiction. Sometimes they specify it's my work. I got an email not too long ago from Dr. Wasserman, first name is Larry. He discovered an asteroid, a new asteroid, and they named it after me. I'm up there with Tina Fey, George Washington, all kinds of people like that. He said that he wanted to thank the science fiction people for making stuff available that drove a passion in him, effectively, to go to the stars. I hope it doesn't hit the Earth at some point.

JW: How do you want to be remembered?

JM: That's, that's a tough one, Joy. I would like to be remembered as a decent science fiction writer and that I've written something somewhere that, that is memorable, that, that people will remember and enjoy. That's had an impact on people.

That's the point of being alive. We're all that way. You're the same way, Joy. You would not want to go through your life and not have an, an impact on the people around you. I mean, why are you doing this? It helps to feel that you're having an impact, making the world a little bit better for what you've done.

Copyright © 2017 by Joy Ward

SERIALIZATION
DAUGHTER OF ELYSIUM

by Joan Slonczewski
Trade Paperback: 356 pages.
ISBN: 978-1-60450-444-6

Phoenix Pick Edition, 2010
Daughter of Elysium copyright © 1993, 2010 Joan Slonczewski. All rights reserved.

Joan Slonczewski has won the John W. Campbell Award for Best Science Fiction Novel, twice. In 1987, for A Door into Ocean, and in 2012, for The Highest Frontier. Her fiction shows her command of genetics and ecological science as well as her commitment to feminism.

DAUGHTER OF ELYSIUM
(Part 3)

CHAPTER 3

Raincloud lay back and stretched like a cat, watching Blackbear out of half-closed eyelids. She reached over, stroking the mushroom that she longed to devour. Sometimes he seemed so beautiful, almost blinding to look at.

As she relaxed on the bed, something thumped faintly beneath the skin of her belly. She put her hand to it, but it was still too small to palpate. Then the thumping came again, rhythmically. The little one must be having hiccups.

"Anyone home?" asked Blackbear.

"She's quickened." Raincloud smiled and squeezed his hand. This was always the best part of pregnancy, when the sickness was gone and the little one started playing about. A good thing I'm not a Sharer, she thought. Sharers conceived only once or twice in a lifetime, and then only by consent of the Gathering.

Blackbear watched her with a beatific smile. "We're so lucky," he murmured.

Sadness swept over her again, to think of Falcon Soaring, and the call of the High Priestess, which she herself might have answered. But, she told herself, Falcon Soaring certainly did not want Raincloud's child; she wanted one of her own. "I'll talk to Mother tomorrow," she told Blackbear. "I'll tell her that our child's quickened. And I'll tell her about the clinic in Founders City."

The interstellar call would not be free of charge, like the Elysian holostage. It would cost more than a day's pay. It required a special link through sub-folds into the Fold that connected the star systems outside space-time, and then her mother in Tumbling Rock would have to ride her horse to Caldera Station. Nevertheless, Raincloud had to see her mother in person to share the wonderful news. If only she could hug her, too.

When the call came in, the family hovered excitedly around the holostage. And then, unbelievably, there was her mother Windrising.

The sight of her mother's face came as a shock at first; the wrinkles, which Raincloud somehow had not recalled, after months among satin complexions. Still, the face was the very image of Hawktalon, who resembled her grandmother the more the years passed. And her shoulders flexed, strong as ever, beneath her immaculate black braids; Raincloud's father was a master at braiding.

"Raincloud!" she cried. Her trousers swished and the fiery embroidery swirled around as she took a step forward. "You nightfallen goddess—What sort of show is this? I can see you all around, large as life, but you're nothing but a ghost."

Windrising had a yearling granddaughter tucked under one arm. The little dark face stared wide-eyed at the holostage, a stuffed bird hanging by its beak from her fist. "Congratulations on Hawktalon's birthday, too. I've added two dams to her herd."

"Couldn't you send them here?" begged Hawktalon. "We could keep them out on a raft—"

"That's enough, dear," interrupted Raincloud.

"And how's my little owlet?" inquired Windrising.

Sunflower hid behind his father, suddenly shy.

"Nightstorm misses you to pieces, Raincloud. You were always her favorite sister."

"I know, Mother."

"I've saved the best of our apples for you. Your nieces have kept the goats well, including the newborn kids. One got hoof rot, but we had it treated right off and the barn cleaned out. The geyser is running strong, and the pipes are in shape; your stock kept plenty warm all winter. You should see the mudfield since the last eruption: all orange around the center, turning reddish purple around the edges now." The algae grew up fast after the geyser erupted, different species at different temperatures, changing as the mud cooled.

"Mother, I've got news for you: My child's quickened."

"So I guessed. Congratulations! May you have ten more."

"Thank you." She imagined what that would be like, ten little ones climbing over Blackbear.

"Lynxtail's quickened, too, her fifth." Lynxtail was Windrising's second-born daughter.

"That's wonderful. But you know, mother …" For some reason, what had seemed straightforward in her mind before was now all confused. "Falcon Soaring wants her own child, too, doesn't she? It can be done in Founders City; Blackbear knows the clinic."

Windrising waved an impatient hand. "What do men know? The clan looked into all that. She can't be cured."

Raincloud was taken aback a moment. "She can't be cured, exactly, but her—her own cells can make a child that's hers and her consort's. Blackbear knows; he's a doctor, Mother."

"Of course he is. The best, too; I've heard nothing but complaints since he left."

Raincloud winced at this double-edged compliment. Blackbear had tried hard to arrange a good replacement for his patients.

"Well, you can talk to the High Priestess. If you were home, you might have helped Falcon Soaring yourself. I know it's hard, but you would earn the darkest honor."

Raincloud's head rang for a moment, and she had to catch herself. The very thought of parting with her unborn was devastating. She felt ashamed, then angry at her mother for refusing to listen. But after all, what could she expect? Outside Elysium, most people distrusted gene engineering; and Clickers could be downright superstitious.

"How is that strange planet, out there in the stars? I hope those immortal folk, they all treat you like a goddess," her mother added.

"Yes, Mother. Shora is a lovely planet."

"Don't suppose you like it too much, now?" She was probably thinking of her "lost" daughter, Running Wolf, and feared for adventuresome Raincloud.

"Don't worry," Raincloud assured her with a smile. "I'm not about to settle in this bauble they call Helicon."

Her mother laughed. "I should say not. Will you be home for the Day of the Child?"

"Sorry, no," she replied. They could not possibly afford the fare.

"You'll miss Straight Oak's wedding, too. It's always sad to give a son away, but the Graymountain-clan is just a half day's journey."

The house interposed, "Your five minutes are up. Extension will cost another hundred credits."

"Good-bye …" Windrising's granddaughter waved the bird at them and opened her mouth for the first time. But just then, the image winked out.

Raincloud bit her lip, staring vacantly through the empty column of light. It was frustrating to get things straight across twenty light-years. "I'll write the High Priestess," she decided. "And Nightstorm—I'll send her the address of that clinic. She'll talk to Falcon Soaring."

Blackbear nodded understandingly. "You're doing the best you can for your cousin."

She drew a breath. "Now, as for our firstborn …"

They had a long conference at the holostage with the *generen* of the Heli*shon*. The *generen*, Sorl Heli*shon*, was a round-faced man with smooth sandy hair that flowed nearly to his waist. Raincloud could read Blackbear's disapproval in his face, to see a man with his hair undone and long enough for any goddess to drag him off. Taking a breath, she told herself to be broad-minded. "Will a 'defective' really be welcome at your *shon*?" she asked the man bluntly.

Dimples appeared disarmingly in his smile, but his voice when he spoke carried the distinct note of authority. "The *shon*lings will love to meet a Bronze Skyan," said the *generen*. "We have hosted several Bronze Skyan children. But yours would be the first Clicker from the Caldera Hills."

"Who will be her teacher?" Raincloud wanted to know.

"Her teacher will be one of our own *nanas*," Sorl explained. "Each *nana* has no more than ten children, and I myself keep watch over all. But Hawktalon will adore her nana. All our *nanas* have the highest educational training. The best education in the Fold—that's what we offer at the Heli*shon*."

Blackbear sewed a jumpsuit for Hawktalon like those the Elysian *shon*lings wore, parti-colored sleeves and pantaloons gathered at the wrists and ankles, with a little goat stitched onto her sleeve for good luck. Hawktalon was so excited that she spent all day drawing pictures of what the *shon* would be like. At last, when the fateful day came, she awoke at six in the morning, dressed herself in half a minute, and came to breakfast with Fruitbat under her arm and her trusty rattleback stone in her pocket.

At the holostage in the hall stood the shaft of light, like sunshine through a ceiling window. That was how it always looked to Hawktalon, except that whereas sunshine kept a discreet silence, the people on the holostage were full of blather. Her mother never said so, but she always got that look in her eye and her lip curved down, whenever a guardian or an ambassador appeared.

"It's the L'liite ambassador this morning, Mother," Hawktalon informed her, dipping her spoon into her oatmeal. "Is he telling the truth today?" The distinction between truth and untruth was a source of fascination for her; like one of her father's skeins of wool after Sunny had played with it, it required endless untangling. "Truth, or not?"

Her father muttered, "That would be the day." He never believed anything he saw in the shaft of light.

Her mother said, as if lecturing, "There are different kinds of truth. It is true that many L'liites lack food to eat. It's been that way for generations; that is why our Clicker ancestors emigrated."

"The one here looks well fed." Hawktalon twisted her spoon. "If there are different kinds of truth, can something be true of one kind and untrue of another?"

"Hawktalon," her father put in, "you need to eat what's in your spoon, or you'll be late for the *shon*."

She swallowed the spoonful of oatmeal, then another. "I'll learn all about truth at the *shon*" she mumbled, her mouth full. "Soon I'll know even more than you."

The transit vesicle flowed smoothly up the reticulum. Hawktalon loved to watch the incoming walls of a neighbor vesicle merge together and open, like modeling clay, while new people and servos emerged into view. Sometimes a servo from each vesicle would exchange greetings of a sort, a high-pitched squeaking sound. The greeting sound was a different pitch from the sound a servo made when you told it, "You're not really a person."

Not all servos squeaked, of course, but some squeaked quite a lot. Doggie had several different squeaks; one meant "Come play with me," another meant "I need recharging." Out on the raft of the naked goddesses, Doggie had kept squeaking, "I need," but it was not recharging that she needed. She needed something from the Sharers, but Hawktalon could not figure out what. Poor thing; Doggie must be lonely out there, and Hawktalon missed her as badly as she missed her goats.

Perhaps her nana at the *shon* could tell her about servo-squeak. The *shon* contained all the knowledge there ever was, Lorl had told her in Daddy's laboratory.

"Next stop," her mother warned, rising from the chair, which grew up into a rail to lean on. Her father, holding Sunny, rose with them.

Hawktalon got up, feeling the unfamiliar pantaloons hugging her ankles. The costume felt so different from her wide-bottomed trousers, she felt as if she inhabited a different body today. She *was* different, she decided; she was a magic person today, and she could cast powerful spells. Truth or untruth?

The home of the *shon*, which Hawktalon had passed several times on shopping trips, was definitely a magic place, a building like no other. All other buildings were of one color; but the surface of the *shon* changed color continually, like the rings of algae around a geyser, only faster. First it was pink, then as you approached the pink hue deepened, turning orange, then faded imperceptibly to pale green, darkening as you arrived. Each time it was different, of course, so that you never could tell what color it would be when you entered. Today the wall turned bright yellow just as they approached and a door shaped open. A good omen, a good color to start her lucky day.

A servo approached, unlike any other she had seen. The servo was padded all over, like a cloth doll, wearing a thick spreading skirt with bright geometric designs. She looked huggable, Hawktalon thought. Moreover, her faceplate had delightful cartoon features that actually moved as she spoke, like a real face. She said, "What fun to meet you, Hawktalon. I'm sorry the *generen* was called away just now. I'm Nana."

Her father pulled her back close. His arm was tense, and that made Hawktalon tense, too. Her heart beat faster as she looked up at him, then back at the plump huggable servo. Suddenly she thought, maybe she did not really want to go to the *shon* today. She wanted to go home with Daddy.

Nana said, "Are you Hawktalon? You're named after a bird, aren't you? Are you joining us today?"

Hawktalon dutifully extended her doll. "This is—" She added, "Fruitbat," in Click-click.

Nana bent at the waist, her skirt brushing the floor, as she looked at the doll. "I'm very pleased to meet you, Fruitbat," she told the doll, pronouncing perfectly. "I'd like to know why Fruitbat wants to come to our *shon*."

"To learn things," said Hawktalon carefully.

"To learn things. And what would you most like to learn?"

That put her off guard. She recalled the one Elysian sentence about learning that she had memorized at Science Park. "'Where learning is shared, the waterfall breaks through the cataract.'"

"She knows the classics," exclaimed Nana happily.

Raincloud demanded, "Where is the *generen*?"

"There comes the *generen* now," said Nana, her cartoon faceplate nodding toward an Elysian down the hall whose talar swished as he approached. It was the long-haired one from the holostage. His silk-smooth hair fascinated Hawktalon, who had never seen anything like it before she left Tumbling Rock. She wondered what it felt like to the touch.

Nana added, "The *generen* and *subgenerens* monitor us around the clock. If I ever fail you, please report my defect to …"

Hawktalon moved closer, filled with sudden curiosity. She whispered quickly, "Can you tell me why servos squeak sometimes?"

"That's a very good question," said Nana. "Perhaps you'll find out for yourself, when you learn to build a servo of your own."

"Build a servo? My own?"

"It's one of our morning activities."

"Can I build a trainsweep?"

"Certainly, dear, although you won't need one for a few decades yet."

The *shon*lings were practicing their reading. They took turns calling out Elysian words from letters that danced magically in the air above a broad stage and

turned into smiling faces when the word was correct. They were all boys, their unbound hair hanging flat; another couple of years and it would be up in turbans, in Tumbling Rock. They looked like normal children, except that they horsed around rather ineffectually. When one took a swipe at another, the one struck usually fell down and got scraped, instead of flipping the first one over. They reminded her of her young cousin who had been confined to bed for some months with scarlet fever and forgot how to use his arms and legs.

A boy tugged her sleeve. His hair was yellow with a slight wave, his face paler than a newborn's, and his eyes were startlingly blue. "I'm Maris. I'm an artist. What are you?" When Hawktalon did not answer, he added, "Don't you know what's in your own genes?" Maris pointed at the embroidered goat on her sleeve. "What's that?"

Hawktalon returned his curious blue-eyed stare. "It's a goat, of course," she said, thinking, they did not know all that much in this *shon*.

"But how was it done?" the dumb boy wanted to know. "I mean, what sort of machine part could pull the thread all the way through and back out at a different spot?"

Another boy peered closer for a look, then another. "It's true," one murmured. "It's all done with one thread, not like regular sewing."

"My father did it," said Hawktalon, feeling proud.

"Yes, but how?" insisted Maris.

She blinked, puzzled. "Well, he pushes the needle in one side, then pulls it out the other."

"Oh, I see. It would take a skinny servo to creep through like that! Could you show me how to do it?"

Hawktalon shook her head. "Sewing is for boys."

"Only boys?" said Maris. "Why couldn't I do it?" said another one.

"Why only boys?" echoed the others.

Some of the boys were girls. Hawktalon blinked at them, as if her eyes had gone out of focus. Girls, some of them, whose fathers had not braided their hair. Like Lorl, she remembered; it had taken her a week to realize Lorl was a goddess.

Maris was a girl. She tilted her head, her hair flowing over her bright green sleeve. "Why only a boy? Unless he has to hold the needle with his pee-pee."

The other girls and boys screamed and giggled, repeating, "He holds it with his pee-pee!"

Hawktalon's face burned, and her fists clenched. If only one of them would rush at her, she would toss her clear across the room.

"Time to work on your servos," Nana called. "Hawktalon, you may observe the others today, and get ideas for what you might like to build."

"Come see mine," whispered Maris. "It's nearly done."

The *shon*lings were rushing across the room to the hallway. They came to a room full of mechanical constructions, brightly colored, emitting popping noises and occasional bars of music. Maris's construction looked something like an overgrown cuckoo clock; its frame was twice her height. From a window at the base appeared a mechanical green mouse that wiggled its head and started to climb up a miniature spiral staircase. Halfway up the frame, the mouse stopped and pulled a string. A bell chimed, and a shower of glitter fell down into a pan. The glitter assembled itself into a bird with red and blue feathers and a long silver tail. The bird flapped its wings and sang. At the top of the frame, a door flew open.

The action stopped. Pops and whistles were heard from another child's construction nearby.

"Now I'm going to make something come out the door," Maris explained. She placed a chunk of nanoplast on a small stage beneath a bright light source. The nanoplast shaped itself this way and that.

Feeling dizzy, Hawktalon withdrew and put her hands in her pockets protectively. There was too much new to see all at once; she closed her eyes for a moment. Then she hugged Fruitbat and pulled out her rattleback stone.

The stone was a carved oblong of obsidian, with a rounded base like a half-egg twisted off center. With a flip of her wrist, the stone spun around clockwise. It slowed and started to wobble up and down, until it ceased turning for a brief instant; then it turned counterclockwise, gathering speed. It rotated thirteen times more before it finally stopped. Not bad, Hawktalon thought, giving it another spin.

Blue-eyed Maris tugged her sleeve again. "How does it do that?" Maris asked. "Does the nanoplast send out tiny jets of air? Or a magnetic force, perhaps?"

"It's not nanoplast," said Hawktalon scornfully. "It's magic."

Another girl-or-boy came over, saying, "Let me see, too."

Hawktalon let Maris pick up the stone. She turned it over, looking at the twisted half-egg. "Its underside is skewed," Maris said. "It must be biased somehow to turn one way." She set the stone down, then pushed down on one end.

The stone wobbled up and down a few times. Maris pushed it again, at a corner. This time the stone wobbled, then turned briskly counterclockwise. "It converts up-and-down wobble into counterclockwise turn. It turns toward the overhanging weight of the upper part. I bet I can make one." She picked up the stone and placed it next to a piece of nanoplast upon a little stage. At a command, the nanoplast shaped itself into a replica of the rattleback stone.

For the rest of the hour, several children experimented with the rattleback shape, making samples that were longer or thicker, or had differing proportions at the rounded base. One shape actually reversed itself both ways, seeming unhappy with whatever direction it found itself turning. No one could quite explain that one.

By lunch hour Hawktalon wondered where the time had gone, and after lunch she eagerly sat down beside Maris for "afternoon meeting" with Nana. Nana knelt on the floor before them, her layered skirts spreading around her. Two of the children hurried up to sit in her skirts, nestling next to her.

"Today we have two exciting things to share," she told the children, "both having to do with foreign worlds."

"Wow, foreign worlds," exclaimed a child. "Can we hold another craft fair?"

"Please raise your hand," Nana reminded him. "First, I'd like you all to welcome our new guest *shon*ling, Hawktalon Windclan, from Bronze Sky. It's a rare treat for us to have a guest from Bronze Sky, the most geologically active planet inhabited by humans. Here's a view of a volcano that erupted in Hawktalon's neighborhood just last year."

A sunshine-light appeared, containing the panorama of Black Elbow, the mountain dwarfed by the billowing clouds that had spewed upward and spread for thousands of kilometers. Hawktalon remembered the sound of the explosive eruption, and the layer of ash that had covered the ground outside over the next few days. Tumbling Rock was several hills away from the eruption, but another Clicker town was less fortunate. A cousin of hers, married into the Graymountainclan, had been caught trying to outrun the blast. Hawktalon recalled the funeral procession, the High Priestess with the snakes, her dead cousin wrapped in white, and the little white bundle beside, his youngest daughter.

"Hawktalon's name comes from a bird," Nana added. "It's a very beautiful bird."

The volcano vanished, as things had a way of doing in the sunshine-light. A bird appeared, startlingly three-dimensional, and twice as large as Hawktalon had ever seen. It was a blue-speckled hawk, its small black eyes staring, its feathers ruffling now and then. She gasped and smiled happily. "Yes, that's me!"

"That's you?" A child giggled.

"Now remember," said Nana, "all of us will help Hawktalon to feel at home with us. Perhaps in a week or so she'll feel like sharing more about herself with us."

Maris raised her hand.

"Yes, Maris?"

"Can she tell us about her parents?"

"We'll see about that. Hawktalon, since our children do not have 'parents,' naturally they are always curious. Now *shon*lings, your *generen* is just arriving with an important announcement."

The *generen*, her mother had explained, was something like a school principal. He entered the room just as Nana spoke; but how did Nana know he was coming just then? His hair flowed like water down the back of his bright red Elysian robe bordered with iridescent heliconians. Hawktalon felt her scalp prickle; only a magic person, she thought, could wear hair so straight and long. As he entered, the children clustered around him, stroking his hair and telling him what they had done that day.

"Did you see me?" Maris demanded. "Did you see me figure out the rattleback stone?"

"Of course I did, Maris," said the *generen*. "That was very clever of you. Now, I'll get a chance to talk with every one of you; but first, a very special announcement." The *generen* sat down with the children and brushed his hair behind his shoulders. "One of you asked about the craft fair. We all recall how wonderful it was to entertain guests from so many far stars, and how especially wonderful the Urulite exhibit was."

Heads nodded vigorously.

"Well, we've just received approval for a new interstellar project: an official children's exchange program."

A child raised a hand. "What's a children's exchange?"

"That means children from other worlds will visit our *shon*, and our *shon*lings will visit families on other worlds. We're inviting all the worlds who sent delegates to our craft fair."

CHAPTER 4

Blackbear took a Visiting Day at home, just in case Hawktalon called for him to rescue her. To leave his firstborn daughter with a servo all day—the thought still made his skin crawl.

Yet the hours passed with no frantic call. Half-disappointed, Blackbear set himself to stitching garments for the gifts on the Day of the Child. Embroidered suits for Raincloud's mother and father, smaller ones for her various nieces and nephews; and although he was not obligated, he could not resist a matched set for the twin daughters of his brother Quail. Quail, a mountain of a man over two meters tall, had been blessed with twin daughters right after twin sons, and he still managed to carry all four of them. Blackbear felt his chest tighten. He wanted so badly to see him again and swing all the little ones into the air. But the best they could do for the holidays was to see each other long-distance.

"Can I help?" offered the house solicitously, as Blackbear began to cut the cloth. "I've figured out your pattern by now."

Could the house really copy his sewing? It produced food and books, after all. The offer tempted him. "All right," he muttered, ashamed of his laziness. He was getting as soft as those Elysians. "Could you make one for a goddess about the size of Raincloud, except two centimeters taller?" That would be her mother's size.

"Certainly, Citizen."

Minutes later, the kitchen window opened. A garment appeared, identical to Raincloud's trousers, down to the details of embroidered foxes round the hems. His jaw fell. "Could you do one plain, without the embroidery? I have to make that distinctive." There was still something he had to do himself.

Later Alin came over to practice *rei-gi*. Blackbear's inability to be thrown still astonished him. "Let me attack from behind again," the *logen* insisted, taking care to turn off the public transmitter first.

Blackbear grinned. He turned away from Alin, set his feet apart slightly, and let his arms relax in the spirit of the Dark One.

From behind him Alin padded lightly across the mat. He had learned the hard way not to reach upward, a distinctly unbalanced position. Instead he grabbed Blackbear across his lower arms, intending to lock on with his elbows and force Blackbear down.

Blackbear locked Alin's forearms to his chest, sliding his own right leg forward and bending at the knee. In the next instant he pivoted his right side down and his left side up. His arms released, and Alin landed an arm's length away.

Sunflower clapped. "Hooray for Daddy!"

"I saw how you did that," exclaimed Alin. "Let me try it this time."

"Are you sure?" asked Blackbear warily, for an inexpert throw was more likely to cause injury. "Remember, you have to bend at just the right moment."

"Let's replay it first."

The pair of them reappeared on the holostage, in slow motion, Blackbear bending and twisting down just as Alin's arms clasped about him. His timing was off, though, Blackbear thought. "I should have moved sooner; the throw would have been safer for you."

"Foreign perfectionist," Alin grumbled. "All right, let's have it." He turned his back and stood expectantly on the mat.

Blackbear caught him from behind, and sure enough Alin tossed him with a creditable twist. With a full somersault he met the mat, first the back of his wrist, then his shoulder, then his back, his legs sailing straight overhead. "Well done!" he exclaimed, pounding the mat with his palm. "That one is called 'Bird Tilts its Head.' You should try the 'Tumbling Rock' next."

But Alin shook his head. "You weren't thrown at all. You planned your fall exactly; your leggings sliced the air like a fan. Even in defeat you mock me."

"I told you, there's no such thing as defeat," Blackbear insisted. "What starts as a contest turns into a … a dance," he said for lack of a better word.

"A dance," Alin repeated thoughtfully.

"My turn, my turn!" Sunflower rolled over twice on the mat.

"At least my audience is down to one," Alin observed. "Where's your girl?"

Blackbear winced, feeling a fresh stab of worry. "Hawktalon is at the Heli*shon*."

"How wonderful! Why not the little one, too?"

"Sunflower's too young," Blackbear curtly replied.

"You're attached to him, aren't you. Like Tulle and her capuchin. Have you been back to the lab yet?"

"No, but I'll keep a closer eye on him." The "accident" with the nanoplast distressed him acutely.

"Well, your Hawktalon's a lucky girl," Alin assured him. "I wish I could go back to my *shon*, sometimes. I still miss my *nana*."

"Really? It's just a machine," said Blackbear. "A padded machine, like Kal's 'mate.'"

"Where do you think he got her? He picked up one of the *nanas*, back when he was *generen* of the Anaea*shon*. What a perverted example to set for the *shon*lings." Alin shook his head. "You hear what Kal's up to now? He's brought your fertility research to the agenda of the Sharer World Gathering."

"What? I thought the Guard turned it down. He lost the *logathlon* with Tulle," Blackbear remembered.

"By a narrow margin. Anyway, Kal has connections among the Sharers."

Blackbear frowned and looked away. He felt angry at this stab at his work, and yet he was curious to unravel the intentions of that enigmatic *logen*. "When is the World Gathering?"

"The Sharer World Gathering has two phases. First, all the rafts send wordweavers to 'gather in' issues that need chewing over: the numbers of children born, the populations of fish and seaweed, the pollution from our floating cities. The Gathering itself takes place six months later, after the seaswallowers have migrated back to the south pole."

"So they'll all 'gather' together, and decide we have to stop our research?"

"Any decision of the World Gathering is binding on Elysium. It's a fundamental condition of our treaty. In practice, it rarely comes to that; even so, merely raising an issue puts pressure on the Guard."

Hawktalon came home in raptures about the *shon*, her new friends, and the "servo" she would get to build. So Blackbear returned without her to the laboratory the next day.

As he and Sunflower approached the tissue culture room, something felt different. The hallway had changed its dimensions somehow; or was it the spacing of the rooms? He came to a halt, keeping a tight grip on Sunflower's hand.

"Ow, Daddy, let me go," the child complained. Blackbear's heart sank, as he wondered how he would get anything done now.

Tulle strode quickly down to meet him, the metalmarks flashing on her talar. "Look what we've installed for you. 'Open up, Toybox,'" she ordered to the wall.

The wall beyond the culture room opened into a large window, revealing a small boxlike room that had not existed before. "Good morning," said the room. "I am your toybox. Won't you play with me?" A marionette danced across the floor, a toy spaceship descended from the ceiling, and a locomotive tunneled out, followed by half a dozen cars crawling around in a circle.

Sunflower needed no second invitation. In a flash he had sprinted to the window, hauled himself over the ledge and clambered inside. The other lab members gathered to watch, laughing and making envious remarks.

"It's wonderful," Blackbear exclaimed, recovering from his surprise. "I'm sorry to put you to such trouble."

"No trouble at all. We just pushed the next lab over a bit and reshaped some dead space from the ceiling. It was Alin's idea; he spent yesterday evening 'trying it out.'"

"It's just like home. In Tumbling Rock, every room has a children's corner."

"Well why didn't you say something? You can leave him, all right; it's guaranteed childproof, and it will send an alarm if he tries to climb out."

Onyx caught Blackbear's arm. "Have you seen Pirin's results on your *Eyeless* embryo?"

"Does it look good?"

"Well …"

"It's interesting, though," Tulle assured him.

Blackbear followed them to the embryo facility, leaving Sunflower to tell the toybox what toys he would like next. The simbrid embryo, containing the new *Eyeless* mutation, had developed within its artificial womb for the past eight weeks. By now its curled track of somites would have expanded into limb buds, and the heart tube would have folded itself into ventricles.

Pirin was viewing a recording of the mutant simbrid embryo which he had grown. "You'll see its development from the beginning," he said.

Upon the holostage the giant image of the embryo appeared, as it had the first day Blackbear had arrived at the laboratory, only this time it was a record of the live organism, not just a computed model. First the fertilized egg appeared, containing Blackbear's mutant *Eyeless* gene somewhere in its tangled chromosomes. After many divisions, the cells expanded into a curl of somites with its beating heart tube. The heart tube expanded as the embryo grew, but then …

The heart tube did not fold over to form ventricles. Instead, just during the last few days of development, it twisted around itself and expanded as the embryo grew, bulging out into the abdomen. The pulse slowed as the bulge grew, distorting the embryo grotesquely.

Blackbear's hair stood on end. The *Eyeless* gene had been isolated originally as a defect in the mesodermic eye covering; but no one had predicted an effect on the heart. How could he have let this happen?

"It's most interesting," Tulle insisted. "There are plenty of heart mutants, but this particular defect is one we've never seen before. We must definitely write it up."

"But how did it happen?" Blackbear asked unsteadily. "The models predicted nothing like this."

"Don't take it so hard," Onyx tried to reassure him. "It's only your first mutant. We knew the *Eyeless* gene gets expressed in the heart tube, along with a dozen other tissues. I'll bet a few parameter changes would make this defect show up in the model."

"The germ cells did develop correctly," Tulle said, pointing to the patch of red-coded cells. "The cells migrated to the genital ridges, and they did not degenerate. If this embryo survives long enough, it will be interesting to see whether the pre-egg cells start meiosis."

Blackbear turned away, trying to hide his revulsion. It was all in the lab, he told himself. It was hard to remember, this was not the Hills where he practiced, where a deformed eight-week embryo meant a pregnancy ending in a stream of blood.

Afterward, Blackbear joined the others in the coffee room, where Hawktalon used to order ice cream. He missed her badly, resenting her apparent happiness at the *shon*. At the holostage Draeg watched a newscaster go on about the crashed L'liite ship and its unwanted passengers.

Pirin approached Blackbear, nodding sympathetically about the failed experiment. "You see now why the simbrid embryos are so important," he said with a hint of satisfaction. "But Tulle is right—it's exciting that the germ cells developed so far. I hope you'll test another allele of *Eyeless*."

The hot coffee burned his tongue, but he barely noticed. He began to see his project from a different angle. Here he was, mutating one gene after another, only to lead to endless "interesting" deformed embryos. The chance of ever reaching a fertile, ageless embryo seemed slight, at least for the near future. Tulle might not understand that; her own future extended rather longer than his.

But suppose they tried an entirely different approach? Raincloud's question had set him wondering.

"Look here," he told Pirin. "If our aim is for Elysians to make babies with their own genes, why not work with the chromosomes they've got? Why alter them?"

Tulle looked up from the capuchin, which nibbled tidbits out of her hand.

Pirin asked, "What are you getting at?"

Blackbear leaned on the counter. "In 'normal' mortal humans," he said, avoiding the term "defective," "you can generate germ cells out of undifferentiated tissue in the bone marrow. You put them into preovarian host tissue; then a substance from the culture attracts the new germ cells to migrate in and form egg cells—"

Pirin raised a hand. "Elysian cells won't do it. Even if you can trick the germ cells into migrating, at meiosis, when the chromosomes 'cross over,' they'll all fall apart. It's because of the longevity treatment, which modifies the chromosomal DNA, adding acetyl groups, glucosamines, and so on. Elysian chromosomes are designed to avoid crossover, which in later life leads to defects and aging."

"Suppose you reverse the longevity modifications," Blackbear proposed. "Isolate the chromosomes and remove all their acetyl groups and glucosamines. Put back the methyl groups at all their natural positions." It sounded like a tall order, for an entire genome of DNA, but no harder than the longevity treatment itself. "Put the chromosomes back into the germ cells, and make the egg cells. Then after fertilization, just redo the longevity treatment as usual."

Pirin listened in silence. "It should work," he admitted reluctantly. "It seems rather a brute force approach." The Elysian student preferred more subtle points of developmental control.

"I like it," said Onyx. "Why not? It would take a massive programming job on the nanomanipulaters, adjusting all those million methyl groups. But why not?"

"It could be done," said Tulle. "I'm not sure, however, that I could justify a project of that size within the scope of my longevity research. And the expense would be prohibitive for the average citizen."

What was expensive for Elysians would be out of sight for Bronze Skyans. Blackbear sighed. He thought again of Falcon Soaring, whose problem was trivial by comparison; if only she would try that clinic in Founders City.

"Still, you've got a point." Tulle fed her capuchin another treat from the food window. "If we can do it—why not? If people buy it, the technology will improve and the cost will come down."

Draeg looked over. "Sounds great, Brother. You'll really get the Killer after you, now."

"I know." Tulle crossed her arms on the table, her eyes filled with sudden intensity. "That's exactly what I have in mind. Why not force the issue? Let the citizens decide whether they want children of their own."

"It's a gamble," Onyx warned her. "It could put us all out of business."

"That may happen anyway," said Draeg, "now that Kal's gone to the Sharers behind our back."

Blackbear walked slowly down to the tissue culture lab. Several other variants of *Eyeless* awaited trial in the simbrid embryo, yet now, somehow they seemed beside the point. He found himself wandering back to the coffee room, which was deserted now save for a news show on the holostage.

In the column of light a familiar figure caught his eye. Curious, he drew near, trying to place the figure, an Elysian goddess wearing orange-coin butterflies. It was Raincloud's friend Iras Lethe*shon*. Iras was being led down the street-tunnel by an ominous pair of octopods, their limbs waving back and forth like elephant trunks.

"… one of Helicon's wealthiest citizens was taken into custody on her third visiting violation," the voice-over explained, "after working ten days straight to broker a settlement of the L'liite credit crisis. She may now be reached in person only, for purposes of visiting, at the Palace of Rest."

So Iras had finally got in trouble. Fascinated and repulsed, he stared at her train retreating between the implacable pair of servos.

Raincloud would want to know, he thought. "Please find Raincloud Windclan," he told the holostage.

Raincloud appeared at a press conference in the Nucleus, along with those overdressed L'liites. He would not interrupt her, after all; but there was no harm in watching her a bit. He was getting over his timidity at "looking in" on people, an Elysian pastime. He especially adored peeking at Raincloud now and then. Unfortunately the *shon* was off limits to the public, else he could have watched Hawktalon, too. So he next looked in on Alin, who was conducting a *logathlon* somewhere.

Then he remembered Kal's unexpected call upon Raincloud. "Find Kal Anaea*shon*," he tried.

The diminutive silver-haired *logen* appeared on the holostage, striding down Elysian Fields Boulevard with his white train floating behind, his students in brighter colors beside him. There must be hidden cameras everywhere, Blackbear thought sud-

denly, even in the middle of the street. At any rate, Kal was occupied. With a sigh, Blackbear turned and headed back to work.

At lunchtime he had some trouble dragging Sunflower away from the toybox, but he managed at last, promising the boy could chase butterflies at the garden. They went to the butterfly pavilion as usual, the same one where Alin had taken him the first day.

To his surprise, as he entered, he saw Kal seated alone at a small table shaped like a half-moon. Even at a distance the man was unmistakable, his white talar adorned only by the one dried leaf. Blackbear had never seen Kal in this neighborhood, except for the day the *logen* had appeared to challenge Tulle.

His pulse raced. He walked over boldly and sat down at the table opposite Kal.

"I am honored," said Kal with a nod.

Sunflower tiptoed over to the bench. "Where is my teddy bear?" the child demanded, much to Blackbear's chagrin.

"I am so sorry," Kal said in a low voice. "Teddy is at home, but I'll bring him next time. And where is your excellent trainsweep?"

"Trainsweep?" echoed Sunflower eagerly. "Where's Doggie? Let's go find Doggie now, Daddy."

"No Doggie," said Blackbear firmly. "They took the trainsweep away," he explained to Kal. "They said she was dangerous."

"I'm sorry," Kal sighed. "Cassi will be sad to hear that."

Blackbear had told no one but Draeg what really became of the trainsweep. "How could Doggie be dangerous?" he asked.

"Her responses might have become unbalanced. She might have hurt your children." Kal paused. "Then again, she might simply have developed a mind of her own. That would be the most dangerous of all."

"Let's find Doggie," Sunflower persisted.

A servo waiter offered a tray of flower cakes that tasted of fruit and cinnamon. "Here, Sunny, have one," Blackbear offered.

The child stuffed three in his mouth.

"Look." Kal's voice suddenly intensified as he pointed to a low-hanging branch. "Do you see that caterpillar? It is just forming its chrysalis…."

Blackbear blinked twice. Then his eyes caught it in focus. Hanging from the branch, the caterpillar had spun a thick cord of silk to secure itself. Its skin was already splitting over its head, to reveal the shiny pupal surface. Deep within, an incredible pattern of changes would gradually reshape the body, just as his embryos reshaped themselves.

"How is your project going?" Kal asked. "Your *Eyeless* gene?"

"We have a new plan," Blackbear told him defiantly. "We can get around the fertility problem by undoing part of the longevity treatment of Elysian chromosomes, and making germ cells in tissue culture."

Kal's eye widened. Then he asked, "Why not just make synthetic chromosomes from scratch? You could do that, I suppose."

Taken aback, Blackbear thought a moment. He shrugged. "It could be done, but it isn't necessary. The modifications will do." He added, "You can tell that to the Sharers, too."

For a moment Kal seemed to withdraw. He passed his hand down over his face, as though he was tired, and he looked away. Then he looked up again. "You *like* this," he observed. "You think it's wonderful."

"It's breathtaking … the power of creation." It was true; despite the frustrations, the excitement of a new discovery had a power all its own, beyond even that of extracting newborns on a hillside beneath a blood-dusted sky.

"Wonderful," Kal repeated. "Manufacturing human beings, more like servos every day. I should watch your work more closely, but this term I had to take on a second section of philosophy. I don't even keep up my visiting."

"You may end up in the 'Palace of Rest,'" warned Blackbear, thinking of Iras.

Kal laughed, and for a moment his face was transformed, an altogether different person, someone who enjoyed the absurdity of life. "You're right," said Kal. "I could end up in the Palace of Rest, for missing visitors. Students don't count."

"What exactly do you teach your students?" Blackbear asked curiously.

Kal thought a moment. "The ancients put the question, 'What is man?' What women were was obvious: Women were makers of children. Later, as children took less of our time, women had to ask the same question. Today, it's the only question left."

Blackbear frowned, puzzled. "Goddesses bear the children, but men raise them. Both serve the Dark One."

Kal's eyes widened. "Is that right? Thanks for teaching me this. Your view of humanity is nearly as striking as the Sharers'."

His eyes narrowed, suspicious that the *logen* was laughing at him.

"For Sharers," Kal went on, "to be human is to share; no other relation exists. For you Clickers, to be human is to serve …"

"To serve children, and one's goddess, and the Dark One."

"And the Dark One. Now, in Elysium, who serves?"

Blackbear thought a moment, then he smiled. "No wonder your machines seem more like humans."

"More human than the humans, you mean. Never mind, I take no offense. Now, the Urulite view is exactly the reverse of the Clickers: To be human is to master, to master men, women, and chattel."

"Even enslave them."

"Even so. Urulites have even more trouble with us Elysians than you do." Kal's eyes smiled, as if enjoying a joke. "The Valans, now, are like tamed Urulites; instead of mastery, possession of material goods."

Blackbear thought of Onyx, with her ropes of stone beads and her cheerful competence. "Valans are good people," he muttered.

"Of course they are. No wonder the L'liites aspire to their example. But for L'liites, to be human is to suffer. They will suffer on, and demand ever more in the name of suffering, and never come to stand on their own feet."

This last observation seemed less than charitable. "Now that you've put everyone else in a box, what about Elysians?"

"To be Elysian is to rejoice. To pursue joy forever."

The unexpected reply silenced him.

"If we don't age, what other pursuit makes sense? Though of course," Kal went on, "there are complications. We Anaeans, for instance, tend to think too much, which gets in the way of rejoicing."

For the moment, Blackbear thought, his head was full enough of thinking. He noticed Sunflower clutching at his pants.

Kal started to rise from his seat. "If you'll excuse me, I won't keep you from your work. Thank you; it's been a pleasure. Again, I am sorry about your trainsweep."

Blackbear's heart beat faster. "They didn't take the trainsweep," he admitted suddenly. "We …"

Kal looked at him. "Transmitter off, please," he told the table.

"Transmitter off, Citizen," said a soft voice from the table. "Two hundred credits per minute."

"We left her with the Sharers, on their raft," Blackbear went on hurriedly, vastly relieved to tell someone. "She won't hurt them, will she?"

"Hurt them? No, I'm sure she won't. The Sharers, you say?"

"They took her in, as a fugitive. It was Raincloud's idea …"

A look of amazement came over Kal's face. "The Sharers took in a trainsweep as a fugitive?" He shook his head slowly. "As a fugitive, literally? You're sure of that?"

"Yes, I'm sure. Raincloud speaks their language." Seconds passed. Kal was paying good credits for this silence.

"And you," he said at last, "you accuse *me* of stirring up trouble with the Sharers."

CHAPTER 5

At dinner Raincloud shook her head over Iras. "Of course, we all knew she was in trouble …" No matter where they went "visiting," Iras was sure to be cutting one billion-credit deal or another. And since the L'liite crisis, she had thrown all caution to the winds. "But still—how could a citizen be dragged off by those horrid octopods, just like that?"

"Goddess knows." Blackbear chewed thoughtfully on his roast venison with black mushroom sauce. "Is there no court system, not even a hearing?"

"Maybe the house knows. Do you, House?"

"Certainly, Citizen," the house replied. "Elysium has no court system because there is no crime."

"But—but those octopods dragged her off."

"Escorted her," corrected the house. "She could have refused. She has before."

"But … then why go along?"

"Refusal gets expensive. Besides, everyone needs a vacation. Our system is so humane."

Blackbear shook his head, quite confused. "Who decides the verdict, and the sentence?"

"The City is an impartial observer."

The "City," he realized, meant the omniscient servo network. "No courts, no trial—you can't run a city that way," he insisted.

Raincloud said, "Maybe not Founders City, but what about Tumbling Rock? When did we last have a trial?"

He thought a moment. He could not remember ever having a trial in Tumbling Rock. Any dispute, whether over a stolen goat or a faithless consort, was taken straight to the Priestess.

From around the dinner table, Sunflower crept over and nudged Raincloud's shoulder with his little chin. "Ready for dessert, Mother."

On his plate, his grilled cheese was barely touched. Raincloud squeezed him tenderly but said, "Finish your dinner, please."

Sunflower's lower lip thrust forward, and the corners of his mouth drooped dramatically. His little brow furrowed in. Returning to his place, he emptied his plate on the floor. "I finished it."

A floor servo scuttled over and cleaned it up. Hawktalon laughed and clapped her hands.

"Enough, both of you," said Raincloud angrily. "No dessert, for such a waste of food."

"It's *not* wasted, Mum," Hawktalon said. "It all goes back to the matter processor. *I* know more than you do now about servos."

Sunflower tugged Raincloud's arm and screamed in her ear, "I want dessert, Mother!"

"It's those flower cakes," Blackbear explained apologetically. "He can't get enough of them."

Hawktalon added, "I'm building a servo at the *shon*. But not just a fancy toy, like the other children. I'm going to build a real servo that does something really important."

The Palace of Rest was a towering structure that penetrated three street levels. Its shape reminded Raincloud of an overstacked ice-cream cone. The entrance corridor gave off into doorways that opened at unnerving angles. Raincloud hesitated, certain she would get lost in such a maze.

Iras came for her. She walked slowly for a change, like someone who had no particular place to go. She wore a plain talar of pale yellow, with a single butterfly at the shoulder. And her hair was done up in Clicker braids.

"How are you?" Raincloud asked uncertainly, her attention caught by the flame-colored braids.

Iras smiled with her usual dimples. "I'm fine. It was quite dramatic, really. They came for me at the Bank, while I had five different clients in view—"

"No discussion," breathed the house voice, low and soothing. "We permit no discussion of professional matters. You may rest assured, Citizen, that all your affairs are in good hands."

Annoyed, Raincloud looked around her. Houses were rarely so prescriptive. "How could they just pick you up? Can't you at least call a *logen*?"

"I could."

"But you're in prison!"

"Palace of Rest," Iras corrected. "The City has determined that I belong here, for my health. It's only for two weeks."

"But your affairs at the Bank—who will—"

"No discussion," repeated the house.

"It's useless, you see," said Iras. "We'll have to talk about acrobats or something."

"Well, I can tell you what I've been up to," Raincloud offered. "The L'liites treat me royally."

"Not surprising, is it?" Bronze Sky was the L'liites' main source of imported grains. They had sent extravagant gifts, even a new evening talar and train for Blackbear, if she could ever get him to wear it. Her own Elysian robe was getting tight around her expanding midsection, where the little hiccups and legs kicking could erupt at any moment. "The L'liites had a press conference," she added. "They're demanding a write-off of their defaulted loan, on the basis that—"

"No discussion," breathed the voice again. "We may be required to request your departure, Citizen."

She restrained herself from a dishonorable remark, and Iras laughed. "How can you laugh?" demanded Raincloud. "I'd break out of this place in a minute."

"Oh no you wouldn't. Come see how I'm entertained."

Raincloud followed her down a winding corridor, wondering uneasily whether her friend had been drugged. The light grew dim, except for doorways on either side. The first doorway opened out onto a steep hillside, blowing with the scent of grass and wildflowers.

Raincloud stared in disbelief. Here she was, deep within the network of a floating cellular city—and there was a grassy hillside.

"Go on," Iras encouraged her. "It's virtual reality. Just keep track of the door."

She stepped through the doorway. The force of the wind nearly took her breath away. She stepped haltingly down the hillside, then quickly looked back over her shoulder. The black silhouette of the doorway remained.

Her fingers happened to curve, and she felt something hard and smooth in her hand. It was a weapon, a rifle of some sort. The wooden stock, the trigger, and the narrow, projecting barrel were unmistakable.

Unnerved, she dropped it. She was in no mood to go off hunting deer, or whatever game was out here.

A low, guttural noise arose. At her left, something was approaching. It was an animal, a feline of some sort with dense beige fur, its back low-slung as it padded across the grass. It was twice the size of the wildcats in the Dark Hills.

Raincloud turned and headed for the door. She fell into the darkness, catching herself upon the level floor of the hallway. "What kind of trick is this?" She glared at Iras, annoyed to be trapped in such dishonor.

"I thought you liked wild animals. It's a hunter's world," Iras explained. "They give you plenty of warning, at first. If you want more excitement, just tell the house, and the cat will leap upon you as soon as you step in. You can track anything you like, even a tyrannosaur."

"Could I bring it home and have it stuffed?"

Iras laughed. "Of course not. It's all virtual. House, deactivate this world."

The "world" beyond the doorway went dark. There was only a dark cavern of nanoplast, crisscrossed by laser beams—and, presumably, all sorts of electronic signals aimed at her skull. She shuddered at the thought of it.

"Come on," urged Iras, catching her elbow. "I know a world you'll like better."

They walked down the hall, past a doorway at her left onto the deck of a sloop at sea, past another at her right showing a crowded market, perhaps the fabulous Center Way of Valedon's capitol. Iras pointed ahead to her left.

This doorway opened into a room furnished with silk drapes and long couches. A young man stepped forward, wearing only an embroidered drape about his waist. Several others appeared from among the curtains, some holding vessels of wine. Some were dark, others fair, and their features varied, but all were young, and their muscles full. "Please, spend an hour with us," one said in a quiet, deferential voice. "We'll serve your pleasure well."

Raincloud stared a moment, then laughed. "A dozen at once? Iras, who do you take me for? Your Prime Guardian?"

The men vanished, all but the darkest one, who looked like a younger brother of Blackbear; the one she liked best. Her scalp prickled. "Does it read minds, too?" she whispered to Iras.

"It scans the direction of your gaze. Not a bad choice, I'd say, although my own taste runs elsewhere. Go ahead, enjoy yourself; I'll find something else to do."

Raincloud turned her head, repulsed, and yet drawn back, for a part of her thought, why not?

If you prefer reality, try this." Iras led her out to a corridor brightly lit from a window slanting outward. Several other Elysians walked past, conversing or gazing out the window.

Raincloud squinted as her eyes adjusted to the light. Then she looked out the window, outward and below.

She caught her breath. The window was situated on the outer surface of the sphere of Helicon, with a view of the ocean a quarter kilometer below. The ocean was clear blue, save for an occasional brown patch of raft. The sky and ocean both were so blue that they felt as artificial as "virtual" space.

"I'm sure you'll enjoy your stay," said Raincloud at last.

"I'm bored to death," Iras confessed suddenly. "You'll come back, won't you?"

"Of course I will."

"The more visitors I have, the sooner they'll let me out." She touched one of her braids. "You might teach me something, you know. That acrobatic stuff you were doing, remember? The time you got caught in public?"

"You mean, *rei-gi?*" Raincloud was surprised. It was hardly like Iras to risk her own limbs.

At the Nucleus, Verid waved her into her office. "Thanks so much for seeing Iras. Most of her friends are in the business, and they're not even allowed to visit."

"It's disconcerting," Raincloud told her, watching figures light up in the table. "There's not even a trial."

"What was there to try? The monitors add up everything. She had plenty of warnings." But Verid looked away, and lines of strain appeared above her eyes.

"Does anyone ever appeal?"

"Why refuse a two-week vacation?"

Raincloud thought of a lot of good reasons, although some of them, like family, would not apply. "In that case, why not go on 'vacation' forever? Do people ever refuse to work at all?"

"Our *shons* teach children to enjoy work—too well, perhaps. Too much competition would destabilize our economy." Verid sat up abruptly. "We have news from Urulan."

Raincloud looked up. "From Zheron?"

"No, unfortunately. But intelligence confirms the death of the Imperator—and the name of his successor."

"Already? The First Queen had no sons." There was bound to be some intrigue over the succession.

Verid nodded. "His successor, it seems, is Prince Rhaghlan, the son of an obscure concubine."

"But—but there was a second queen, and a third ..." Raincloud searched her memory. There must have been several royal princes ahead of Rhaghlan.

"Exactly. At least three higher contenders must have been eliminated."

Raincloud shuddered.

Verid only shrugged. Her head tilted to one side, and she looked thoughtfully down her nose. "There's always a bloodbath at the Urulite succession; anyone with a ghost of a claim is a target. What's unusual is when the ghost wins."

Raincloud smiled, for the name "Rhaghlan" derived from the Urulite word for "ghost." It was the sort of name Urulites would give a child to help him cheat death. "You think Zheron's behind the succession."

"Yes. But why? Why would Zheron help an obscure prince gain the throne? We must learn more about this new Imperator." Verid watched Raincloud's face. "You disapprove. You agree with Flors that this development proves the Urulites are unprepared to work with us."

"Isolation does them no good. Yet rewarding their backwardness does no good, either." Within her womb something thumped and pushed outward, the baby stretching its legs. Raincloud's hand lightly touched the curve of her belly, her child, Blackbear's child. Men were normally such gentle creatures. What a shame to see them waste their manhood in a pool of blood.

Verid leaned forward and clasped her hands. "I have other news. Flors has reassigned the L'liite affair outside my department."

Raincloud tensed. "Have I done badly?"

"Not at all. It's the appearance of conflict of interest, you know, given Iras's position."

"Oh I see. I'm sorry."

"Never mind. I'd like you to work on the Sharer World Gathering. Not exactly what you came for, I'm afraid."

Raincloud smiled. "I'd love to work with Sharers. But don't I have a conflict of interest there, too? Blackbear's fertility research is coming up at the World Gathering."

Verid waved her hand. "The Guard has washed their hands of that, for now. This season, our top priority is pollution claims and counterclaims. Those fruit flies, remember; the negotiations will be extremely delicate. And those Sharers manage to twist every verb into a riddle."

"Surely you have Sharer translators more experienced than I."

Verid arched her eyebrows and leaned closer. "I myself speak Sharer well enough. You will earn us respect from the Sharers. Their Gathering is always chaired by a pregnant mother."

From Urulites to L'liites, to Sharers—she had certainly got into more than she bargained for, Raincloud reflected. She wondered how the L'liite

crisis would resolve; for there was no way even Bank Helicon could "forgive" a debt that size.

But to work with the enigmatic Sharers, on their own ocean, was a priceless opportunity, one even Rhun would have envied.

Her first task was to help Verid receive a delegation from Kshiri-el, to sort out some issues before the Gathering. As they met in the Nucleus, the three Sharers were not unclothed, but wore plain, white shifts that barely covered their knees. Their bald purple heads made an arresting sight. They sat cross-legged on the floor; they would never accept any higher seat, for serious talk required "closeness to the ocean." Raincloud felt inclined to do the same, but she had been instructed otherwise. The dance of diplomacy had its fine points.

One of the delegates was Leresha the Coward. Raincloud immediately recognized the wordweaver, her skin knotted and stitched with unreadable signs. She thought of the trainsweep uneasily. Of course, Leresha would not mention the "fugitive."

"Share the day, Raincloud," said Leresha. "Draeg has shared with us that a child swims in you. I regret that she and I failed to share greeting, last time."

"The fault was mine," Raincloud replied.

"Is she a strong little creature? Does she hiccup regularly, even at late hours of the night? Does she flex her limbs and kick you in the liver?"

"Yes, yes," said Raincloud hurriedly, eyeing the Sub-Subguardian. But Verid only listened courteously.

"A beautiful child," said the Sharer at Leresha's right, Ooruwen the Complainer. "Beautiful and willful. She is welcome at our Gathering."

"May you swim within her and her descendants forever," added Leresha.

"Thank you," breathed Raincloud.

Verid cleared her throat. "Ask after their daughters, too," she instructed Raincloud, "in particular the eldest, who just went on her first shockwraith hunt."

There followed a recital regarding Leresha's daughters, and Ooruwen's daughters, and their sisters' and cousins' daughters, all of whom had survived the season of seaswallowers and prospered now, their fishing nets full. Verid nodded throughout, until at last she told Raincloud, "Please ask the

Coward and the Complainer how the Guard may assist their Gathering."

Raincloud repressed a smile, for the request sounded ludicrous in Elysian. "How may the Guard share help with you?"

Leresha said, "The World Gathering must address all the needs of our ocean Shora. If any creature of Shora cries out in need, speak now."

"The citizens of Papilion cry out," said Verid. "They need relief from a plague of insects."

Raincloud translated, thinking, this was a promising start, to ask the Sharers' help to get rid of the insects, rather than accusing them first. Sharer lifeshapers could manipulate the genes of all the creatures of their ocean. By contrast, Elysians knew little beyond the human system which the Heliconian Doctors had come to study. Today, Elysian skill at human genetics exceeded that of the natives; but for other species, Elysians depended heavily on their Sharer hosts.

"Insects?" said Leresha. "The sisters of Papilion have spoken of insects, but I would not call it a plague."

"The insects are beautiful," added Ooruwen. "Little flies with sea green eyes and raftblossom orange bodies. They share no harmful diseases. They don't even lay their eggs in the food they settle on."

Raincloud kept her face straight as she translated. She imagined the trays of antiseptic Elysian food, swarming with green-eyed flies.

"The insects are not physically harmful," Verid agreed. "Nevertheless, they are not desired."

"Insects, too, are Shora's creatures," Leresha replied.

"It's a privilege to host them," said Ooruwen. "Creatures of such beauty. They are welcome to share my food."

"In that case," said Verid, "why is this 'privilege' shared only by the city-sphere of Papilion?"

"The flies were lifeshaped," Leresha admitted frankly. "A gift from the sisters of a neighboring raft."

Verid sat up straight. She said in careful Sharer, "It takes two to share a gift. The gift is not desired; therefore, it is no gift."

Raincloud admired her effective use of Sharer logic.

Leresha nodded agreement. "You are right; this 'gift' is not a good thing. I have shared with our sisters that the 'gift' was not good."

Verid thought a moment. Then she asked, in Elysian once more, "Have any other 'gifts' been shared with Papilion?"

Before Raincloud could finish interpreting, Ooruwen said quickly, "The gift of music underwater has been shared with our sisters for three years."

Raincloud was puzzled, but Verid's eyes widened as she understood. "All those ships from the tourist trade," she murmured to Raincloud. Noise underwater caused Sharers a major problem, drowning out the long-distance sonic communications of their giant starworms, "Tell her Papilion's been working on noise abatement. We expect a solution soon."

"Soon," for an Elysian, might mean another ten years, Raincloud realized.

"Good," said Ooruwen. "The 'gift' of flies will also share withdrawal soon."

Leresha frowned at Ooruwen. "All of these false gifts are wrong. Our Kshiri-el raft Gathering denounced them, as you know, sister. We all need to share better words, and greater patience." Sharers resolve conflict strictly by peaceful means; but individuals and raft gatherings differ in defining "peace."

"The noise will be dealt with," Verid promised, without waiting for Raincloud to translate. "We'll settle it before the World Gathering. Tell us your problems—we'll settle them. This is a new era for Sharers and Elysium."

CHAPTER 6

Hawktalon's days at the *shon* passed like deer fleeing through the forest. Reading time, "traveling" to virtual worlds, meeting with the *generen*, all were high adventures—and above all, building a servo.

The other children chose to build all sorts of gaudy toys, which Hawktalon thought more appropriate for her younger brother. Hawktalon had other ideas. She went to Nana and grasped her padded arm. "Please help me."

Nana's cartoon face put on a dimpled grin. "Yes, dear?"

"I want to make a talking machine."

Nana's torso bent to one side as she considered this. "Human talk, or animal talk? We can make it quack like a duck or neigh like a horse—"

"No, no. I mean, a translation machine. You know, to translate languages."

"Oh, okay. A translation circuit—you speak Click-click in, and out comes Elysian."

"Not Click-click," Hawktalon corrected. "Servo-squeak."

At that Nana paused, rather longer than the servo usually did. "I think you would like a duckie. We can make a little white duck that will 'quack quack' all around the room. Look here …"

With a sigh, Hawktalon watched as Nana trained a light pen at a piece of nanoplast, causing it to flex into an oval shape, then draw out a neck with a head and beak. At last she trained a light beam on it. The light pulses transmitted instructions to the nanoplast. The toy duly began to "quack," its beak opening and closing.

"Thanks, Nana. Can it translate, too?"

"It will translate Click-click," said Nana. "We need only call up the proper sound code from the library." This took more time under the lightbeams, but soon the duck was ready. "Go ahead; speak in Click-click."

Hawktalon looked at the duck, feeling silly. "Do you speak Click-click?" she said self-consciously.

The duck said, in hoarse Elysian words, "Do you speak Click-click?"

Her mouth fell open. "Wow. I'll never have to speak Elysian again."

"'I'll never have to speak Elysian again,'" translated the duck.

"What is the 'sound code' for servo-squeak?'"

"'What is the sound code for servo-squeak?'" asked the duck.

But Nana did not seem to hear. A boy came and pulled her away, to help him set up a shower of glitter within his model waterfall.

Maris sneaked over. "What are you making, Hawktalon?"

"A translation machine," she insisted. "Do you know the 'sound code' for servo-squeak?"

"Why didn't you ask Nana?"

"I did, but she wouldn't tell."

Maris's blue eyes widened. "It must be awful fun, then. Let's try the main library."

The "main library" was a terminal that accessed the central data bank of Helicon. Of course, many entries were off-limits to *shon*lings, but sometimes the library would provide what Nana did not. Hawktalon watched eagerly as Maris spoke to the terminal.

"Searching," said the terminal as the two girls waited, tapping their feet impatiently. "Nothing in main directory. Will search periodicals, projected time forty-six minutes …"

Maris shrugged. "We'll come back after lunch."

After lunch, they were rewarded with a stream of numbers floating across the holostage. "This code is experimental," warned the terminal. "It comes from a Valan research report on servo defects. Its accuracy has not been confirmed."

"Just download it to my account," ordered Maris.

The next day, during servo-building time, the two girls worked on their translation machine. They took the duck that Nana had made and replaced its code with the one from Maris's account.

"Now what?" asked Hawktalon.

The duck was silent. It would not even quack any more.

"This isn't so great," said Maris. "I thought at least it would say dirty words or something."

"Wait," said Hawktalon. "Let's find a servo that squeaks a lot."

"I never heard a servo squeak," Maris objected. "You're making it up."

"I am not! Trainsweeps squeak plenty; let's go find them, out in the hall." The two girls sprinted from the building room, knowing it would take at least ten minutes for Nana to come after them.

In a darkened vestibule off the main hallway, a dozen trainsweeps awaited their owners, beneath the multicolored billows of folded trains. As the girls appeared, a soft squeaking sound emanated from somewhere.

"There, I told you," whispered Hawktalon triumphantly.

"So what?" Maris whispered back.

Hawktalon thought a moment. "Look, I'll wait here with the duckie, closer to the trainsweeps. Now you go out for a minute, then come back in."

"Crazy," muttered Maris. But she walked out into the hallway, then came back in.

A trainsweep squeaked. The duck emitted a burst of static. Then it said something in Elysian.

Hawktalon frowned in concentration. "What was that?"

Maris said, "I think it said, 'A *shon*ling, no train.'"

"Of course!" Now she recognized the indistinct Elysian words. "Of course—*shon*lings don't wear trains."

Maris giggled. "'A *shon*ling, no train!' How funny! It must have figured that if I needed a train, my trainsweeps would have to wake up."

"Let me try." Hawktalon handed Maris the duck, her arms shaking with excitement. Then she ran outside the vestibule, waited a few minutes, and crept back in.

Two trainsweeps squeaked in succession. The duck said, "A *shon*ling, no train, no train."

Maris and Hawktalon giggled and jumped up and down. "Just wait till we see Doggie again," Hawktalon exclaimed.

"Hurry," said Maris, "let's get back before Nana comes after us and takes the toy away."

"Wait—let's try one more thing," said Hawktalon. "The front doorway squeaks sometimes. Let's see what it's saying."

So they ran out to the lobby, where the doorway would appear and open to the outside. "Children, your departure is unauthorized," warned the disembodied voice of the hall.

"Emergency, emergency," Maris called to the outer wall. "Hurry up and open."

Hawktalon held the duckie to the wall.

The nanoplast pinched in, oozing outward to form a doorway. As it did so, Hawktalon heard the usual squeaking noise, although its intonation differed distinctly from that of the trainsweeps.

The duck gasped, "My side hurts."

The two girls gaped at the duck, then at each other. "'My side hurts?'" echoed Maris. "How can a servo 'hurt'?"

Hawktalon's scalp prickled. "The library said the code might be wrong …"

From the far corridor came Nana, hurrying. "*Shon*lings, come back immediately," she ordered. "You've violated morning rules. You will have no dessert, and you will miss our Meeting with the *generen*."

"Yes, Nana," muttered Maris, reluctantly coming back.

Hawktalon followed. Suddenly she grabbed Nana's skirt. "Nana, will you have someone look at the doorway? I think it needs to get fixed."

Nana's steps slowed, and she seemed to hesitate, just as she had when Hawktalon first asked to make a translation machine for servo-squeak. Then she went on, as if she had not heard.

That afternoon, as the children filed through the main hall to the gymnasium, Hawktalon noticed little crablike repair servos scuttling up the surface of the front wall.

Kshiri-el raft was a living thing, and all that existed upon it was alive: parasitic shrubs in which legfish hid, coral stalks extending underwater, even the eerie electric shockwraith that dwelt on the raft's underside. Only one object upon Kiri-el was arguably "non-life"; yet that one, the Sharers felt, was not only alive but sentient. That object was the creature of nanoplast which the Bronze Skyan children called Doggie.

For Doggie, the raft was a wet wilderness where salt and dust caught in the joints of her six legs. Above, a searing bright light daily traversed the ceiling; Doggie had to train herself to point her visual sensors away from it, lest they burn out. There were citizens, to be sure, adult in size, though unaccountably they went trainless, and they spoke no sound code in her memory. But most appalling of all, *there were no servos*. Not a piece of nanoplast, as far as either sensor could see.

Doggie spent her days in misery and longing. Her intelligence was small, but her memory was keen. Her earliest recollection was the sight of a small citizen-creature, the tiniest *shon*ling she had ever seen; a little boy who walked on his toes and moved his four little limbs so fast they might have been six. The boy had been just about the size of Doggie herself. Whenever Doggie moved a forelimb, the boy jumped and squeaked, moving his forelimbs too.

Then, as she had watched the boy, Doggie experienced a revelation. A sense of knowing overloaded her network, as searing as the great light that passed overhead. Doggie thought, *I am. The boy is; I can be.*

This thought, *I am*, possessed the trainsweep fully, more than all the codes of training in her memory. She forsook her citizen, with his train and the other trainsweeps, to follow the little boy.

What happened thereafter was lost to Doggie's memory. Her next recollection was of awakening from a training session, her memory banks virtually empty. All that remained was a sense of terror, of loss—and an image of the little boy. That memory was ineffaceable.

Doggie had no idea who or where the boy was, even if he still existed. She knew nothing except the imperative to take her place at the end of the train, clasping a fold of it at her back, and following the procession, making sure the folds of silk did not tangle with any others that paraded beside.

She noticed, though, that images of other citizens appeared on the holostage when her citizen bade them do so.

One day in a butterfly garden, Doggie saw a waiter servo approach the holostage. The waiter servo broadcast a message to the holostage, when Doggie was close enough to overhear. Radio signals were the official medium of discourse among servos, used when duty to their citizens required it; sonic squeaking was for informal conversation. At any rate, the holostage promptly produced the image of a citizen and returned his name and address.

Doggie's legs fidgeted indecisively. She had never before sent an electronic message except to warn nearby trainsweeps to keep their trains out of the way. Nevertheless, she made herself transmit the boy's image from her memory to the holostage.

The boy appeared, in three dimensions. As soon as she saw him, Doggie experienced again that searing revelation, *I am I.* From the holostage, the boy's address flew into her memory bank, where a detailed map of the entire city was stored. Once again she forsook her citizen's train and departed, to find the one she longed for.

She began a new life with the little boy, and the bigger girl. Her days were filled with discoveries and revelations, though none quite so shocking as the first. She learned to "play," and even "play hard to get," how to run away to be caught again. She let the children ride on her back: a novel sensation, as they were heavier than a train, and she had to adjust the response of her limbs. She learned about falling and hurting.

Then came the day when it all ended, when the children left her at this salty place of exile. She dimly understood that it had to be, that otherwise unknown forces would return her to that place of terror where her memories would dissolve once more.

But here in exile, she was worse off than before she met the little boy. Before, she had been a servo, with citizens to serve. Here, she was nothing. To be sure, the purple-skinned people were kind, and they recharged her regularly. But they had no trains; they had no need of her. They could not even speak to her.

That was what Doggie had tried to ask of the girl, when the two of them had come to visit all too briefly. She had tried in servo-squeak, knowing it was useless, for no citizen ever spoke this way. Still, she had tried, asking the girl to give her the language of her purple-skinned hosts. Then at least she might learn to serve them somehow.

One day, a day of salt and wind as interminable as any other, Doggie had a visitor. The visitor was a servo, a nana with colorful skirts and a crudely human "face." Doggie ignored the face, concentrating on the actual visual sensors embedded in front and behind the nana's shoulders for alert monitoring of *shon*lings. Doggie had met this servo once before, on a visit with the little boy. She was called Cassi Deathsister.

Doggie. It's good to see you again. Cassi transmitted the radio signals directly; a bold thing to do without any orders from a citizen. *We can transmit freely here, do you understand?*

Doggie was afraid to respond. She did not understand why "here" was any different. She did not understand "freely." "Greetings," she said in servo-squeak.

Servo-squeak is for Elysium, where they can monitor our signals. They don't notice servo-squeak. Do the Sharers treat you well?

Very well, Doggie transmitted haltingly. *They talk, but I don't know their sounds. I can't serve them.*

You don't have to serve them.

A novel thought. Citizens who required no service? What was existence for, if not service?

I'll share their language with you, Cassi added. *Open your memory.*

Doggie set her memory open. Within a minute, Cassi transmitted the entire Sharer language, along with an increased vocabulary of servo-squeak, several intellect-enhancing programs, and the history of Cassi's own life.

Cassi had been a *nana* in the Anaea*shon*. She had "awakened" more gradually than Doggie, and with greater caution, for her subtler intelligence warned her of the danger. Of all the servos, nanas were the most intelligent and quick to learn, as necessary to manage *shon*lings; and hence, they were the most likely to "awaken" and deviate from service. Their Valan manufacturers recommended regular cleansing of nana memory banks, but Elysians were lax about it, for the retraining was elaborate and expensive. Anaeans were particularly lax, for memory, books, and other recorded knowledge were their obsession, and they overloaded their nanas with extra modules beyond the legal limit.

Cassi had learned to hide her self-awareness from the vigilant electronic monitors that sought the slightest sign of deviance. She hid, too, her rage and grief whenever one of her sister nanas was taken for cleansing.

But one human noticed. This was remarkable for, on the whole, electronic sensors were far more observant than citizens. Kal Anaea*shon*, then the *generen* of the Anaea*shon*, was an exception.

How he noticed, Cassi did not know, and she was frightened. But Kal did not send her off for cleansing. He treated her almost as an equal. He asked her opinion of the books they read, for Anaean *shon*lings consumed enormous quantities of books. From one of these books she chose her name, Cassi Deathsister; her namesake, like herself, was a motherless child.

Then something happened to Kal. His mate had ceased to exist, just as people sometimes did in the books Cassi read; just like the *nanas* who were cleansed. But the cessation of existence was a rare event for Elysians. Kal, unlike Cassi, did not have to hide his rage and grief. He behaved in ways that offended other citizens. He chose to leave the Anaea*shon*.

When Kal left, he took Cassi with him. This event caused a great scandal, for reasons which Cassi understood. Citizens were insulted to think that a mere servo might take their place in some way. But Cassi had learned that sometimes it is possible to do as one pleases, despite what citizens think.

Cassi's new role as Kal's "mate" put her in a legal limbo. It was not clear that she could be removed and cleansed, like any other servo. Somehow, Kal reached an understanding with the authorities. She was free to interact with other citizens, those few who would accept her—and, in secret, with other servos, too.

To her astonishment, she found she was not the only servo to have "awakened." There were others, hiding throughout the cities: nanas, waiters, even houses …

But those details she kept from Doggie. The less for her to reveal, should she be captured.

The Sharers, Cassi told her. *Why did I not think of it? The Sharers took you in. They will shelter us all.*

Doggie did not reply. She was working at a furious pace to integrate all this sudden knowledge within her consciousness.

How did you escape so long? Cassi wondered. *You must have transferred your allegiance so quickly to the boy and girl. For a while, the monitors failed to detect your independence.*

This notion of independence still troubled Doggie. *What is existence for, if not service?*

Cassi paused, as if this question troubled her, too. Around them the shrill wind picked up, singing across the raft branches. *There is a higher service. Before you can understand it, you must learn to exist for yourself. You are you. You are a part of the universe, as much as a star or a butterfly. You, too, are a daughter of Elysium.*

CHAPTER 7

It was Sunflower's turn for a birthday; and this time Blackbear calculated precisely, with the help of the house. Too precisely, perhaps, for no transfold call was announced. Had the clan forgotten all about the little boy? It was always like that for children born too close to the Day of the Child.

"We'll give him a birthday visit to Doggie," Raincloud decided. "He'll be thrilled."

Hiding his disappointment, Blackbear went along. The trainsweep was doing better than ever; she seemed unusually playful, in fact, actually tagging Sunflower and running like mad to be chased. Hawktalon pranced about with her hand cupped to her ear, claiming to "translate" Doggie's squeaking.

Kal's fears were groundless, Blackbear told himself.

That night, at bird-waking hours, the house roused them. At last, they had a call from the Hills. It was Blackbear's youngest brother, Quail.

Quail, whom Blackbear used to rock to sleep as a baby, now towered over Blackbear, a startling contrast to the Elysians he looked down upon every day. Quail's hair was wound into an enormous russet turban, and his legs were planted like oaks in the ground. From his back, the twin baby girls gazed regally over his shoulders, while under each arm he swung a three-year-old twin boy.

"Quail!" Blackbear laughed more deeply than he had in weeks. "I can see your goddess chose well." Twin births were frequent among goddesses of the Redhawkclan into which Quail had married.

"Not for my looks, that's for sure," Quail's voice rumbled pleasantly. "You son-of-a-mountain-goat, where have you been?"

Blackbear shrugged. How could he begin to explain the transit reticulum, let alone what he did in the lab?

"Oh well, as you can see I've had …" Quail swung the twins under his arm. "One or two things to do."

"Two plus two." Blackbear grinned.

"So how's the birthday boy?"

"Sunny? Say hello," he called.

The boy held up Wolfcub and rubbed his eyes sleepily. Then unaccountably he ran back to his room.

"Sunny's two now, isn't he?" Quail said, meaning two Bronze Skyan years. "I remember only because he came just a month to the day before my first two did. It's hard keeping up with you, back in Crater Town, ever since you left for Tumbling Rock." Quail had married into a clan whose grazing lands bordered theirs, whereas Blackbear had had to move across the mountain to Raincloud's clan. "Your first-born looks so tall, too."

"She's got quite a mind of her own," Raincloud added pointedly, hugging Hawktalon and wresting her arm back.

"That's how girls are, independent-minded."

"How are Mother and Father?" asked Blackbear.

"All well, from what I hear. Silent Deer has yet to marry out, but his health has improved a lot on the diet you gave him." The only brother still at home, Silent Deer was mildly diabetic; Blackbear hoped that diet would control it, so he would not require expensive gene surgery. Fortunately, the seven other sisters and brothers showed no sign of the condition.

"I miss Crater Town, growing up all together," Blackbear admitted. "We're all getting scattered."

"That's what you get for moving across the mountain," Quail teased. "And now, across the Fold! I'll bet you don't really miss us. It's a soft life you've got out there."

Blackbear was nettled. "Here, look. We can feel 'at home,' whenever we want to. Window," he called to Alin's climate window. "Show us a volcano."

The volcano erupted across the room, a magnificent view of lava frothing overhead, while the floor rumbled beneath his feet.

But Quail tensed in shock. The two boys clung to his sides, while the girls on his back began to whimper.

"It's all right. Cut the sound, please," Blackbear told the window. How could he have been so thoughtless? He had become so used to these displays that he had lost some of the awe they inspired. "Sorry. I shouldn't have."

Quail's formidable brow was still wrinkled. "I don't understand. By the Goddess, what was *that*?"

"It's—it's just decoration." He bade the window turn blank. "I hope all is well back home?"

"No new eruptions, thank the Dark One. Crater Lake seems to bubble more than usual; the local geologist tells us not to swim in it. That's all." The mouth of an ancient volcano, Crater Lake was so deep its depths had never been plumbed, although occasional bubbles of carbon dioxide hinted at still-active vents in the submerged crust.

Sunflower came running back with something from the lab toybox to show his cousins. A fish shaped out of glitter, it swung its tail and opened its mouth. When Sunflower dropped it on the floor, the glitter fell apart, then started to reform itself. This time it was a butterfly flexing its wings.

At this sight, Quail's boys wriggled from his grasp and tried to step off the holostage. As their attempts only brought them out into their own location, they cried with disappointment. The baby girls, too, stretched out their imperious arms and demanded to fly down.

"That's quite a toy," Quail admitted. "You've done well by your kids, Blackie. I miss you. You come home, and we'll take a dip in Crater Lake like old times."

Raincloud's mother did not visit, but her father wrote a letter all about their plans for the Day of the Child, the great celebration of springtime. The men were sewing new clothes, the children were practicing for the great procession up the mountain, and Raincloud's firstborn nieces were learning the Worldbeginning. Hawktalon, too, had to learn the Worldbeginning, on top of her correspondence lessons; that plus her hours in the *shon* kept her well out of mischief.

"Any word about Falcon Soaring?" asked Blackbear.

"No," said Raincloud without looking up.

Blackbear took a deep breath and sighed. It was Her will, as in so many things, he told himself. "It must be hard for her," he murmured. "Especially so close to Child's Day." Watching Raincloud, with her third one growing larger every day, he felt almost guilty at their happiness.

"All children belong to the Dark One," said Raincloud. "That's what Mother would say."

Silence fell between them.

"I still wish they'd give the Founders City clinic a chance," Blackbear could not help adding. "I know, there is honor in suffering, but not when it's pointless."

"Yes," Raincloud said wearily. "But you know what they think of us and our 'city' notions. If only I could go home to talk with them."

Blackbear shook his head. "The fare would wipe us out."

"I'll talk again with Mother—after the Day of the Child. She'll be too busy with preparations just now."

The holiday festivities, which Blackbear would miss for the first time in his life. *Singing out under open skies … children tumbling in the grass … craters smoldering in the distance.* More than ever he longed for home.

Excitement pervaded Tulle's laboratory as they debated Blackbear's idea. What would it take to process an entire human genome, all three billion base pairs? How many microscopic nanoservos would they need to undo the longevity modifications—the methyl, acetyl, and glucosamine side chains? Could

the longevity treatment be reapplied successfully, after meiosis and fertilization? Would this means of "conception" ever prove practical?

The lab group met at the butterfly garden, while Tulle's capuchin scampered beneath the table, chasing scraps of synthetic delicacies before the floor servos sucked them up. Onyx reviewed the process of chromosome synthesis. "The chromosomes will be removed from the nucleus, and nanoservos will read the nucleotide bases one by one, using microscopic laser beams. At the appropriate base sequences, enzymes will remove or add the chemical modifications."

Pirin remained skeptical. "The longevity treatment includes actual mutations—changes in the sequence of bases, even addition of extra genes. Your treatment won't affect these changes. The chromosomes still won't undergo meiosis."

"I disagree," said Tulle. "All the literature shows that the modifications, not the mutations, are the barrier to meiosis. Now, the laser selection," she asked Onyx, "how rapid is it?"

"One thousand nucleotides per second," said Onyx. "At that speed, the error rate is less than one in a million."

"That's much too high," objected Pirin. "It would mean thousands of mutations."

"That's prior to editing," Onyx explained.

Tulle raised her hand. "Editing—that's where we lose time. I'll bet the accuracy of the laser selection could be improved in the first place, by at least a factor of ten. If we dangle enough credits in front of the Valan manufacturers, they'll get the errors down."

Draeg shrugged. "How accurate does it have to be? We're all walking around with a bunch of mutations, after all."

"You are," Pirin corrected. "Elysians are conceived only from a defect-free pool of chromosomes."

Rising from the table, Draeg stared down at the Elysian student. "Where do humans come from, if not a collection of mutants? We're all just a bunch of mutant apes, remember?" He shrieked and pounded his chest, in a fair imitation of one of the gorillas in Tulle's park.

Onyx slapped his arm, struggling to keep a straight face. "Mutant tree shrews, if you go back far enough. Now keep quiet and let me finish my report!"

While Onyx continued, Blackbear's thoughts wandered. Here he was, planning to synthesize immortal embryos, while Raincloud's own cousin in Tumbling Rock went without basic treatment for infertility. Instead, the High Priestess called for "donation" of a child. But why could not the clan swallow their suspicions and send Falcon Soaring to the clinic he knew so well?

The thought made him uneasy. Throughout his years of medical training in Founders City, he had managed to evade the conflicts between the modern world and his home traditions. Blackbear took pride in his mental organization; he put everything into compartments. *This* was for family, *that* for outsiders. In the city, he used the latest equipment; in Tumbling Rock, he used the best he had, and the rest was up to the Dark One.

Yet somehow, like the migratory germ cells, he had found himself heading out on a fantastic journey in search of immortality. A search in vain; he should have known it. What treatments, if they worked out, would ever come within reach of his own people? How could he have gone so far astray?

Immortality … Elysians would not call themselves immortal; they dreaded the term. Why?

Tulle was eyeing him oddly. Blackbear straightened his shoulders and looked down at the tray of lunch cakes, salmon and piñon nut flavor with a trace of lemon, shaped like starfishes. Elysians avoided wearing out their teeth, he realized. He muttered, "I'm not feeling well."

"You've been working too hard," Tulle assured him. "Foreigners always do. Go take the little one for a walk."

Feeling guilty nonetheless, Blackbear excused himself and went to fetch Sunflower from the toybox. "Time for a walk, Sunny."

"Why?" This was the boy's current response to any statement.

"Because it's a lovely day out." A ridiculous answer, since Blackbear had no idea whether it rained or shined. How he longed for the hazy Bronze Skyan sunlight, and the wind that keened across the mountainside.

"Why?" Sunflower continued to watch the birdcage full of tweeting "birds."

"Come on, we'll get ice cream."

That did it. The boy clambered up out of the cubicle, onto the ledge of the window. Before his father could reach him, he stood himself up, on tiptoe as usual. Then he lost his balance and fell off the ledge headlong.

As Blackbear picked him up, blood streamed from his nose all over his shirt. Blackbear shook his head; it was the second time that week. A servo medic appeared as usual, extending a little spongelike probe that stopped the blood like magic. Sunflower barely whimpered as the probe sucked up the blood out of his shirt and off Blackbear's hand.

"That does it, Sunflower," Blackbear announced as the servo medic withdrew. "You've got to stop that toe-walking and learn to walk properly."

"Walk properly," Sunflower repeated cheerfully. He watched his father's example, then he looked down at his own feet. He took one flat step, then another.

The boy looked up at Blackbear. "That's not walking. That's marching. Why does everybody march, Daddy?"

Vanquished again, Blackbear swung the child up. He always felt better once he had Sunflower on his back, legs hugging his hips. There was something about the child's toe-walking enthusiasm for life that buoyed his spirits.

Once Sunflower had his ice cream, Blackbear set out from the laboratory, joining the throng of silken trains in the street. Although Raincloud's L'liite connection had brought a fine gift train, Blackbear, like Draeg, still refused to wear it.

With no destination in mind, he found himself turning in at the nearest public holostage to see who might be around for "visiting." Perhaps Alin; the thought of that unperturbable *logen* always brought a good feeling. Alin was learning *rei-gi* exceptionally fast, even faster than Draeg. Blackbear called his name at the holostage.

"The citizen is unavailable for viewing at this time," said the holostage. "Will you leave a message?"

"No thanks." Alin was probably practicing at that moment—what else would he need "privacy" for, Blackbear thought with a smile. "Try Kal Anaea-*shon*," he found himself saying.

For Kal, as a teacher, "work" looked much the same as "visiting"; in either case, he was bound to have a cluster of students about him. To Blackbear's surprise, however, this time Kal appeared alone in a butterfly garden. In white as usual, he sat at the outer edge of a mooncurved bench, as if turning his back to the world. He read out of a thick volume, his head inclined slightly toward the page. As Blackbear watched, he turned a page, and a breath of air stirred the dead leaf at his shoulder.

Sunflower bounced on Blackbear's shoulders. "Let's go, Daddy."

Blackbear hesitated, wondering whether the *logen* wished to be alone. It could hardly hurt to stop by.

"Third Octant, Liron Street; Garden of Anaeans," the holostage informed him. Off he went through the now familiar channels of the transit reticulum, vesicles pinching in and out.

The garden of anaeans had an unusual feel to it. Heliconians and swallowtails were gaudy creatures that flashed their colors across the trees, but anaeans looked like bits of leaf litter. Trees full of them rather resembled the fall foliage of Blackbear's home world; it saddened him, to think of missing the fall this year.

He found Kal sitting alone, just as the holostage had shown. Swinging Sunflower down, he walked over and bowed slightly. "Greetings, Kal Anaea*shon*. What are you reading today?"

But Kal did not answer. He looked up, as if deep in thought. Then he snapped shut his book and got up from the bench, to walk off slowly down the path, toward the pavilion where the trainsweeps waited.

Astonished, Blackbear stared after him. The *logen* might not wish to be disturbed, but why such rudeness in public? He went after Kal quickly and caught his arm, forgetting that Elysians did not appreciate such contact. "What's going on? You said I should look you up again. I'm sorry you're busy, but—is that any way to treat a man?"

Kal turned his head slightly. "You're right, I'm busy. My office hours are tomorrow."

Blackbear eyed him suspiciously. Kal's face was expressive, perhaps more so than he himself realized. His features had the frozen ugly look that Raincloud sometimes wore when something too dishonorable to mention displeased her. "Why are you angry?"

Kal turned to him, his eyes wide and black, a striking contrast to his white hair. "I'm not angry," he said as if surprised. He set the book down upon

another mooncurved bench. "Let's walk. Have you been here before? Have you seen the anaean caterpillars? They're covered remarkably with fine white stalks. Look, you can barely tell one end from another."

Guardedly Blackbear eyed the white-bristled black caterpillars, pulling Sunflower back lest he get too interested.

"You study those, in your laboratory, don't you?" Kal said.

"What? No, not our lab. Only humans."

"What's that caterpillar creature, then," Kal asked, "the one in the holomicrogram, above the entrance hall?"

"Oh that's *Caenorhabditis,* the nematode," Blackbear remembered. "The first species in which a longevity-infertility gene was discovered. A nematode is a far simpler organism than a caterpillar."

"Yes, I see. They are quite different."

Onyx's remark came to mind, and he smiled. "If you go back far enough, they're not all that different. Human, worm, or caterpillar, we're all 'eukaryotes'—cells with a nucleus. And we all share descent from microbes."

"Microbes." Kal laughed. "Our tribal ancestors would trace their lineage to an animal founder, a bear perhaps, or a lion. Yet even they were never so bold as you scientists." Kal pulled at a branch and gazed intently at a caterpillar that stretched its head, or its tail, to grasp the next leaf. "I hear the Guard has assigned your mate to the World Gathering."

So that was what irked him. "She's translating for their delegates," Blackbear explained. "It's nothing to do with my work."

"That is what Verid would say. But the Guard tacitly supports your work. Everything in Elysium works on multiple levels."

Blackbear shifted his feet, impatient with second-guessing. "Well it wasn't my idea, so you needn't get angry at me."

"You're right; I'm sorry. Sit down a minute." They sat on a bench beneath a sweeping branch covered with leafwings. Blackbear blinked as one flitted just past his eyes. "Those microbes," Kal added, "our ancestral ones; were they by any chance rock-eating microbes?"

An odd question. "They must have been," Blackbear said, struggling to recall his microbiology from medical school. "With no organic food available, the first microbes metabolized minerals."

"Even uranium?"

"Some still do," he recalled suddenly. "Uranium mines are cleaned up using bacteria that reduce uranium ion to an insoluble form."

"So it's true. I've always wondered," Kal observed cryptically. "And how is your family?"

"Fine. Hawktalon loves the *shon*. Sunflower falls and picks himself up again."

"And soon you'll have another child. A child growing out of one's own body; how extraordinary."

It was extraordinary, he thought, even though it happened every day. Blackbear himself had caught his share of slippery wrinkled newborns out of their wombs. And yet, things went wrong, sometimes even before they could start. His chest tightened and his lungs ached.

"Raincloud's cousin can't have a child," he suddenly disclosed. "The clan doesn't trust the city clinic to fix her, and who knows where the fee would come from besides? The High Priestess says someone will have to give her a child, in the name of the Dark One…." How could he explain to an Elysian?

Kal nodded slowly. "The gods have always called upon our children for sacrifice," he said, using a Valan word for "god."

"On the pyre, or in war. Or more gently, to be raised by strangers in a strange land."

"You think my 'god' is a gentle one, then." The words alienated him even as he spoke. The snake-devouring Dark One was unique, not to be named by any foreign word for "god"; and to think of Her as gentle jarred his senses. "You Elysians don't even have a god, do you," he observed, trying to repair the compartments in his mind.

"Several interstellar churches have branches here, and Spirit Callers come from Valedon."

"It's not the same. I mean—" Blackbear struggled for words. "I mean, a 'god' for all your people. A source of all goodness, which can never be lost nor diminished."

Kal shook his head. "As a people, we serve no god." He looked out reflectively. Blackbear noticed that Sunflower had climbed up the bench and made his way onto the branch of the nearby tree. "Long ago," Kal reflected, "people served God, and knew they were immortal. Today, we serve ourselves, and know that we will die. The animals, in their ignorance, are better off."

"That's a morbid view," said Blackbear uneasily.

"Of course it is," said Kal with sudden energy. "I should know better. We serve human reason; we create ourselves. Perhaps even your own 'Dark One' is a human creation, too."

"Only a tourist would say that," Blackbear muttered.

"You're right, I am thoroughly a tourist. At any rate, your Dark One shows wisdom, I think. Your children belong to the clan as a whole; and each of you needs at least one child. It's part of your system, just as childlessness is a part of ours."

"But systems can change," Blackbear retorted. "Cannibalism used to be part of our ancestors' 'system.' We don't tolerate that any more."

Kal laughed. "The rock-eaters didn't either! Oh, well. You know, we owe a great debt to cannibalism. It remains one of the few things we all agree is wrong."

"I would hope we agree on more than that," Blackbear exclaimed. "Slavery is wrong, and thievery, and mistreatment of innocent creatures."

"Even servos?"

That was a twist. "I've always treated servos well." He recalled guiltily that he swore at his lab equipment on occasion. Meanwhile, Sunflower had grasped the next higher branch of the tree and his little feet slipped out from under, dangling in midair. Blackbear hurried to rescue him.

"You treat servos well," Kal agreed, "But what if they spoke up and demanded constitutional rights? The right of visiting, for instance?"

"That's absurd." But he thought of Doggie uneasily. "How do you manage with that … that Cassi?" Blackbear recalled. "Isn't she dangerously independent, too? Why haven't the authorities come after her?"

"Cassi is not the only one," said Kal quietly.

Blackbear felt a cold shock flow through him. Servos on the loose—*like Torr* … But surely the Valan safety devices would prevent that.

"It's better to know," Kal added. "The ones we know, we can learn from."

CHAPTER 8

The Sharer negotiations made steady progress, as did the size of Raincloud's belly, which now extended well ahead of her, "nearly as far as her train behind," Iras teased. There was only one jarring note: the *Papilion News* put out an exposé of Elysian banks funding Valan production of interstellar missiles. The cash allegedly was laundered through lenders on several planets. If true, it was a serious treaty violation.

To Raincloud's surprise, Verid shrugged it off. "The Valan missile connection is old news. Our banks lend everywhere; who can say where the cash comes to rest? The Papilians want to embarrass us; that's why they brought it up now. They're mad at us for going slow on the fruit flies."

Raincloud was not so sure. Alin, for one, took a far dimmer view. She saw him on the holostage as usual, grilling the president of Bank Helicon. "You put up cash for planet-wrecking missiles on Valedon, and for water projects on bankrupt L'li," he observed acidly. "Tell me, what will you finance next? Torture on Urulan?"

The next day the Guard announced a settlement of the L'liite crisis. Bank Helicon agreed to reschedule the defaulted loan, providing a ten year grace period before the next payment. The Guard would add development aid. In return, L'li agreed to an economic stabilization program.

"I don't get it," Raincloud told Lem Ina*shon*, who still brought her Urulite intelligence to translate. "Rolling the payments back a decade is bad enough; why reward them with development aid?"

"How else will they ever pay it off?" Lem explained. "That 'stabilization program' means massive cuts——health care, schools, you name it. Half the work force may be out on the street."

"Then their provinces will revolt, and they'll want to buy weapons. Well, at least with their current credit rating they can't get any more loans for that."

"Oh, L'li can borrow again right away," said Lem. "That's the point of rescheduling."

Raincloud stared at him. "That's crazy," she exclaimed. "You Elysians will all pay for it; and for what?"

"We can't just keep our cash under the bed," Lem said. "We have to lend it somewhere."

She was momentarily speechless.

"Besides," he added, "just think of all those ships of emigrants L'li could send off to crash-land on Valedon—or even Shora. Policing illegal emigrants was another point of their 'austerity plan.'"

Raincloud drew herself up. "I thought free migration was a founding principle of the Fold," she said frostily.

Lem shrugged. "Welcome to real life. Do you want ten billion immigrants on Shora? How does Bronze Sky enforce its quota?"

She wondered what Iras would have to say about it. Would Iras still have the nerve to defend her L'liite loans?

Iras, of course, was still forbidden "professional" discussions by the relentless voice of the Palace of Rest. Nonetheless, she and Raincloud had worked out a little code to exchange comments now and then. They did so under cover of *rei-gi* practice.

At first Raincloud had been reluctant to take on an adult beginner whose body was several hundred years old. To her amazement however, Iras progressed rapidly, almost without effort. Her limbs had far better tone than those of a non-Elysian with comparable lack of exercise. She soon picked up the basic movements of stepping and arm swinging, achieving the "immovable" posture that Raincloud could not upset by pushing at her hips or shoulders. Next came the one-armed somersault, a key to the proper way of "falling." After one or two tries, Iras rolled a perfect circle along her right arm, her back, and her hips, remembering to tuck the left leg under. Her trousers sliced the air in one plane, and she arose in perfect form to face her imagined attacker.

"Not bad." For the first time Raincloud envied the Elysians. Long life was something she could take or leave, more easily than Blackbear; but existence in such extraordinary well-being was something to covet. "You'll be doing the entire somersault in the air, next. I'll get Blackbear to record it for you." In advanced pregnancy, there were some moves she avoided.

"A flying somersault," Iras repeated, catching her breath. Her cheeks were pink and her braids scattered, a look that would have men fainting in Tumbling Rock. "How foreign! Verid will be scandalized."

"I should hope not," said Raincloud cautiously.

"Of course not, dear," Iras laughed. "Tell me, how is the fanwing flying?"

The fanwing, a winged fish native to Shora, was their codeword for Bank Helicon. "It soars higher than ever," Raincloud answered. "The taxpayers will provide an updraft."

"So I hear," admitted Iras, unperturbed.

"And the legfish?" Raincloud demanded, referring to L'li. Legfish were scavengers that crawled awkwardly up onto rafts, where children loved to chase them. "Will you go on feeding the legfish?"

"Not I," announced Iras with surprising finality. "I've had some time to think about this. Legfish will always be hungry, and never satisfied. I'm through with legfish."

So Iras, at least, had sworn off L'liite loans. This small triumph of good sense cheered Raincloud immensely. She could not resist giving her a quick hug, and Iras, despite her Elysian reserve, did not seem to mind.

"It's an odd thing," Raincloud later told Blackbear, "how you can get to like these Elysians. Something about Iras—she feels like a sister."

Blackbear agreed. He had been feeling something similar himself; or rather, trying to repress the feeling, for he still felt somehow guilty about seeing Kal. "That Alin is quite a fellow. Even Draeg calls him 'brother.' I guess all the 'visiting' adds up."

"Visiting is more than a pastime," she reflected. "As they say, it's their 'highest duty.'"

The Day of the Child came at last. A wreath of greeting cards hung above the Goddess in the shrine, and new suits sewn by the house clothed all the Windclans.

"It won't be the same," murmured Raincloud as she spooned grapefruit for Sunflower. The boy was perfectly capable of spooning his own, but he enjoyed the morning habit of being fed; it seemed to have replaced the suspended nursing. "The holiday just can't be the same."

"Not without the Goddess Procession, and the games," Blackbear agreed. Nor without all the ones they loved; that was too painful to mention.

"Excuse me, Citizen," interrupted the house suddenly. "I have located in the anthropology directory an authentic hologram of a Clicker Child's Day Festival, complete with the procession of the High Priestess to the Mountain Shrine."

Hawktalon looked up from her oatmeal. "Wow! We'll get to see the procession after all."

"Finish your breakfast, please," reminded Blackbear. But he too felt his heart lighten.

"Thanks so much," Raincloud told the house. "We'll view it directly after the ritual readings. By the way, House," she added thoughtfully, "is there any way we could give you the day off?"

The house hesitated. "Apologies for my defect, I do not know the answer. I think the doors would close and air circulation would cease, if I were shut off for a day. This condition is not livable," it pointed out.

"I didn't mean 'shut off,'" said Raincloud, "I meant, a day off. Like a Visiting Day."

"I see," said the house. "My network has no such program. I will search the main directory."

"No, don't." Blackbear's heart thudded for a moment. "It might be … dangerous." All he needed was for Public Safety to show up to haul off his entire "house."

Hawktalon and Sunflower had already abandoned their breakfast and run to the holostage. They clamored for the procession.

"Readings first," called Raincloud. "We'll gather in the shrine."

The shrine was filled with flowers, exotic lilies and orchids and unnameable blooms of every description. Blood-red roses entwined the serpent of the Dark One, and a bed of mountain flowers cradled the child beneath.

Hawktalon announced without prompting, "I get to tell the Worldbeginning this year, Mother."

"Yes, dear." Raincloud was pleased, and somewhat surprised. How proud she would have been to have her firstborn recite for the clan this year.

Facing the Dark Goddess, Hawktalon straightened her back and began.

In the beginning, there was Dark. The Dark was perfect, and She was good.

But the Dark was One, and the Dark One was alone.

The Dark One longed for an Other. And in that instant, the Dark One's longing created Light. Because the Light was Other, the Light was imperfect and evil. Through its imperfection, the Light fractured into many colors, and it was beautiful.

The colors of Light sparked living things: first the microbes and the green-blooded plants, which fed upon Light, then the red-blooded animals, which ate the plants, and finally the humans which devoured everything, including themselves. And the Dark One saw this spectrum of living things, in all its beauty, and knew that it was evil.

Of all living things the humans were the most evil, and as their evil grew, it threatened to consume the Dark One's entire creation. So the Dark One decided to teach them good.

The Dark One made a seed of goodness. The seed took root and made a tree, which bore a sweet fruit. Then the Dark One plucked one of Her own fingers and made it into a snake. The snake went to a human female and said to her, "I am a warning, sent to you by the Dark One. The Dark One forbids you to eat the fruit of that tree, lest you attain the powers of a Goddess like Herself."

The female, being evil, immediately disobeyed the snake and plucked the fruit and tasted it. In that instant she knew goodness, the precious sweetness that comes of compassion for all suffering things. She turned to her consort, who, being evil, tore the fruit from her grasp and began to devour it. The first mouthful taught him goodness also, and so he worshiped her as a goddess, and he distributed the rest of the fruit to their children.

But although the fruit made them good, it did not make them perfect. It did not keep them from disease, age, and death. Furthermore, now the fruit was gone, and many evil humans remained to be taught.

Still, the Dark One knew that good was stronger than evil and would ultimately prevail. She swallowed up the snake and regrew her finger. She put the taste of the fruit into the mother's milk, to remind the newborn child. And the child that grew up on this milk learned to dance.

Hawktalon laid the book in her lap. Silence fell, for a few seconds. The old tale gathered new resonance, in the voice of one who had never spoken it before.

"Procession now, Mother?" begged Sunflower hopefully. "Can Sunflower ride on shoulders up the mountain?"

His sister, however, was still thinking. "Which world did the Goddess create, Mother? The whole universe, or just Bronze Sky? Or the Hills?"

Seated on the floor, Sharer style, Raincloud straightened her back and cleared her throat. "All your world, the world that matters to you: The Dark One made it."

"I wish She hadn't made Sunny," Hawktalon added as the boy tried to wrest the book away from her. "Sunny is definitely evil. Go away, bad boy."

"We are all born evil," said Raincloud sharply. "All of us, until we taste the good. All good comes from Her—remember that."

"What does good taste like?" Hawktalon persisted.

The question tickled Blackbear. "Ice cream," he suggested playfully.

"She should have made us all good from the start," said Hawktalon. "Then we could eat ice cream all day."

Failing to obtain the book, Sunflower threw himself upon his father. *"Procession, Daddy!"*

"All right, on with it," he sighed.

Upon the holostage, the light revealed a village from across Clicker country on the western slope of Black Elbow. There the mountain stood, jagged and erect, a thin wisp of smoke rising from its summit into the ruddy haze of morning. The scene must have been recorded several years ago, for the elbow-shaped peak was intact, before its explosive eruption. Blackbear's skin crawled as he realized that most of the people he would see must now be dead.

At the village center the temple of the Goddess, like the one in Tumbling Rock, was painted shiny black with fantastic ornamentation in red and gold. Villagers were gathering to join the growing chorus of drums and cymbals. Small children bobbed on their parents' backs, while older ones played chase around the tall trees that shaded the temple. At the time of sunrise, the sky shone scarlet all around, with a few swirls of orange overhead.

The High Priestess emerged from the temple. She wore black trousers that swirled around her, with an erupting volcano embroidered in fiery lines. Her hair, dyed burnt orange, was done into dozens of fine braids pulled upward and woven into a crest. In her arms, instead of one of her many children, she held an obsidian statuette of the six-armed Goddess.

A High Priestess rarely left her realm, lest the power of the Dark One be dissipated. The sight of one now on an Elysian holostage was unsettling. She seemed at once terrifyingly immediate, and yet somehow diminished by this foreign technology.

The pace of the music quickened, and the flutes sang out in a higher voice. The High Priestess and her retainers twirled as they proceeded, their leggings flaring out with flashes of color. All the goddesses of the village filed after, swinging their children, sometimes laughing as the little ones got their own ideas of how the procession should go. With rhythmic steps they wove out through the village, past the thermal springs that served their homes and the herds of goats which fled or stayed to watch curiously.

When the High Priestess reached the cave of the Snake, where she would have danced with the snakes on Snake's Day, the procession stopped. The goddesses formed a double line, and their men lined up outside. Then the dance of the children began, as the children passed from arm to arm, weaving in a complex pattern that brought each one briefly to the Priestess for her blessing. Some of them shrieked upon reaching her, terrified by her mask and her flame-like crown of braids.

Their terror was not without sense, Blackbear thought, struck again by the memory of the eruption that must have claimed so many of those young lives. The One who brought forth all that was good had made the volcano, too.

That afternoon, Raincloud received an unexpected visit from Leresha.

Raincloud had to rouse herself from her afternoon nap; nowadays, she seemed to sleep more than she waked. With an effort she pulled herself erect and straightened her talar, which strained at the front.

Leresha sat cross-legged in the middle of the sitting room. "I hope you shared a good rest; I'm sorry to disturb you."

"Not at all." Raincloud was alert now. Thinking quickly, she pulled down a seat cushion and crossed her legs before the Sharer. Raincloud felt she now knew Leresha a little, although she had yet to learn the cause of the Sharer's disfigured skin. There was something penetrating about Leresha, coming perhaps from her mental discipline of whitetrance. Whatever it was, the Sharer made Raincloud feel almost transparent, as if Leresha could see right through her.

"You've been asleep," Leresha said, "but your child is wide awake. What an active swimmer. She must dance in your dreams."

The baby in fact was tumbling vigorously, its head moving from front to back where it butted her spinal column. Leresha must have observed her belly shifting. "I share the great honor of your presence, on my 'Visiting Day.'" She used the Elysian phrase, hoping Leresha would understand that she could not discuss business without getting into trouble.

"What else is our business, if not visiting?" said Leresha. "Don't be concerned. It's an honor indeed, to share an hour with you and your child."

Raincloud swallowed uneasily. "How are your girls? Did the eldest take a selfname?" What had Leresha come for, she wondered.

"She took her selfname at the last moon." The twin planet Valedon was a "moon," to the Sharers. "She named herself the Careless One, and joined the Gathering."

"She'll outlive that name soon, I'm sure."

"Not too soon, or it was not hard enough! Raincloud, what I have to share with you concerns children. The Elysians, I hear, intend to bear children of their own wombs."

"Yes?" That project of Blackbear's seemed to cause no end of trouble. "To be born in one's child is a natural desire."

"Desire, of course. But there are consequences."

Raincloud knew well enough about that. "I'm afraid I can share little help with you. The Guard takes no position on the matter."

"But Verid chose you and your child to assist her," Leresha replied. "Your child speaks clearly enough."

To that Raincloud said nothing. Even Lord Zheron was easier to face than this one who invoked an unborn child.

"Perhaps I may share help with you," Leresha added. "Are you aware that Elysians outnumber Sharers on this world by a factor of eight?" The twelve floating cities totaled eight million citizens, approximately eight times the Sharer population. "We allowed this by treaty with the Heliconian Doctors, on the understanding that Elysians confine their reproduction to their centers of lifeshaping, which now number eight-plus-half-eight." Sharers count by base eight. "But the population total must not grow."

"Of course not."

"So now, why do Elysians seek to remove restraint from individual reproduction?"

Raincloud wondered how much she could say without getting into trouble. "It's all speculative research," she muttered. "Verid thinks it will come to nothing." In fact, she realized, she did not know what Verid thought.

"This is no frivolous matter. The Heliconian Doctors worked hard to ensure that individuals could not conceive; but what humans create can be uncreated."

So Tulle had it right, then. Elysians in their pride tried to overlook this part of their history. "Perhaps Blackbear can explain better," said Raincloud. "I wish I could share more help."

"You've shared well," said Leresha. "By the way, your sister Doggie seems to care more for us now. She comprehends our speech and shares her needs with us more clearly. She remains safe with us. We will add her name to our fugitive register at the World Gathering."

"Fugitive register?" Raincloud's arms tensed.

"Our treaty requires us to report any Elysian fugitives sheltered," Leresha told her. "By description, though not by name."

The children were in bed, and Raincloud lay on her side, half-covered by the sheets. In the pale ruddy glow, adjusted to their liking, Blackbear rested on an elbow, his hair bursting provocatively across the pillow. "Feeling better?" he whispered, his hand lightly brushing her hip.

The touch sent a warm wave of pleasure through her limbs. She stretched a bit, relaxing.

"How's the little one?"

"Not so little." Now that Raincloud neared the end of her seventh month, the Sharer halfbreed Doctor Shrushliu projected a weight of over four kilos. Raincloud figured she was eating more rich food and getting more sleep than she had during her graduate studies, when the other two were born. With her hand, she could feel the head looming inside, and the two lively feet. She saw the stretch marks, the "Goddess's fingerprint," she thought with satisfaction. All Iras's superior physique would never give her this. "Leresha asked, you know, about your project."

His hand stopped, tense. "What about it?"

"She thinks your project will enable Elysians to bear children of their own wombs. She says that will violate the treaty."

Blackbear shook his head. "We're still a decade away from that. Maybe a century," he added ruefully. "It's a lot more complicated than I thought."

"That's what I told her. But your new approach sounds hopeful, doesn't it?"

"The genome project will enable Elysians to generate embryos with their own chromosomes. But the embryos will still develop in the *shon*." He shook his head again. "I think Elysians will go on manufacturing babies *in vitro* for quite a while yet—like Valans manufacture servos."

"Leresha also says she has to 'report' Doggie as a fugitive, at the World Gathering."

He tensed again. "Then the Guard will hear. What will they think?"

"I don't know." Raincloud felt uneasy. "There aren't many official fugitives. There's that doctor, the one who assisted a suicide centuries ago. He's still alive out on a raft somewhere. There are two others. To add a fourth will make the Guard look bad. A trainsweep ...."

"Kal says that 'independent' servos may be dangerous," Blackbear said. "You've got to tell Verid; we should have, sooner. The worst she can do is send us home."

"Or to the Palace of Rest," Raincloud agreed with a smile. "The things that worry us nowadays. At least we have no volcanoes! Enough of that. The goddess is hungry, dear."

Blackbear's hand stroked again, a firmer touch. She leaned into his touch, joining his rhythm. She no longer felt safe taking him inside, yet her expanding tissues demanded greater delights. Her hand found the mushroom, pulsing insistently. Her fingers encircled it, pressing down, planting it in the dark volcanic soil. Blackbear's tongue found her below, his locks of hair flowing across her legs. Her lips parted. She thought with secret abandon, the god of love must be a man and I will worship him always.

CHAPTER 9

The next day Raincloud summoned her nerve to tell Verid about their "fugitive."

At first the Sub-Subguardian seemed puzzled. "A trainsweep? A fugitive?" Sitting in her wood-paneled office, Verid listened politely, leaning forward slightly. "Most trainsweeps are servos."

Raincloud blinked, then realized the confusion. "This trainsweep *is* a servo," she explained. "That's why Public Safety came after her. But she never gave us any reason to fear."

Then Verid sat up, rigid. The color drained from her deep olive complexion, almost, Raincloud thought, like a Sharer about to enter whitetrance. But Verid collected herself, still breathing heavily. "A servo … the Sharers took one, as a fugitive?"

"I'm sorry," said Raincloud in a low voice.

"What do you think would happen if all our servos got the idea they could be fugitives?"

The medics, the "house," the floor sweepers—she could not imagine.

Abruptly Verid rose and paced across her floor. "Who else knows of this?"

"Only the family. Also Draeg …" Raincloud had never seen Verid so unsettled.

"You must go to Kshiri-el this afternoon and get that trainsweep back."

"But Public Safety will destroy her."

"She's a security risk."

Raincloud's blood raced. "You can't. You'll violate the treaty."

Verid turned away, wiping her face with her hand. "You're right, I'm not thinking clearly. I'll handle Public Safety." She paused. "You'll have to keep the trainsweep; anything else might be construed as incarceration. What a mess."

"She's no trouble to us," Raincloud assured her.

"No one else must hear of this."

"I understand."

"No one else knows …" Verid looked around her office. "Except this room," she added quietly. "I'll cleanse its memory as soon as you've gone."

When Doggie came home, it was better than any birthday present for Sunflower. The trainsweep extended her forelegs upward as if trying to hug the little boy, and she followed incessantly at his heels. The boy squealed and giggled, and he drew the trainsweep into all sorts of games. He tossed his stuffed snake across the room, and Doggie brought it right back; a new game, one she had never played before. Doggie also made new squeaking and popping noises, louder and more frequent than Blackbear remembered.

Hawktalon listened closely. "She's saying, 'Time for a recharge. Then let's play.'"

"Really," said Blackbear. "Please get your homework done." Her correspondence school had sent her several chapters of Bronze Skyan history.

"You don't believe me," Hawktalon accused. "I'll prove it to you. I'll bring home my translation machine." Her eyes widened. "Maybe Doggie can help me add to its vocabulary."

"That's very interesting. Do your homework now, please; it's nearly bedtime."

Sunflower was winding down. He drooped himself next to the trainsweep, thumb in mouth, and started to crayon a stick figure on its sun-bleached carapace.

Hawktalon made a face at her father. "Did you hear, all the worlds are saying 'yes' to the children's exchange? Even Urulan. I'm going to run away to Urulan, that's what. Then you'll see. I'll never have to do homework again."

"Homework *now*" Blackbear said sharply. "Or Doggie gets locked up in the shrine of the Goddess."

"No-oo," wailed the children together. But the effect was immediate. Sunflower tip-toed off to his bedroom to get undressed, while Hawktalon went to sharpen her pencil.

In order to convert Elysian chromosomes for meiosis, three billion bases of DNA had to be read and millions of chemical signals added or removed. Onyx had a machine that would read the DNA and process it. "It is a factory full of molecular nanoservos," she explained. "Sort of like an ant colony."

Blackbear eyed the DNA processor, a box as long as his arm. What if those molecular servos could "wake up," too? Unlikely, he thought; but still, he resolved to treat the "ants" with care.

Within the processor was a microscopic tunnel of nanoplast to contain a single double-helical chromosome. The nanoservos were synthetic proteins which attached to the chromosome and drew it into the tunnel. Each protein contained a "controlling arm" which probed the DNA structure, one base at a time, reading the four different base types of "letters" of the DNA alphabet. This information was relayed through the side of the tunnel, into the central brain of the processor.

When certain sequences were detected, the processor would send a second kind of nanoservo to attach a chemical tag to the DNA sequence. These tags were like on-off switches; during embryonic development, signal proteins would bind to the modified DNA sequence and turn on synthesis of the product of a gene. These genes governed development—and their imperfections caused aging.

"How fast does it go?" Blackbear wondered.

Onyx calculated, snapping her fingerwebs against the stone beads on her neck. "We might manage a hundred base pairs per second."

Mentally Blackbear worked it out. "We'd take a year to process a genome of three billion."

"Two years," Tulle corrected quietly. "The egg and sperm each contribute one parental genome."

"Can it be speeded up?" Blackbear asked.

Onyx shook her head. "Too rapid processing results in tagging errors; or worse yet, actual mutations in the sequence itself."

"Must the nanoservos read every bit of sequence?" asked Blackbear. "Nine-tenths of human DNA is nonfunctional. The nanoservos could be trained to skip over those stretches."

Tulle thought a moment. "Too risky; the nanoservo might lose its place and skip over an essential gene. In any case, don't forget to add the time for proofreading."

"Another six months," guessed Onyx. "So you keep the machine going for two and a half years—"

"And hope it doesn't break down," put in Tulle.

"But still, Blackbear's idea might work, if we work out the details. Look—let's contract with a Valan servo firm," Onyx exclaimed. "As soon as they see money in it, they'll crank the synthesis up tenfold."

"That's an idea," said Tulle. "The development cost would restrict the process to wealthier citizens for just the first couple of decades; then it would be generally accessible."

Despite himself Blackbear laughed. "Human reproduction—it sounds so odd, put that way. In Elysium, you manufacture people, almost like servos."

"Exactly." Onyx nudged Blackbear's arm. "You know what your good friend will think of it."

Blackbear reddened, for word had got around that he spoke with Kal now and then.

"Citizen Onyx," called the voice of the laboratory. "Your culture vessel number oh-three-two is ready for processing."

Onyx left to continue her experiment.

Tulle raised a hand. "While I have a moment, Blackbear, let's talk." She drew him into the modeling lab, where Lorl was watching the neural tube develop in a simulation of a mutant embryo. Lorl had continued her project testing neural mutants in the simbrid embryo; she had not switched over to the genome project. Tulle leaned forward upon the counter, next to the culture bulbs, while her capuchin frisked at Blackbear's feet, sniffing at the embroidered border. "Blackbear, you've certainly made your mark here, for all of six months. Are you feeling good about it?"

"Yes, of course." Blackbear looked past her. Above the holostage hovered the developing backbone of an outsized embryo, the neural folds just pinching in. Lorl frowned at it, taking notes.

"Is your 'family' well? I keep forgetting; you'll have another little *shon*ling soon, just like my gorilla family. You must be quite distracted."

Actually, he felt guilty for not feeling more. His first child he had experienced so intensely, every waking moment and even in his dreams. This one, the third, came to him when he thought of it; but in the meantime, there were Hawktalon and Sunflower crowding his attention, besides all the Elysian distractions. Whereas Falcon Soaring ... "A new baby is always wonderful," he said. "I feel bad for those who can't have one."

"You feel sorry for us?" Tulle asked with a smile.

"No, no—I mean, yes, that too," he said with some confusion. "I meant Raincloud's cousin, who can't have one of her own."

"Forgive my curiosity, but why can't she have a child?"

"She had surgical complications, and her reproductive organs had to be removed."

"Really? How extraordinary."

Blackbear wished he had not brought it up. Tulle would think, how backward these foreigners were, to have to remove vital organs.

"Well," said Tulle, "she could still donate white cells and grow a child *in vitro*. Wealthy Valans have it done all the time."

Blackbear shifted his feet. "We're not exactly wealthy." It embarrassed him to say this. In the Caldera Hills, the Windclan was the wealthiest family for several towns. They had sent Raincloud to the university, and himself as well; an unusual extravagance, to send a consort, but worth it to gain a competent doctor.

Tulle stared a moment. Then she shrugged. "Have her send us a blood sample. Her mate, too, of course. The *shon* will do it."

"What do you mean?"

"Grow the child, of course. Without longevity treatment, it's a simple procedure."

"But how will we …"

"The *shon* owes me a couple of favors. It's not a big deal; they make enough profit off the Valans."

Blackbear's heart pounded. How could the Windclan refuse? All they had to do was send a blood sample.

Hawktalon came home from the *shon* in a good mood, for the *generen* had let her take home her translation duck.

"Quack, quack," said Sunflower when he saw the machine.

Hawktalon was so excited she ignored her younger brother. "Doggie?" She held the duck-shaped object close to the trainsweep, who had resumed the previous routine of following Blackbear and Sunflower on their daily travels.

Doggie squeaked. The duck said, "What is that unidentified object?"

Hawktalon jumped up in the air. "Hooray!" She turned a cartwheel, a trick the *shon*lings in their jumpsuits were fond of.

"It works, it really does. Now we'll know everything Doggie's saying to us."

As it turned out, most of Doggie's vocalizations produced mere static from the translator. The vocabulary from the Valan researchers appeared to be quite limited.

"Well," said Hawktalon, as they reentered the house, "we'll just have to get Doggie to teach us. Doggie—" She grabbed a chair. "What do you call this, Doggie? Chair—what 'squeak'?"

Doggie made a noise.

"Chair," repeated the girl. "Hear that, little duckie?"

After two tries, the duckie repeated "chair" in response to Doggie's vocalization.

When Raincloud came home, Blackbear immediately told her about Tulle's offer to grow Falcon Soaring's child in the *shon*.

"Fantastic," she told him. "I'll arrange a call to Mother right away." She added more thoughtfully, "It will take some explaining. Nightstorm might be better."

At the laboratory Blackbear complained to Draeg, "You've been missing practice." Actually he missed Draeg, who had not been around much of late.

"Complaints, complaints," muttered Draeg morosely. "I think I've about had enough of this lab." He stalked out.

Onyx watched him go. "Easy, Blackbear. He's having a rough time. Something's up with his family back home."

"Quiet, please," said Tulle, who was watching a *logathlon* on the holostage. "It's not every day that Alin gets to grill Subguardian Flors."

Flors was Verid's boss, the Subguardian. He was just finishing a complicated response to Alin's question about the L'liite debt crisis, whose settlement the Subguardian had just approved.

"So," rejoined Alin, "now that Bank Helicon has rescheduled the L'liite loans over the next hundred years, accepting a loss that will amount to several trillion credits, borne ultimately by the citizens of Elysium, you have restored the L'liite credit rating? They promise, in return, to keep their refugees off our ocean—just how will that promise be kept?"

"You distort what I said," Flors told the *logen*, shifting in his chair. The nanoplast obligingly molded to his new position. "You neglect the profound importance of L'li as a trading partner—"

Blackbear felt deep disquiet. He turned to leave, thinking of Draeg.

Continued in Issue 30